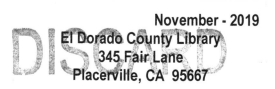

THE ATHENA PROTOCOL

THE
ATHENA
PROTOCOL

SHAMIM SARIF

HARPER TEEN
An Imprint of HarperCollinsPublishers

For Hanan, my own goddess of justice and wisdom

»»»

And for Ethan and Luca—quiet warriors and natural mystics

1

SOMETIMES, I WONDER IF THE world might just look better through a riflescope. Crisper, clearer, narrowed down. Less messy.

In my crosshairs, a boy soldier, just a teenager, not much younger than me, is asleep. Mouth slightly open, hand flung over his eyes to block the glimmering dawn light that's started to spread into the sky. I can even see the tired threads on the frayed collar of his stained camouflage jacket. I shift my rifle to the left, where, farther back, behind a stand of thorny trees, is a squat concrete building where this militia group's leader, Ahmed, sleeps. Then I swing right, over to the caged area where the fifty or so girls they kidnapped three months ago are trapped. Everyone is asleep: the soldiers, their hostages, their leader. I wait and listen to the other two women beside me.

Lying so close to me that the lengths of our bodies are almost touching, is Hala. I feel her shift, and behind us Caitlin coughs, quietly, suppressing the sound, although we are way too high up and far back from the camp for anyone to hear us. I cough too. The air here is dry; scratchy dry—catching in your throat every time you breathe. The smell of scorched earth rises up to my nose again—the smell of West Africa. For a moment, I think about the tarnished metal smell of rainy streets in London, at home. But it doesn't last long, and I cough again.

"Short delay on the incoming trucks," Caitlin says softly. "Three, four minutes."

Hala and I relax off our riflescopes, and I turn to look at Caitlin over my shoulder while I use my water bottle to knock away a dead cockroach that lies next to me. She's listening to a feed in her ear.

"I'm hungry," Hala says. Hala is always eating, or thinking about eating.

Caitlin reaches into her small backpack and tosses us each a protein bar. I'm not thrilled with it, but I doubt she has fresh croissants in there, so I keep quiet and take it. Hala eats hers fast, without comment. Fueling up. I swallow mine with less enthusiasm. The cold slide of sweetness in my mouth is disgusting. I try to remember that millions of children are starving in Africa and that I have no right to complain. Especially since we'll be back home tomorrow.

"Let's get set up again," Caitlin orders kindly. Something about Caitlin's American accent, which is a complete drawl, like something out of a cowboy movie, makes me feel even more British.

Hala and I obey, leaning into our riflescopes, eyes focused once more down on the militia camp below. We're all in the same positions we took the first night we were here, when we were just watching, tweaking the plan. Christ, that was a rubbish night. When I finally got to sleep, I was thrilled to dream of something else.

We have these contact lenses that zoom in and out depending on how you blink, so even from up here we had a perfect view of the soldiers. I hadn't expected them to be so young. You see videos about child soldiers in Africa, but these weren't kids—and yet they weren't men either. Probably recruited willingly by Ahmed and his terrorist militia. If you're stuck in a village working the land all day to plant crops that may never actually grow, maybe Ahmed gives you something to believe in—and guns to play with. We watched them that night, laughing, teasing each other the way boys do, scrapping in little fights that rose up like boiling water and then evaporated as fast. The bloodied noses, shouts and shoves; I could handle that.

But what they did to the girls . . . These fifty girls they had captured from a distant village, in an attempt to blackmail the government into releasing prisoners . . . None of us could watch what they were doing, and none of us could look at each other. When I caught Caitlin's eyes by mistake, they were welled up, which somehow made me even angrier, that she was suffering. I wanted to do something right then, go down there and end it all at gunpoint. I think I even scrambled up, because Caitlin put a hand on my arm to grab me and she held it there, calming me down for a minute. It had ended by itself, by two in the morning. The human urge for sleep overtaking all the other urges. And the camp fell quiet, just as it is now.

Lying on your stomach on hard, baked earth is no picnic. We've been stretched out there for nearly an hour because Caitlin likes to be early for everything, doesn't like the stress of cutting things too fine. My legs are getting stiff. I wiggle them and wipe a smear of sweat off my nose. Sunlight has lifted the ink color of the sky behind the rough line of trees far ahead, and the heat is already there, weighing us down. I'm tense, nervous; because once this raid starts, we can't make a mistake. I start to fidget and I feel Hala turn to look at me with irritation.

"What?" I demand.

But Hala turns back to her own rifle, looking through the viewfinder. Hala doesn't talk much at the best of times, and on top of that, she doesn't like speaking English. She speaks it fine—really well, considering she only learned it properly in the past couple of years. But she keeps to herself, and I'm pretty sure she never had much to say in Arabic either. Usually I appreciate that about her, not having to do a ton of small talk all the time, but now, her perfect calm feels annoying.

"Damn, this heat," I say, just to break the tension.

Caitlin's soft Southern tones are soothing, like oil on water.

"This ain't heat. Iraq in August, carrying fifty pounds of combat gear. *That's* heat."

"You're not the only one who's been military-trained," I tell her.

"And I can't compete with what you got up to, Jessie," smiles

Caitlin. "I was just a foot soldier. Nothing special."

Acknowledging people's feelings is Caitlin's favorite response to everything. They must have taught it to her in officer training once, and it stuck. I learned it in a leadership course a couple of years ago in England, in this special training school I was in, but I was only sixteen then and I usually preferred head-on confrontation to worrying about what the other person *felt* all the time.

Still, this isn't the army, or a government program, and, in our little team of three, Caitlin sets the tone and gives the orders. So I subside. I shift a bit because she always sees through me, knows my need to boast, but now her smile fades. Her eyes turn to where two trucks are coming over the horizon toward us. The camp below is still silent, scattered with the outlines of the sprawled, sleeping boys.

"Seven minutes." In Caitlin's eye, the lens gives her a reading on the trucks' speed, their distance, and their ETA.

"Ready?" Caitlin asks.

I feel a pulse of adrenaline rising through me.

"I was born ready."

I can hear the swagger in my own voice, can feel Hala rolling her eyes, but I can't help it. Hala, of course, just nods.

"Line up your first shot."

We both bend our heads to our riflescopes. Hala focuses on sleeping soldiers to the right, I take the left side. We wait for Caitlin to give the order. Time moves slowly now, and every whisper of movement has paused, even our breathing.

"Now," Caitlin commands.

The first squeeze of the trigger is a surprise to my fingers, as if I always forget the exact pressure to use. Perhaps because that pressure has changed a bit with the modifications on these rifles, because they shoot drugged darts, not bullets. Still, it's easy for me, hitting targets. One, two, three, four . . . I pick off unsuspecting soldiers in a steady rhythm. Because steady matters. Steady means not rushing, because rushing could mean a mistake that could swallow us all.

One eye is on the riflescope, and with the other I watch through my zoomed-in contact lens as the soldiers feel the sting of the darts. They rouse themselves for a couple of seconds before they crash into unconsciousness. One after another they are hit. Twenty, thirty . . . and my side is done. Hala is still finishing off hers. She's slower, but she's an excellent shot. Now everything is still. The trees rustle under a cough of wind, and in the cage, the women shift a little, but the expanse of dirt that forms the main part of the camp is silent.

Hala glances at me with a look that's almost happy. We did a good job. But then, Caitlin's voice interrupts.

"Two o'clock."

Hala and I both swivel. A single soldier is up, running toward Ahmed's room. Thin legs and a torn jacket that flaps against his skinny frame. He's smart—darting from side to side, making it hard to take aim.

Except for me. Still caught in the momentum of his run, he drops forward onto his face, sprawled in the red dust. And everything is silent once again.

Caitlin sighs with relief and throws me a smile. Hala just shakes her head as if she can't believe the shot.

"Let's go," says Caitlin. "The trucks are coming."

I can just make out the low thrum of their engines as they head in, carefully timed, from the west. Those trucks are the only assistance the government of this place is giving us, once we've done the hard part. I scramble up, fold away my rifle, grab hold of our weapons, and follow the others down to the camp.

We step carefully among the soldiers. Mouths slack in forced sleep, defenseless. Hala sweeps over them with her weapon to be sure none of them has escaped our darts. Then she heads to the cage where the women stand staring, openmouthed, silent. We are all dressed in dust-colored, fitted combat clothes, with holsters, weapons, and boots. Our heads are now swathed in keffiyeh scarves that we've pulled up over our faces. Only our eyes are visible. Cell phones are everywhere, even out here, and we can't let anyone know who we are.

While Hala smashes open the cage door to free the women, Caitlin and I hurry past, toward Ahmed's hut. But the women are hesitant. Hala tries to reassure them that she is there to help.

"Try smiling," I mutter, and I know she's heard me in her earpiece because she shoots me a dirty look. Smiling is never her strong suit, but she gives it a try and it works. Now the women start to sidle out of the cage, toward the incoming rescue trucks.

At the hut, the two soldiers who were standing guard for Ahmed are down, asleep from our darts, and with any luck, Ahmed is snoring inside, so we can drug him too. We each have a dart gun—and a handgun, just in case. Our orders are to capture Ahmed alive and hand him over to the government forces, who'll take credit for finding him. That's the price we agreed to for securing the kidnapped women.

But as we are preparing to burst in on Ahmed, one of the trucks honks, again and again, as it approaches the camp. I look over, stressed. The escaped women have been running up to it, almost under its wheels, so the driver probably hit the horn on instinct—but the sheer volume of the sound is something else. There's no way Ahmed won't have heard it.

Anxious, Caitlin nods, and we move in—quickly, for every second we wait gives Ahmed time to turn the odds against us. The door is unlocked, and Caitlin opens it so I can enter, my handgun out in front of me. I feel Caitlin step in right behind me, solid, covering the other side of the room.

I stand there, gun out, feeling like an idiot. Because we planned, we plotted, we laid on the ground for an hour to make sure we weren't seen coming in, and we didn't count on this. That Ahmed might have girls in his room. The very people we've been sent here to save.

There are two of them, and they can't be more than fifteen. Had Ahmed still been asleep, it might not even have mattered. But the commotion outside has clearly roused him. And those extra three seconds have lost us the element of surprise. We're just not fast enough to get the girls out of the way before Ahmed has them in front of him, using them as handy human shields. Now my pistol is aimed at the girls instead of him while Ahmed's own gun grazes their heads from behind.

"Stay on him," Caitlin murmurs.

We keep our guns up and pointed at him. A standoff. But I can tell that he feels better, more in control, now that he has chips to bargain with. He is good-looking beneath the straggly beard. Somehow, I hadn't expected that, as if the vileness of his deeds should be reflected in his face. Sweat coats his forehead as his close-set eyes watch me back. The girls are sweating too, a sheen of moisture over the bruises on their faces, and one of them starts to cry.

"Quiet!" Ahmed commands her. But she's terrified, almost hysterical. The other girl whispers to her to stop, but the sobbing continues. It's making Ahmed edgy. He pushes her away, and with relief, the girl runs to a corner of the room and continues crying there.

"Let us take her," Caitlin says, trying to get at least one of them out of there.

But Ahmed's gun sweeps away from one hostage and toward the other. Before I can move, a shot blasts out, echoing off the walls like thunder. I jump, startled. The girl in the corner hits the floor. I stare at the wall behind where she stood. It's sprayed with blood. There is a moment of stillness. Then Caitlin makes a sort of gasping noise from her throat, and I feel my blood rise, the crimson bleeding of it blocking the rest of my sight.

Only Caitlin's voice brings me back, just. I can feel her arm brushing my own as she talks to Ahmed, and it feels right—Caitlin's arm and her voice—as if something good still exists in this brutal room.

"Take it easy. We're not here to kill you," Caitlin is saying.

My eyes glance at the dead girl on the floor. The remaining hostage pants with fear, her eyes screwed up tight, her head shaking beneath his pistol. Ahmed looks out the window, where more trucks holding government soldiers are arriving.

From above, I hear something, just a faint rustle, and into my ear and Caitlin's comes the sound of Hala's voice.

"I'm on the roof," she says.

I start to breathe again. A tiny shred of hope. She must have heard the shot and our exchange and done what she does best—climb. The building is topped with a poorly thatched roof, the wall beneath brown and smooth. It seems impossible that anyone could scale that wall, but Hala has. Her nickname back home had been *il bisseh*—"the cat." That was one of the first things she'd told me when she first started talking to me, in that depressing room in the detention center.

I know Hala must be struggling to get a shot on Ahmed, but I also know that her bullet is our best way out of this. I don't want to get caught in her line of fire, so I take two steps back, nice and easy, my eyes fixed on the girl's. If there is a God, I seriously doubt he'd let Ahmed exist. So now I'm just praying for Hala to sort this out.

"Bring him forward," Hala's tense voice whispers in my ear.

I watch Ahmed, his finger itching on that trigger while the girl gives a slight whimper. With my left hand I take a small grenade out of my pocket. Ahmed is wily, eyes like a fox. He sees something in my hand.

"Live grenade," I say, and toss it gently toward him. On instinct he lets go of the hostage and moves forward to catch it. When he does, he realizes the pin is still in it—and the pistol is blasted out of his hand. Hala's bullet takes a finger or two with it and he screams, a high whine that pierces the throbbing in my head and makes me feel better somehow. I move forward and take hold of the girl, while Caitlin knocks Ahmed to the ground with the butt of her pistol, retrieves the grenade, and handcuffs his hands and feet.

I start to become conscious of sounds again. It happens like this sometimes, when I focus hard—one sense drains away, leaving me oversensitive to another. But now the room is flooded with sound—with the whirr of helicopter blades, which must be our own chopper, sent to collect us; and the diesel throb of more trucks arriving outside. Ahmed, too, is aware, for his head turns toward the single window. Through it, I can see government troops jumping out of the trucks, dragging the drugged soldiers into the cage where the hostages had been held.

Beneath my hands, the girl's shoulders are thin and shaking. Her eyes fearful and distrustful. I hold her gaze for a moment and put an arm around her, trying to let her know that she'll be safe. Gently, I guide her toward the doorway and hand her over to Hala, who has appeared from the roof. Hala's glance goes to the corpse of the other girl. She flinches, then gives me an anguished look. I get it. Another life wasted. Another image to haunt us. I reach out to grasp Hala's shoulder. She accepts the touch, then turns away.

While Hala walks the remaining girl outside, I pull a limp, stained sheet off the bed and cover the body of the other girl. Her face is a mess, and I feel my stomach turn. But I don't want to throw up—it feels disrespectful—so I look away and take a couple of breaths, and then I kneel down, touching my hand to her forehead.

It's still warm, still real, and I check her neck for a pulse, but I know there isn't one. Her eyes are wide open in frozen fear, and I slip my fingers down to close them. Blood, her blood, gets onto my fingers. I look at the smears of red on my hand and gently wipe them away on my jacket.

Meanwhile, Caitlin is talking to Ahmed.

"You'll be arrested and given a fair trial—"

Ahmed interrupts her with a snort.

"They had to send *women* to get me." He smiles. "I'll be back in a year. And, little by little, I will take over this land."

As I listen, I feel an actual pain in my chest, but it's not physical—it's like what they call a heavy heart. When you know someone is right but you don't want to believe it. For the first time since we arrived here, I can see things clearly. Because we care about these kidnapped girls, we have come to help a government that is too weak to deal with terrorist factions themselves, in a country too divided. Long term, they can't fight a man like Ahmed; persistent, ruthless, arrogant. And maybe we can't either. If we play by rules that criminals like him just ignore.

I feel it bleeding back behind my eyes, the crimson, and it brings with it a sharp pain in my head. My skull feels like it's bursting.

Slowly, I stand up, away from the dead girl, and I pull my gun out of its holster. I turn it on Ahmed. I'm not rushing, but every movement is deliberate, impelled by something a little bit outside of me. Caitlin stares at me, her head shaking slightly.

"No, that's not the order."

But the sounds around me become grainy, disconnected. Ahmed's eyes are smirking, and in my ears there is the white noise of pulsing blood. I look at Ahmed—handcuffed, defenseless—and I hesitate to pull the trigger. And that hesitation makes him smile, because he feels safe. An arrogant smile that splits open his mouth and shows pearly teeth. Then, I don't think of anything except how easy it is to squeeze my index finger around the trigger, how smoothly the gun kicks back, and how quickly Ahmed slumps down, his chin on his chest.

Suddenly, Caitlin is shouting, Hala is at the door, taking in the mess, and the gun is snatched from my hand. I am pushed against the wall.

"Disarm her," Caitlin commands.

I don't try to argue. I can't think at all, so I obey. I place my hands up high on each side of my head and lean against the wall, while Hala uses her boot to push my feet wider apart. I feel Hala's methodical hands moving along my sides, my back and my legs. My breathing is quick and ragged. Part of me can't believe what I just did. I glance over my shoulder to look at Ahmed. It was a clean shot, of course, straight through his forehead. I stare at him. He was alive, and now he's dead. How easy it was—how fast—for me to snuff out a life. It's the first time I've ever done it, and, without warning, I feel sick. Bile rises in my throat, but I swallow it down with a dry heave. Taking a deep breath, I turn back to the wall and stand up tall. He raped these girls, and I just watched him kill one of them. So why should I care? And yet, somehow, I do.

"Disarm complete," says Hala, showing Caitlin an armful of weapons. *My* weapons.

Hala's eyes meet mine disapprovingly, and I pull a tiny jackknife out of my boot lining and pass it to her to prove she missed something. The petty, silent exchange with Hala gives me something else to think about for a second. But then the tiny piece of foil in my ear canal comes to life and a disembodied voice speaks sternly from thousands of miles away:

"What just happened?"

I bite my lower lip so hard that I taste blood. Caitlin touches the lapel camera on her clothes.

"Peggy, it's hard to explain—"

"We're hooked up to your cameras," Peggy interrupts, echoing in my ear. "We can see he's dead. Why?"

Caitlin hesitates. She doesn't want to be the one to state the obvious. To drop me in a pile of shit.

"I took him out, Peggy," I say, to save Caitlin the decision about how to reply.

"Was he a threat?" asks another voice that I recognize as Kit's. Despite the fact that she's my mother—or maybe *because* she's my mother—I immediately feel the impulse to annoy her.

"Yeah, to humanity."

The voices in London go quiet, and I know that I'm in serious trouble.

"Clean it up," Peggy says into our ears, and Caitlin nods to Hala, who swings a backpack off her shoulders. Reaching in, she extracts a pack of white gel blocks that look like those detergent tablets you put into dishwashers. Moving fast, but without seeming to rush, Hala covers the room, placing the blocks in all the corners and beneath Ahmed's body. Then she takes a tube from her bag and traces a line of gel between each tablet.

"Be careful," Caitlin tells her.

With a slight push to my shoulder, Caitlin guides me toward the door. I move quickly. Outside, our chopper waits, unmarked, blades turning, the body of it small and black against the red baked earth. Caitlin follows me outside, and we both break into a jog, heading for the open door of the chopper. We climb inside and wait, tensely, for Hala to emerge. When she does, she's running so fast she seems to blur in the glare of the sun.

"Go, go, go!" Caitlin calls to the pilot.

As she reaches the chopper, Hala ignores my outstretched hand but reaches for Caitlin's; she pulls her inside as the helicopter lifts smoothly away and, below us, Ahmed's building erupts in a roar of pure, cleansing flames.

2

AFTER THE CHOPPER, WE BOARD a private plane at a small airfield somewhere on the outskirts of the capital city. It's a long flight, but I don't sleep much. I'm dull-headed with exhaustion, but every time I fall asleep, I dream about Ahmed, so it's better to stay awake after a while. Hala is out like a light, but Caitlin's restless, at least until she goes for her pills. I feel her glance at me, but my eyes are mostly closed. I'm pretending to be asleep so she doesn't feel like she has to talk to me about killing Ahmed and analyze me to death; but even so, she pops the foil on the pills while they are still inside her backpack, and then she goes to the bathroom to take them. She saw a lot of stuff on her tours in Iraq, not just the usual horrors of war, but abuse handed out to Iraqi prisoners by the US soldiers. She tried to blow the whistle, but they threatened her with a dishonorable discharge and she backed down. Personally, I think that's why she takes the pills. Not that she can't stand what happened, but that she can't stand that she couldn't change it. On top of that, her early life in Kentucky was like a bad country-and-western song. If she needs some help dealing with it all, so what? But she won't admit to it. It's funny when people need to pretend to themselves that they have their shit together. Caitlin reminds me of the Athena leaders that way. She's older than Hala and me—late twenties—and sometimes she feels more like one of them than one of us.

That gets me thinking about them, the women who are our bosses, the women who started Athena. The ones who recruited us, trained us, and who pay us to execute orders. You won't find a more accomplished group of high achievers anywhere, and I'm pretty sure a couple of them have been in similar situations to the one we're in now, though they never talk about it and it's not on their résumés or Wikipedia pages. They're all successful, driven, and disciplined in their own ways (even Kit). They didn't get where they are by tolerating people who don't listen, and I know that, one way or another, I'm in for it big-time when we land.

Which is why I creep into the house at 2:00 a.m. even more quietly than usual. I really don't want Kit to hear me. Most of the time it doesn't bug me to live with my mother, but at moments like this I wish I had my own place. The house is big though—one of those old, white stucco homes in Notting Hill. Kit bought it fifteen years ago, when she was still a pretty well-known music star, and it's probably the best investment she ever made. I avoid the front door entirely, because it always creaks and you can't shut it without making the whole house shudder. Instead, I use a drainpipe and a wisteria branch to climb up to the window of my room. You can edge a little knife blade under the frame and lever it open. I drop my bag onto the wooden floor and slip inside.

It smells like home. Like furniture polish and that expensive lemon room spray Kit likes, and like pasta sauce or something with tomatoes. My stomach grumbles with hunger, but going downstairs might wake up my mother, and that would mean a postmortem about Ahmed. I decide to risk a shower because I can't stand the smell of dust and sweat any longer. And just in time, I'm in bed. About five minutes after I'm lying down in the dark, my bedroom door opens. Luckily, I'm turned on my side, away from it. I keep my eyes closed and breathe softly and deeply. Kit stands there for ages, and I just wait, wondering if she ever bothered to check on me like this when I was younger. I don't remember it, and maybe I would have been asleep anyway. But the truth is, Kit wasn't home much when I was a kid. Her career took priority, and that meant a lot of touring.

Finally, the door shuts. Pretending to sleep has made me drowsy. I drop off within minutes and wake up at seven the next morning— finding, with relief, that I've dreamed of nothing at all.

I roll onto my back and look at the ceiling where a strip of sunlight ripples across the white paint. There is a pit of tension in the base of my stomach because there's a meeting at Athena headquarters this morning, and I'm pretty sure I'm going to be court-martialed. Or whatever you do to operatives who work for a private agency that nobody else knows exists. I think over where everyone is now.

Hala and Caitlin will be home in their respective apartments, getting dressed, drinking coffee. Or mint tea, in Hala's case. Li, one of the three cofounders—along with Kit and Peggy—is doubtless meditating in her spotless white living room, or on a conference call with her technology company in Shanghai.

I hear footsteps outside my door. Kit knocks softly and puts her head in.

"I didn't hear you come in," she says.

"I tried not to wake you."

She nods. She doesn't mention that she checked on me. She steps into the room, and I sort of sit up in the bed. She is fully dressed—skinny black jeans and cowboy boots—and in one hand she has a cup of green tea. There's always an air of glamour about Kit, which is in no way diminished by her working-class accent. She makes everything look easy, and always moves with grace. If she wasn't famous or you'd never heard of her, you'd still turn to look when she walks into a room. I can't work out if it's something that you pick up when you become a star or if it's why you become a star to begin with. She sits down on the edge of my bed and just sort of examines me for a few seconds. Is she looking at me, her daughter, and seeing a killer? I look down and swallow. Which spurs her into speech.

"I know you probably want to talk," she starts.

Yeah, right.

"But I think it's better if we wait till I meet with Peggy and Li."

I nod.

"I'm going to get a coffee," Kit says. "Want to come?"

I shake my head, feeling miserable. So we can sit and make small talk about the weather while I wait for the Athena ax to fall? I think not.

"Well, there's bread downstairs. Have an egg. For protein."

I still can't get my head around the way Kit has turned into the mother of the year, but only since I left to join the Program, which was when I was fifteen. And it's continued since she brought me back, to join Athena. She's always after me to eat eggs, finish my vegetables, and wear warm clothes. Where was she when I was six years old and actually needed that stuff?

It's as if she can read my stubborn defiance, even though I haven't said a word. She gets up and leaves, and as soon as the door clicks shut, I reach for the TV remote and flick on the news. I lie back in my bed and watch the end of a report on a gun attack in Los Angeles. The next item is a reporter outside the Houses of Parliament bringing us all up to speed on some boring piece of legislation. My eyes start to close again, lulled by that peculiar pattern of speech that all news people seem to have. And then I hear the word *Cameroon*. The African country we've just returned from. I scramble to the end of the bed and turn up the volume. The studio newsreader hands over to Jake Graham, who is reporting from outside the Cameroon High Commission in London. He's well-known, Jake. Lean and rumpled, with hair that always looks a bit overdue for a cut. A good journalist, one of the earnest ones, a real crusader type out there in the trenches. I'm not thrilled he's been given this story.

"It's a happy ending for the young women who were kidnapped

by religious militants three months ago," Jake explains on air. "The daring rescue ended with the assassination of militia leader Ahmed Dawood."

I watch, dry-mouthed, as Jake squints into the camera and the sun.

"The United States and major European governments say they were not involved in what looks like a lean, almost vigilante-style operation. And so the question remains—how did this happen?"

Jake looks out from the screen directly into my eyes.

I'm tense. I didn't expect this—and I can imagine that Li, who's all over everything that gets onto every news channel, will be freaking out, especially about that "vigilante" comment. My only hope is that somehow it will all blow over. Nobody here had ever heard of Cameroon before the kidnappings, and they'd forgotten all about those captured girls till this morning. Don't tell me they're going to give a toss by tomorrow.

Irritable, I head to the bathroom to get ready. But I avoid looking at myself in the mirror. I just can't. It's like I'm not the same person today as I was yesterday. Before Ahmed. Which is just the kind of revealing psychological detail the Athena therapist would love. Maybe I'll save it to tell her, and make her day, since those sessions bore me to tears most of the time. Quickly, I get dressed. In the light of day, away from the chaos of the mission, I feel guilty about taking a life when I wasn't being threatened. But then I remind myself whose life it was. Ahmed kidnapped and abused those girls, so didn't he have it coming? The thought is not as reassuring as I'd like it to be. I grab my backpack and head out.

■ ■ ■

The tube is crowded. It's hard to believe that it was only yesterday morning when I was faced with miles of land and nobody in sight. I shift slightly, turning my head away from the smell of shampoo mixed with early-morning perspiration that always fills the underground train in summer. My stop marks the very beginning of the City, as in the City of London—the part where most of the major financial corporations and some of the tech companies are based.

I push my way out with the tide of commuters and stick to the left-hand side on the endless escalator, taking it two steps at a time, leaving behind the underworld of crowded tunnels and warm rushes of fetid wind. With a swipe of my travel card over the automated machines, I am out and breathing the morning air within seconds. The breeze from the river carries a faint tinge of exhaust fumes. As I walk to the office, I turn to look at the gray water, sparkling in the unfamiliar sun, and the bridges and the buildings that rise, gleaming, above them. Never in a million years would I have imagined coming to an office here. These buildings, the people rushing to work, have always felt so corporate. But here I am—though hardly a nine-to-fiver, I suppose.

I walk past my place of work, keeping to the other side of the street. The building is a sleek, rising tower with chrome letters six feet high: CHEN TECHNOLOGIES. CT is a real company—or group of companies—and a powerhouse in the technology world, started by Li Chen in Shanghai, and now spreading globally. Turns out it's also the perfect, legitimate company to hide our much smaller, unsanctioned organization. As I pass the massive front doors of the building, Li herself arrives in a black Tesla. Which is cool enough that passing traffic slows down a bit to look. Her driver stops precisely by the entrance, and the car doors rise up vertically. Li doesn't like to waste those minutes between arrival and reaching her desk, so her assistant, Thomas, always meets her as she pulls up, and briefs her on the day to come. Thomas is also one of the few people she trusts to know about Athena. Meanwhile, legitimate technology employees flow past her and into the building, a wide stream of faded jeans, backpacks, and paper coffee cups. As if Li is Moses or something, the stream parts to let her walk through in her tailored suit and designer shoes. I continue on, past the office, then cross the road, turn left into a small back street, and then left again into an alleyway that winds back to the rear of the building.

We joke that this is the tradesman's entrance. Li can come in through the main door—the building has her name on the front and houses eight hundred of her employees. Kit and Peggy get driven in through the underground garage, to a private entrance and a secure lift that takes them directly up to the Athena floor. But the rest of us come in this way. A quiet back alley that leads to a plain metal garage door, operated using a hidden fingerprint pad down low near the ground where no one would think to look. When I touch my index finger to the pad, the door stays resolutely closed, and for a moment I hesitate. Have they actually locked me out for what I did? I wipe my hand on my jeans because it's sweaty, try it again—and the door slides up.

Inside is a garage and another door at the back, which leads nowhere, and then a door to the right, which is the one we use. A tap on an unmarked metal plate with an innocuous-looking credit card gets me through that, and into our elevator. There are no buttons in here, only a screen. I step up to it, hold still, and wait for my iris to be scanned. The pale-blue light slips over my eye and confirms it belongs to me. The screen then displays a menu of bland choices, none of which would make sense to anyone—things like *Option 1* (which goes to the main Athena floor, where the operations room is, and where Kit, Li, and Peggy have their offices) and *Option 2*—the tech cave. I can't remember why we call it the tech cave, because it's not underground. Maybe because Amber, who's in charge of it, guards it like a bear. . . . It has a great view over the city, but the windows are one-way only—we can see out, but from the outside it looks like mirrored glass. It's where all our weapons, passports, spare clothes, and body armor are kept under lock and key by Amber—and her beloved new technology is also tested out on this floor, somewhere.

I use my eye like a mouse—moving the screen cursor over to Option 1 and then blinking twice to choose it. Apparently, it's unbreakable security. Finally, the elevator starts to move up. And as it does, I feel my stomach drop to the bottom of my shoes.

By shooting Ahmed, I compromised the secrecy of Athena, and I know that secrecy is the one thing we cannot survive without. To the outside world, Athena does not exist. We're not some black-ops division of British Intelligence or a CIA experiment. What Peggy, Kit, and Li have done is start something that *nobody* sanctions. The upside is, they don't report to anyone, and they don't get tied up in red tape. The downside is obvious. We'd all end up in jail if anyone figured out what we're up to. So I know I've really messed up.

It's funny but, of all of them, it's Peggy I feel worst about letting down. Maybe because she's the one who would be the most understanding. She's just one of those kind, really decent people, who never judge without hearing you out. Peggy is American. East Coast, Ivy League, smart as a whip. I doubt there were many other African American women knocking around Harvard doing law degrees thirty years ago, but it's not something she brags about. Always super well-turned-out, she looks like she spends half her life going to the opera and ballet, and the other half at high-end charity luncheons. She was the US ambassador in London for a few years— and she was also CIA in her time. One way or another, she seems to have contacts in every country. She met Li when they were both UN Goodwill ambassadors.

Li grew up during the Cultural Revolution in China. She never mentions it, but she was taken from her family as a girl and forced to work for the government. Which is where I imagine the story gets interesting—the rumor is that Li became something big in Chinese Intelligence. More than that is a mystery. I know how to trawl online for obscure details as well as anybody, but you can't find any information on Li anywhere, beyond the bland *Fortune* and *Forbes* magazine profiles.

As for Kit—well, what do music stars do when they stop selling records and start panicking about getting older? In my mother's case, she came out as a campaigner for women's rights. To be fair, Kit was an activist and feminist from her teens, and, boy, did she like to tell me all about it when I wouldn't come with her to a rally or sign yet *another* petition. She used to lecture me about being part of a lost generation of self-absorbed kids who didn't care the world was going to hell. Most of those talks were held late in the evening when she was halfway through a bottle of vodka, which sort of reduced the impact. Then she spent a year traveling around Eastern Europe, Africa, and India, taking publicity shots for the UN with women and girls who were living in poverty or overcoming the odds. It definitely gave both Kit and the UN some good coverage in the press.

Until what happened in Pakistan. Nobody saw that coming, and it changed all three of them. It was the start of Athena, which was something so unique, so off the charts, that I didn't even hesitate to jump ship from the Program and be part of it. If you'd told me I would ever work for my mother, I'd have laughed in your face. But here I am.

Thomas meets me as the lift door opens. He knows to expect me because Amber put an app on his phone that pings, or barks, or something, every time one of us scans in through the alley door.

We turn left, toward the situation room and the founders' offices. Those all sit behind another sealed door. To the right is a corridor leading to the operations room. Ops is a big space, filled with screens: those clear, floating screens that are kind of projected into a space. At various times, they hold headshots, heat maps, research, analysis patterns. A lot of boring online search stuff too. Caitlin, Hala, and I do a fair amount of background work ourselves on the missions that Athena is considering pursuing. Other than us, we have only a few analysts, and I've never met them. I guess they're a small core of employees that Li feels she can trust—or maybe people she has something on. Who knows for sure? Li is really careful to silo people. If you're in tech development, that's all you work on. And when I need something from the tech team, there's only one person I deal with—Amber. So I suppose that none of us really know the true extent of Athena.

"You're late," says Thomas. "Did you oversleep?"

He walks alongside me. In fact, just ahead of me, giving me the feeling that he's escorting me on purpose.

"I never oversleep," I tell him.

"You just *chose* to be late today of all days?"

When I'm in trouble, he means.

Thomas is about thirty and has worked with Li as some kind of über-assistant since he graduated from university. He shares Li's obsession with perfect grooming. There are no unruly eyebrows or loosened neckties anywhere near Thomas, and no one ever shortens his name to Tom. He consults his smart watch compulsively. It seems to display a constant stream of instant messages from Li—except, I suppose, when she is busy meditating or doing yoga, both of which she swears by and tries to get all of us to do.

We're almost at the situation room, where a meeting is just underway. Inside the glass panels I can see that Li has just arrived. Hala is munching on an apple, and she and Caitlin are listening to Peggy, who is sitting opposite them, alongside Kit. With a flick of his security card, Thomas activates the door of the situation room, which slides open for me to enter. The click of the door makes everyone look up, and I swallow, but not so that anyone would notice. I turn to glance back at Thomas, but his eyes have moved to Hala, with whom he exchanges a quick smile. Not for the first time, I wonder if he carries a torch for Hala—and yet, the two of them together just seems so unlikely. Behind me, the door slides shut, and Thomas walks away, leaving the room in silence. Caitlin and Peggy nod at me, Hala avoids any eye contact, and Li and Kit exchange looks. I sit off to one side, pour some coffee, and look up at the expansive, floating screen. On it is a headshot of a handsome man with flecks of gray at his temples.

Moving past the interruption of my entrance, Peggy directs everyone's eyes back to the screen, where, by all accounts, they are briefing the next assignment. We've all done some background prep on it before we went to Africa—especially me—so it's familiar, but now that it's time for the mission to be run, Peggy will be looking to do a recap and give everyone the concrete steps and timeline to execute it. I don't want to get too comfortable, but I'm relieved. At least we're moving on and not picking over the carcass of the old mission. And they let me in here. Maybe they're not that fussed that Ahmed took a bullet after all.

"You're all familiar with Gregory Pavlic by now," Peggy is saying. "He owns casinos and restaurants, but he makes his real money trafficking women out of Eastern Europe."

"Him and a hundred others," says Hala through a mouthful of apple. She wipes her mouth on her sleeve. Discreetly, kindly, Peggy hands Hala a tissue. Hala looks surprised. She puts it in her pocket, then uses her sleeve again, and I try not to smile. Really, I can't imagine Thomas could actually go for Hala. I mean, she's a nice person under that scowl, but her table manners are terrible, while he looks ready to take tea with the queen every day.

"Yes. But if we get Gregory, a lot of the others go down with him," Kit says, looking at everyone in turn—except for me.

"Gregory plans long term," Li says. "He's spent years building relationships with scores of Eastern European politicians, showing them the high life. Between gambling, sex, and drugs, he has incriminating digital files on almost all of them."

I watch Li as she talks. She's in a neat navy suit, and she's wearing her digital glove. Li adores that glove, uses it to do things that she could easily manage with the click of a mouse. It does look good though, encasing her hand in a delicate mesh of fabric, shot through with copper-colored wires. With a flick of her index finger, Li switches the photograph of Gregory Pavlic on the screen with another. An elegant man with a wry smile, a little older than Pavlic. I notice Peggy's eyes soften as she looks at the picture.

"Aleks Yuchic, Serbia's justice minister," Peggy says. "One of the few politicians who's stayed clean."

"How do we know?" Caitlin asks. She hasn't seen the research on Aleks—she focused on studying Gregory.

"Well—on a personal level, he and I were great friends when I was ambassador," Peggy explains. "He knows all about Gregory's business but has no way to close it down because so many high-ranking judges and officials are implicated in Gregory's files. We'll get him those files to prove Gregory's blackmail tactics, along with hard evidence of what Gregory's doing, and then he'll find a long-term solution."

Once Peggy's given us the cuddly, friendly version of why she trusts Aleks, it's Li's turn to chime in and confirm that every possible background check has been run on Aleks and there isn't a bank account to be found in any offshore haven that could possibly connect to him.

"Jessie did most of the work on him," Peggy adds. "I thought it would be useful for her to brief us all on that."

A few eyes turn to look at me. It's true, I've been working on Aleks, long before we left for Cameroon. We usually research one mission ahead. Peggy nods at me to elaborate. Typical of her to be kind, to try to include me. I clear my throat and explain.

"I sent a virus to his computer and—"

"How?" interrupts Hala. I shift in my seat. It's not the kind of question that matters in a high-level briefing like this, but Hala's clearly making a point to hit out at me.

"I embedded it in a take-away menu from his favorite restaurant. When he opened the email, I had access to his entire hard drive. Then I used Li's celltrax software to get into his phone, and, since you're so concerned—"

"We've been watching everything he emails, texts, and receives ever since," says Peggy, lightly, stepping in to calm my rising indignation at Hala. "He's clean."

A wave of Li's glove brings up a 3D plan of Gregory's home that zooms in and around the room where they have found the digital files are being kept in a safe. I lean forward. How we get into Gregory's home and his safe is the part that Athena has been working on round the clock—and the part we agents haven't heard about yet.

"I guess we can't just walk in the front door," Caitlin says.

"Actually, we can," says Kit. "Turns out Gregory's a fan of mine, and I told my managers I want some cash from a private gig. So they got the word out, and now Gregory thinks it was *his* idea to pay me a fortune to come out of retirement and play his fiftieth birthday party next week. That's why we moved the date of this mission forward."

I sputter into my coffee. Not entirely by accident. Finally, everyone looks at me—except Hala.

"How is that a safe plan?" I ask. Seriously, I can't believe what I'm hearing. My mother, who hasn't played a gig in ages, is planning to stroll into the home of one of the worst human traffickers on the planet and *sing* for him while we steal data from his safe? I stare at Kit in disbelief. Her eyes move down, and that tiny muscle in her jaw flickers—a sure sign that she's angry. I wait for her to say something, to defend this daft plan, but Caitlin steps in.

"We're trained to do this job, Kit." Even she thinks it's a mad idea. But she's more polite about it than me.

"Yeah, but you can't sing my greatest hits," Kit returns. "You need me to get into Gregory's estate." My mother is looking mainly at me, exerting a bit of authority. I sniff and look away.

"It's unusual," Peggy says, "but overall, our analysis is that it's far safer to have Kit there with Caitlin as her bodyguard—as Gregory's guests—than to risk trying to break in. His security is impressive."

With an elegant wave of the glove, Li turns off the screen and instructs Caitlin and Hala to go down to the tech cave to see Amber for further preparation. They get up and move to the door, and so do the others. I shift.

"What am I doing?"

I hadn't meant to ask that. It sounds childish and indignant. But actually being ignored by my team terrifies me. To my surprise, out of all the women in the room, it is Hala who responds.

"Good question," she says. "What *are* you doing? Except disobeying orders?"

I liked it better when she was ignoring me. But I let her have it.

"I'm *thinking* about what we do here. What did you think Ahmed's soldiers were going to do when they woke up? Start a feminist group?"

Hala throws me a superior look.

"You're not paid to think," she says. "Just do your job. For a change."

What? I fly at Hala before I realize what I'm doing. She's surprised but dodges and lashes back. We're in it now, hand-to-hand, fast and hard, hits, kicks, blocks . . . but then my legs give from under me and I'm on the floor. Caitlin stares down at me, appalled, and I realize she's swept at my legs with her feet and brought me down. Now, she grabs Hala's shoulder and steers her toward the door.

"I vouched for you when you needed asylum and everyone thought you were a terrorist," I call after Hala.

She doesn't answer, but Caitlin gives me a look to shut up, and I do. I dust myself off as the Athena leaders exchange glances, glances that feel long and meaningful and which Kit answers with a nod. None of that silent interaction thrills me. But I'm upset with Hala. I know she's a stickler and she's upset I broke the rules, but when she was locked up in a UK detention center, it was *me* who helped get her asylum application through. Not to mention brought her on board with Athena. A little gratitude would be nice.

I take a breath as Peggy walks out, and then Li. Only Kit stays back, and I wait for her to leave, but she doesn't. Instead, she indicates the chair next to her own.

Reluctantly, I sit, and the chair is very close—too close. For a long moment, Kit says nothing; she just shuffles papers. Probably giving me a minute to settle down after the drama with Hala. I sit quietly, and—without wanting to—I catch that smell that is only Kit's: a combination of skin, hair, and perfume that slams me back into the past. For a moment, I'm seven years old again and being carried upstairs to bed after falling asleep on the couch while my mother and her friends talked and played the guitar until late. The same scent that touches me now, I had known then, my face buried in Kit's hair, my legs wrapped tight around her waist.

"I know you managed to follow orders in the Program," Kit says.

With a blink, I snap back to this room, and it's as if the short distance between us on the chairs has suddenly become a gulf that I don't know how to cross. I edge my chair away a little, as if I'm trying to get more comfortable, but, really, I want to put some space between me and that scent, and those memories.

"Sorry, what?"

"You followed orders in the Program," repeats Kit. She stresses the word *Program* with something like sarcasm.

I finished school early, when I was fifteen. And I mean *finished*, like, ready to go to university. I was always good with math and physics and stuff. I like the order and logic of those subjects.

But I was too young to start college. And another private school got in touch, saying they focused on gifted kids. When I started there, it turned out that it wasn't just academics but also physical stuff, like target practice and three-hour runs—which should have given us a clue they were up to something more. That school turned out to be a feeder for the Program—this elite training regime, meant to create a modern "army" to fight cybercrime and all that by contracting out their employees to the government and big corporations.

Part of me liked it. Being in a place where there were rules and boundaries and a place you always had to be. There were no rules in our house growing up. I could stay up late, eat what I felt like. Kit didn't want to stifle my creativity, but I didn't notice that hers got any better when she was blind drunk and awake half the night. On the surface, my childhood sounds like what every teenager would want, but when you've had it all your life, you just want someone to care enough to tell you to go to bed, or eat an apple, or whatever. By the time I was fifteen, I felt as if I was floating the whole time. In limbo. And the Program felt like the opposite. Plus, after basic training, I got to specialize in electronics and bomb defusing, and all the things that I came to love.

"Athena isn't the government," I say. "I quit the Program because I hated having my hands tied."

"You're right about Athena," Kit says. "We're not elected, and we're not legal. If we're exposed, we all go to jail. We were on the morning news, Jessie."

I nod, because I know that's true, and I feel terrible about it. Kit looks down.

"Jessie—you're fired."

I just stare at her for a moment. I actually feel my mouth open and close, like a fish.

"You—you mean suspended?" I stammer, at last.

But Kit shakes her head. "We've talked about it, and your work with Athena is over. You'll need to brief the others on what you know about Aleks and this mission before we all leave for Belgrade. But that's it."

Then she stands up and stretches out her hand. I look at the palm blankly, at the familiar silver rings on Kit's middle fingers. What is she doing?

"I need your pass," says Kit.

She doesn't meet my gaze, which is good, because the lack of trust hurts more than I want to let her see. I reach into the back pocket of my jeans and pull out the small electronic card that gives me access to these offices. I place it into Kit's palm, and as her fingers close over it, I feel my frustration forcing its way out, bursting through cracks.

"You never wanted me in the field," I say, and to my annoyance, Kit nods in agreement.

"That's true. You're my child, Jess. But I thought at least at Athena, I could keep an eye on you."

"So you want me tied to some desk job somewhere? Why? You never gave a toss about me when you were on tour my whole life."

Kit glares at me. "This is about what you did to Ahmed."

I just want my job back. And I also just want Ahmed's face *not* to be there every time I close my eyes. I wish I hadn't done what I did. Deep down, I know this is how it should be, that it's even fair—but I can't make myself admit it to my mother. Kit clears her throat. I look up, hoping for reprieve.

"A team is only as strong as each person on it," she says seriously.

Oh my days. If there is anything I can't stand, it's when my mother sounds like a quote from an inspirational calendar.

Kit picks up her designer bag and prepares to leave. Without waiting for an answer. Infuriated, I follow her to the door.

"I'm your best agent," I say.

"Others are being recruited," Kit returns.

Well, that's a shock to me. As far as I know, it's only the three of us agents here. Caitlin was brought in because she worked for Peggy at the embassy after leaving the army. I recruited Hala myself. And it's because I'm Kit's daughter that I'm trusted here. *Was* trusted.

"How do you know you can trust them—these new agents?"

"We don't. Not yet. But if they ever make it onto this floor, they won't disregard orders. Or get into physical fights with their team-mates. I'm *embarrassed* that you—"

That knocks me, and maybe Kit sees it, because she bites off her anger and stops talking. Both of us are silent for a minute, then I glance at her again, looking for a chink, a way back in, a way to convince her. But there isn't one; I can see that. Once, when I was much younger, I saw Kit slam the front door after a fight with a boyfriend, then pick up a guitar and smash it onto the floor. At the time it had scared me, but, looking back, I had despised the behavior of my mother, the tantrum of a rock star trading in clichés. Kit turns, and I can see the same flinty spark in her eyes; I can see the effort she is making not to raise her voice again.

"You're special, Jess," she says at last. "But you're so immature. And nobody's indispensable."

And my mother opens the door and walks out without giving me another glance.

3

THAT PHRASE "DRAGGING YOUR FEET" has never meant much to me, because I've always loved what I do. Until now. Now, I listen to my own steps shuffling along the gleaming wooden floor, and it's the sound of misery.

I always knew Athena was important to me, but now that I have to leave it, it suddenly feels like it means *everything*.

It all began, in a way, in Pakistan. Kit was supporting a school for girls, in a northern province where Taliban influences still lingered and girls were hardly ever educated. She contacted Peggy for help pushing it through the UN's slow approval process. She knew Peggy pretty well. They had met first at a White House lunch, I think, because they were both into women's and children's causes. But they ended up becoming real friends, especially once Peggy moved to London to be the American ambassador. Anyway, Peggy got on board with the school and got Li to sponsor it. That was Li's first shot at major charity work apparently. What a start. No wonder she's less than thrilled with government agencies now.

Anyway, they all met up in Lahore and drove for hours to open this school formally. It was a big deal, from what Kit said. UN officials, the whole village out in force, TV cameras. So they open the schoolhouse and attend the first lesson—more than twenty girls, all as excited as anything. Then they eat with the villagers who've laid out this huge feast for the three of them. And then they drive back to their hotel to get a good night's sleep and wait for the flight home the next day. Except Peggy switches on the news in her room while she and Kit are having a congratulatory drink—and they see that there's been a fire in a northern village. Kit said she didn't even connect it with *their* village till she recognized a guy on the TV screen, hauling buckets. A villager who didn't want his twin girls to attend because the local tribal leader was taking money from the Taliban and he feared for their safety. Kit had spent ages persuading him to send the girls to school. And he did. And now she's watching him on the TV news, trying to douse ten-feet-high flames with a bucket.

They hustled a car and driver to take them back up there immediately, and by the time they made it, there was nothing much left of the school. Or the girls. Kit has never spoken about the rest of that night to me—about what she saw or how they faced the villagers— and neither has Peggy or Li. But I saw news pictures online, later. The one I'll always remember is rows of white sheets, each of them covering a small body. It makes me sick just to remember the photo. I can't even imagine how Kit felt. So when she came back from

Pakistan and hit the bottle harder than ever, I cut back on the sarcasm and stopped the fights. I didn't have a better solution at the time, but I suppose she did.

Or, rather, Peggy did. Because somewhere in the ashes of that brutal fire, the idea for Athena was born. Li had the money to bankroll a private agency that would fight for women and children. And after growing up under Chinese communism, she'd probably had enough of waiting for governments to solve the world's problems. Like Peggy, she was completely disillusioned in Pakistan. And like Peggy, she probably had some skills and experience with intelligence work. Kit was the last on board, and I'm pretty sure that was because Peggy wanted to help her out of the darkness that she was stuck in after Pakistan. And soon after that, Kit asked me to help her—and I was happy that she asked. Not that I wanted her to be as crushed as she was—just that I wanted us to be there for each other, like a real family. So I agreed. Everything I was learning in the Program— weapons, coding—could only be useful to Athena, and this would be something where, as Peggy told me, I wouldn't be just a hired operative with no idea of whose wars I'd be fighting and why.

Except now. Now, the fight will go on, but I won't have anything to do with it.

At the elevator, Thomas is waiting. His glance slips away from mine as I approach.

"I've arranged a ride home for you," he says.

I'm about to snap at him that he can keep his ride, that I'll take the tube back, when Peggy's voice interrupts.

"Got a minute?"

Peggy bustles toward us. She wears a gray tweed suit flecked with pink. Her hair is immaculate, her accessories perfect. She must have had *lessons* on how to dress, growing up in New York on the Upper East Side. Which is fine if you want to look like Jackie Kennedy or Michelle Obama, I suppose, but sometimes all that perfection is just annoying. I'm also sure Peggy went to etiquette school, or something, somewhere along the way. But she's not snooty about any of it. It's just who she is; kind, decent, correct.

As Peggy reaches me, she gives Thomas a nod to get lost, and he glides off. Then there's an awkward pause, and I try to keep my eyes on the floor, but Peggy takes advantage of a moment of slippery eye contact.

"Your mother's worried about you," she says.

"First time in history."

Peggy's gaze holds enough disappointment to make me feel ashamed of myself briefly. My sarcasm's become a habit, I realize. I remember Kit's regular admonishments that good habits lead to success and bad habits lead to failure. Another maxim my mother appears to have picked up in the past couple of years, no doubt from a support-group meeting.

"If you won't talk to her," Peggy says, "talk to me."

"About what?"

"How you're feeling."

Peggy's tone is so kind that I actually want to cry. Maybe she sees that, because she takes my arm and guides me aside, into a smaller office where we are really alone, away from all the glass. But I refuse to cry here, in front of Peggy. I'm not unhinged or traumatized, even though the others think I am. I turn to Peggy, newly energized by anger.

"You really want to know how I feel?" I say. "I'm happy. Happy Ahmed is dead. Happy he'll never abuse or kill another girl."

"You don't look happy," Peggy says. She hesitates. Then she speaks again, her voice lower.

"Your first kill is never easy, and it always gives you nightmares."

Right, then. So maybe the CIA job was more than just desk work and surveillance. I shift a bit under her gaze. It's like she knows everything about what's really going on inside me.

"That's why we have a protocol, Jessie," Peggy continues. "To *protect*, not to kill. Unless absolutely necessary."

"Yeah, I read the manual," I tell her. "It sucks on the ground though."

I feel Peggy inhale and hold back a reply, and I take the chance to ask a question—something that's been bugging me since this whole Ahmed thing began.

"Peggy, what if you can't finish people like Ahmed by putting them on trial? What if you have to fight fire with fire?"

"An eye for an eye?" The soft brown of Peggy's eyes turns to steel, but I shrug.

"That's what Ahmed understands."

"Perhaps, but this isn't about him; it's about Athena."

"I get it," I tell her. "We have orders, and I broke them."

But Peggy shakes her head.

"No, I mean Athena, the Greek goddess of war. Also, of justice. And wisdom."

I'm not imagining the emphasis Peggy puts on that last quality. Clearly implying that I lack it. We all know this classical reference because it forms the backbone of the work we do here, but I'm not in the mood for the Athena pep talk.

"Take me to Belgrade," I say desperately.

Peggy studies me. "I'm as unhappy about this as you are," she says. "We've prepared for this mission for months, and it was planned with three operatives. We didn't expect to be down to two."

"Then take me with you. I've learned my lesson."

"You just told me you were happy Ahmed was dead."

Me and my big mouth.

"You know, we were on the fence with you," Peggy continues. "Whether to fire you or just try desk duty for a spell. It's not great for us to lose your skills. But, Jessie—fighting with Hala in the situation room? In a meeting?" She shakes her head, reproachful. "Self-control is nonnegotiable in what we do."

"You don't know what it's like," I say. My voice comes out as a whisper, my eyes are on the floor.

"What do you mean?" Peggy says.

I stare at my shoes, looking for words. But I can't explain it. Peggy and Li and Kit can't get what it's like to constantly fight physically against people who'd kill you in a heartbeat. Something savage, kind of raw, flips a switch in my mind and I can't just turn it off and think clearly the moment I'm done. None of us can. Caitlin and Hala are just better at hiding it than me.

Peggy's still waiting for me to speak. But I can only shake my head. She reaches out a hand and pulls me toward her. Before I know it, she has me in a hug. I relax into it after a moment.

"Come with me," Peggy's voice says by my ear. She pulls back to look at me.

"Where?"

"To the Cameroon High Commission. I need an assistant to take notes, and you can see how you've changed the lives of those girls you saved."

Ten minutes ago, taking notes like someone's PA in a stuffy embassy would have been my idea of boredom. But right now, I don't want to go home and stare at the walls and think about the rest of my life. I nod, and Peggy walks me back out to the elevator and down to the basement garage, where her car and driver are waiting.

While the rest of us finish a job and then go straight on to the next one, Peggy usually ends up still working on the previous mission for some time. Her idea coming into Athena was that it's fine to rescue women and girls, but then what? Most of them don't have the education or training to move forward, so they end up vulnerable to the same people we've tried to get them away from. So Peggy uses her political contacts and her charity connections to arrange long-term solutions in each case. *Sustainable* is one of her favorite words, and everyone thinks that Peggy is nothing more than a do-gooder; a well-meaning retired ambassador with too much time and money on her hands.

Peggy starts explaining how she's raised funding to provide counseling for the girls Ahmed kidnapped. It's pretty amazing to hear—and yet, I stop listening after a bit because my mind is replaying that moment I pulled the trigger on Ahmed, trying to remember what I felt.

I blink, watching a different London pass by outside the car window, more spacious and genteel than the heart of the City, with its clustered, modern buildings. Now we're cruising through leafy streets lined with trees, past redbrick homes similar to Peggy's own Chelsea apartment building.

One minute, I wish I hadn't killed Ahmed; the next, I can remember only that poor dead girl on the floor—he took her life, and so many others, so brutally—can it really be a bad thing that he's dead? My mind is racing all over the place; I'm relieved when the car pulls up. But, if you can believe it, who's standing there but Jake Graham, the TV news guy. Talk about bad luck. We get out of the car, and there he is, in this iron-railed London square, right outside the Cameroon High Commission. He reported from here two hours ago, so what on earth is he hanging around for? Behind him, a cameraman winds up cables. If we'd arrived ten minutes later, he would probably have been gone.

Peggy hands me some files, and I follow her to the steps of the building. We are already partway up when Jake strides over and steps up next to Peggy. His eyes flit across me briefly and I turn away, moving ahead as if we're late. Peggy giving me the files was a smart move, and I'm grateful I bothered to put on my blue jacket. It dresses up the jeans and shirt enough that I might be some meaningless assistant.

"Mrs. Delaney," he says. "What are you doing here?" His tone is pleasant, but he's on her like a ton of bricks.

"Lovely to see you, Jake," Peggy responds. "Good report this morning."

"Thanks. I've been waiting around to get a comment about who killed Ahmed and saved those girls."

Peggy's poker face gives nothing away.

"And? Who did?" she asks. Really, I love the way she looks at him, like butter wouldn't melt in her mouth.

"Nobody's talking," says Jake. "Which usually means somebody's lying."

"Is it an occupational hazard to be so cynical?"

Jake grins. But he doesn't let up. "What are *you* doing here?" he asks again.

"The ambassador is a dear friend. I want to see if my charity can help get those poor girls some counseling and back into school."

"Apparently, they've been well taken care of already," Jake informs her. "They've had first-class medical treatment, new clothes . . ."

Peggy looks mildly interested but starts up the wide stone steps toward me. I'm standing by the door, looking at my watch, like I'm trying to keep her on schedule. But Jake follows her up. Like a dog with a bone.

"This wasn't the Cameroon government," Jake is saying. "They're taking credit, but I heard reports that women soldiers were involved. They don't have female soldiers in Cameroon."

"Well, perhaps they should." Peggy's voice holds slight irritation now, as she turns to face Jake. She stares him down, just a bit. As if daring him to keep going. I've been on the receiving end of that look before, and it's one you remember. Jake backs off.

"Sorry," he says. "This has nothing to do with you, but I felt there was more to it."

"You're a good reporter, Jake," Peggy tells him. "You got there by following your instincts. Don't feel bad about it."

A brave double bluff. He shakes Peggy's hand and walks back down the stairs. I've already stepped into the shadows of the interior door, keeping my head buried in those files but, in any event, Jake doesn't look at me. By the time Peggy joins me, I can see she's worried. But she gives me a smile.

"He's got nothing," Peggy says.

I nod, grateful for her words, but I've never felt worse. I've jeopardized my team so badly that I'm not going to complain ever again about being kicked out of Athena.

Home is a weird word. I know the house that it refers to. Large and light, with white-framed platinum albums on the wall and signed pieces of art from Kit's contemporaries. At times, home has meant a place full of guests, music, and Kit's effusive affection.

But mostly, it means a quiet, echoing place—just me and the

housekeeper, and stretches of silent loneliness. I was always encouraged to have friends over. But I was two years ahead at school, so I never had that many friends my age. I guess I've never been social in the way Kit was. To me, books and coding were easier to deal with than people—something Kit never understood. But now, in the past few years, Kit no longer tours, or records very much. She's also quit drinking, and at least three evenings a week she sticks around indoors, reading or watching a TV show. It's like I always imagined home should be.

But now, after just half a day of hanging around the house, my resolve not to feel sorry for myself has evaporated and I'm about ready to spit. I've flicked through a hundred TV channels, watched some YouTube videos about coding, taken a nap, and made myself a sandwich. A blanket of boredom settles over me like a misty rain, and the feeling soaks through me. All I can think about is that the others are busy preparing to take down Gregory Pavlic's trafficking empire while I'm cooling my heels here.

I head upstairs, flip open my laptop, and turn on some music. I don't use headphones because I want to be able to hear Kit when she gets home, which could be anytime. The Athena founders come and go, combining their work for the underground agency with their regular day jobs. For Li, that's running her tech empire. Peggy is still one of London's go-to people for charity and diplomacy. And Kit continues to support different women's causes.

Out of habit, not to mention boredom, I try first to log into the Athena communications system. It's a closed I2P-style network that is really almost impossible for anyone outside the Athena team to trace or monitor because it doesn't use any external server or software. I go to the correct URL and enter my credentials—but a red skull comes up in the center of my screen to tell me that the computer I'm on is no longer authorized.

Annoyed, I do some surfing online, but I use a VPN to mask my IP address and a browser that is hidden. Just in case Amber or one of her tech heads have taken it on themselves to try to watch what I do on my own private computer. I start looking up Gregory Pavlic but, really, the level of information out there is too basic. What I really want is to get into the Athena files on him—all the research that I was a part of.

I run some software that might be able to talk to the Athena servers. I've left enough innocent-looking code on them that might not have been scrubbed away in the weekly tech cleanup that Li insists they run on all systems throughout her companies. Sure enough, after about ten minutes, I get a hit.

A program on the key server has gotten root access so it can hide itself in the operating system and intercept keystrokes that pass through the kernel. Put more simply, I just have to wait for someone with authorization to log on at the Athena office, and then I can see what the latest passwords are—and use them.

It's Thomas who logs in first. I feel a pulse of excitement as I trace his online movements. And, within another few minutes, I'm in, with access to all the research on Gregory, his money trails, known associates, and all the rest of it.

Two hours later, and there's still no sign of Kit as I pad downstairs to grab a bowl of cereal, which is something I haven't eaten in months. As part of our ongoing training, we each get a diet plan every week, prescribed by Li and her nutritionist. It varies a little for each of us, to take into account our body types and metabolic rates and all that stuff, but the gist of it is, lots of lean protein, plenty of vegetables, and some complex carbohydrates to give us high-quality fuel for burning. My breakfasts are mostly some variation on eggs with avocado, or smoked fish, or things that are supposed to give you some protein and also omega oils for your brain function. So that we can think our way out of trouble as well as fight our way out, I suppose.

Two hours after that, and I've spent ages with the aching boredom of tracing Gregory's web of offshore bank accounts. Let me just say, it's not as sexy as they make it look in the movies—when you tap a few keys and thirty seconds later you zoom in on a hidden address that no one else noticed before. No. What I'm doing is raking over the grunt work that another analyst has already done, and they seem to have done it well. The accounts link together, one to another, in a pattern like a daisy chain, and tracing the pattern takes forever, and then adds nothing to what we already know. After a bit, I see in my mind that there's a way to make the work go faster. I start coding—a short program to run the links faster. We have a program already, of course, but this new one takes the data and looks at it from a different angle. Sounds fancy, but it's not that hard, and it works faster than I can manually. I've had it running for a while, but nothing's come up yet. And, now, there's the sound of a key in the front-door lock. I turn down the brightness on my screen so it's completely blank and head downstairs.

Kit is in the hallway, swapping her high-end cowboy boots for a pair of acupuncture slippers that are supposed to cure everything while you shuffle around the house.

She looks up at me as I trudge downstairs.

"Hey," she says. "You okay?"

Lost my job. Made my first kill and I wasn't even provoked. Having the time of my life.

"Yeah."

I follow Kit as she heads into the kitchen, where she pours herself a glass of water from the filter tap.

"I'm starving," she says. "Jeanette left a casserole in the fridge. Did you find it?"

Jeanette, our housekeeper since I was eight, so loyal to Kit, and with whom I've spent more time over my life than I have with my mother.

"No."

"What did you eat all day?"

"A sandwich. Cereal."

Kit makes a disapproving sound and takes the foil-covered dish out of the fridge. Then she peers at the oven, as if it's this big mystery she has to solve. I go over and switch it on.

"I'm not hungry," I say, edging toward the door. I see rejection in Kit's face, so I give her a quick, apologetic smile, but she's not having it.

"You just don't want to talk," she starts.

Perceptive as always.

"I'm leaving for Belgrade tomorrow morning, with Caitlin," Kit says.

"Why so early?" I ask. "The concert's only at the weekend."

"Rehearsal," Kit says. "I haven't played a gig in a while. Most of the band is new, so we need a couple of days. Plus, a day for a tech recce—checking the sound, speakers, equipment."

I listen, but the truth is, it has nothing to do with me anymore. The fight has drained out of me for the moment, or perhaps I'm just tired. I continue on, toward the stairs.

"Well, I'll see you in a few days," Kit says, and her voice changes. "Can I get a hug?"

I step across the living room and present myself, and she gives me a quick embrace.

"You take care of yourself, Jess."

"You're the one walking into the lion's den," I say. "Playing a concert for Gregory Pavlic."

I'm worried about her, and she can feel it. She looks at me for a long moment till I shift, uncomfortable.

"What?"

"I'm not sorry you're out of this whole thing," Kit says. "I think I was mad to ever ask you to join Athena."

"Why did you, then?"

That throws her. But, now I think about it, it's a good question. What kind of mother would send her child out to do

God-knows-what for a secret spy force? Probably one with deficient maternal instincts.

Kit hesitates. "I thought I had a responsibility to develop your gifts" is her lame reply. "And I thought it was something we both believed in."

Well, she's right about that. We were both excited to be part of something where we could really make a difference. But I can see that Kit's mind is somewhere else already. Perhaps she's finally imagining a future where I have a proper job, commuting home to eat pasta and watch a bit of TV with her before starting again the next day. The idea of it stifles me to the point where I almost have to gasp for breath. I tell her I'm tired, and I get upstairs and into my room before she can say anything else.

4

THE NEXT MORNING, THE HOUSE has that awful, empty, echoey feel to it. Last night, I had wanted to tell Kit not to go to Belgrade—because it's dangerous, what she's doing. And also, if I'm being honest, because I didn't want to wake up alone. But I won't tell her stuff like that anymore. I did when I was younger. I remember being about nine or ten and begging her—literally *begging* her—not to go away. She was off on a tour to the States. And why I remember it so well is that she didn't even seem to feel bad about it. She just hugged me and then peeled me off her, sort of irritated, like she was worried I would crush her clothes. She told me I would get used to it. And she just went. The door closed. And there was only silence. For four months.

I flick on the TV to break the quiet now. Jake Graham's on again, this time with a story about a girl in Syria who's been brought here for medical treatment. I look at this kid—probably twelve years old—who's made it through years of war and is fighting to stay alive, and I feel like a brat for whining about waking up alone in this massive, rock-star house.

I jiggle my laptop mouse to wake it up, and while it kicks into gear, I head into the bathroom and go over what I know of the Athena plan. A car came to collect Kit for the airport at 6:00 a.m. Apparently, Gregory's chartered a private jet to fly his guest performer to Belgrade. Caitlin, who's posing as Kit's security, will be flying with her. Peggy leaves later this morning, probably slumming it in a normal airline's business-class cabin. Hala will have already landed in Belgrade, and is even now probably meeting one of Li's contacts to arrange weapons on the ground. Kit and Peggy will stay in a rented house with Caitlin, having declined Gregory's offer to arrange accommodation. The last thing they need is a mansion with security and surveillance arranged by the thug they are trying to bring to justice. Hala will most likely be put into a room or apartment somewhere else, though she will take some time to sweep the place where Kit is staying for bugs. She'll also jam the security camera feeds, if there are any, and kill any cell phone signals inside the house. She's good at that stuff, very diligent. Doesn't leave any openings or vulnerabilities. Which is more important now than ever. Until now, none of the Athena founders has come near us on a mission. No sense in making connections between us all if we don't have to. But, I suppose, this job is the exception.

In the kitchen, I consult my diet sheet out of habit and scramble a couple of eggs for breakfast, washing them down with coffee. By the time I go back up to my room and settle in front of the laptop, it's not quite 8:00 a.m. The first thing I notice is that my code has yielded something. Something significantly new.

Gregory's financial and corporate network is in the Balkans. Maybe once, he dabbled in Ukraine. But now, two of his newest shell companies show money coming in from Moscow. And both those companies are registered to a particular art gallery in Belgrade.

Now, Athena knows about this gallery—it's run by Gregory's daughter, Paulina. But I don't think anyone made the connection with these shell companies before. My fingers fly over the keys and bring up a photograph of a young woman—a girl, really—a bit older than me. Paulina Pavlic. High cheekbones, almond-shaped eyes, great smile. Completely stunning to look at, if you want the truth.

It takes me several more hours, but eventually I've tracked the shell company that owns Paulina's gallery back to one parent company, called Lavit. I had to pass through four other entities to reach it, and I still can't be sure it's the right connection, but it feels that way. Just enough of the names, bank details, and fake addresses mesh together.

Next, I dig up whatever I can on the directors of Lavit. There are three. One is dead. And I mean super dead, like, since 1963. His records come up on the Serbian state registry. Not uncommon for criminals like Gregory to use dead men's identities to set up untraceable companies, but it takes the wind out of my sails a bit. If they're all dead, I've got nothing to track and no one to find. I try the next one, this time a female name, Katarina Volim—Serbian as well—but I can't find that she's bit the dust. What I do dig up is a Facebook page, but the girl on it is in her twenties, posing with sunglasses and a cigarette. Not likely to be her, but I keep it on ice, just in case, and move on to the last one.

That takes longer but leads somewhere unexpected. This guy is fifty-three, Russian, and a businessman, but his name, along with young Katarina's, also turns up somewhere that feels like it must mean something. He and Katarina are on the board of directors of a super-high-end private clinic, just outside Moscow. The website is only in Russian and is slick as anything. Pictures of happy middle-aged men and women pushing buggies, and babies being cuddled by blond nurses. It looks like a bizarre advert for designer kids. Which makes me think: Where do those babies come from? I log out of everything and take my laptop down to the safe in the basement, securing it inside with a cable lock. Then I grab a jacket and head out.

Since my access to Athena has been revoked, I have to wait for Thomas to come and let me in. As usual, he looks immaculate, and the barest hint of cologne creates a fresh fragrance around him, even this late in the workday.

"This had better be good, Jessie," he says.

"It's exceptional," I reply.

"Li's on her way in, she's finishing a call with China."

I nod, happy that Li's agreed to see me. I'm just a bit proud of the new connections I've figured out, and, deep down, I'm hoping that Li will be impressed enough to wonder if she and the others have been too quick to fire me. . . .

Politely, Thomas lets me out of the elevator first but then briskly passes me, leading us into Li's office. Li has just gotten there herself—she shrugs off her suit jacket and drapes it on a padded hanger behind the door. Then she settles in behind her desk and nods at me to sit down.

Swiftly, I summarize what I found out about Lavit, the company that owns the gallery run by Gregory's daughter.

"Paulina Pavlic is squeaky clean," Thomas says. "We've checked her thoroughly. She graduated a year early from a top boarding school here in the UK, and she's a photography nut, hence the gallery. Daddy can afford to give her whatever she wants."

That interests me. Someone else who graduated early from school. It's not easy being noticeably younger than your classmates. It leaves you with a superiority complex in one way, but mostly, you feel left behind while everyone else is friends and looks at you like you're a freak. Of course, I don't bother communicating any of this to Thomas or Li. Anyway, Paulina isn't my main concern here.

"Paulina aside, the same company, Lavit, is connected to the Victory Clinic, outside Moscow."

"Connected how?" Li asks.

"Two of Lavit's company directors are on the board of the Victory," I explain.

Li flicks a frown at Thomas. "Did we know this?"

He hesitates, hating that he and the others might have missed something, then shakes his head. This is exactly what I was worried about. If they hadn't picked this up, could they have missed other stuff?

"And why should we be concerned about this Victory Clinic?" is Li's question. I pull out some pages that I printed off the website and slide them over the desk, toward her.

"It's like some scary, designer-baby factory," I continue, eager to press the advantage. "I think Gregory's up to something new. I think he's using these girls he traffics to supply this clinic with harvested eggs."

"Have you any evidence, or is it pure conjecture?" asks Thomas.

Pure conjecture? Who actually talks like that? Meanwhile, Li looks at the pages, then at me, thinking.

"Even if it is true—and this is not much in the way of hard proof—it doesn't change anything we're doing," Li says at last. "Whatever his endgame, our plan is still to stop Gregory."

"But if Aleks prosecutes him for the wrong crimes, he could walk free—"

Li interrupts me. "You don't work for Athena anymore."

Thanks for mentioning that. I'd almost forgotten, as I sit here like a schoolgirl trying to get out of detention.

"I'm trying to help . . . ," I say.

"Where did you get all this?"

"It doesn't matter." I try to move on before it crosses her mind that I might have hacked the Athena servers. "What matters is that I can help with this mission."

But Li holds up a hand. Her cheeks are flushed with anger.

"Jessie, you took a man's life without cause *and* put us all in danger."

"Haven't you ever made a mistake?" I sound petulant, even to myself.

"Everybody does. It's what you do afterward that counts."

I meet her gaze but keep silent. For once. I want to tell her that I know I did something wrong and that I'm trying to make it right— but I can't find my voice under her glare. Her eyes stay on mine.

"Thomas will see you out," she says.

I don't need an alarm to wake up the next morning, because I've been sleepless over Ahmed and my meeting with Li. As I toss and turn, I wonder if people like Ahmed, or Gregory Pavlic, ever lose sleep over the innocent people *they* kill. What's the point if all we do is stop them for a bit till they make a new plan and rise again, stronger than before? Taking a life is no joke, but haven't I saved many more innocent lives with that one bullet? Maybe the whole Athena ethos—trying to do the right thing—is just tying our hands, putting us at a disadvantage against men who have no ethics or morality.

I've also been thinking through the Gregory/Lavit/Victory thing all night—and by 5:00 a.m., I give up trying to sleep and get back on my computer. Flicking idly through the society pages of Serbian news sites, I discover that Paulina broke off an engagement with some eligible young guy last year after her affair with another girl. Judging by the press response, it caused quite a stir in the local gossip columns. I look at Gregory's daughter on the screen, and

Paulina Pavlic's eyes smile back me—beautiful and unreadable.

While being enigmatic is not enough of a reason for me to suspect Paulina of anything, the fact that her gallery is owned by Lavit, and that Lavit connects to Victory, still bothers me. I keep digging and what I find, by piecing together photos and posts from Paulina's social media accounts and cross-referencing them with the flights taken by Gregory's private plane (which Athena has tracked for a while) is that Paulina has visited Moscow twice in the past four months. Could she have been visiting the Victory Clinic? If so, why? She's young. Not likely to want a baby or to need treatment if she does. I sit back in my chair to think. When two unlikely things collide just once, it's probably coincidence. But when you have a shell company taking big payments, with the same company directors as this dodgy Russian clinic, and the daughter of a notorious criminal linked to it . . . If Paulina is dirty, maybe she has a copy of Gregory's files on the local politicians. And that would save throwing Kit and Caitlin into a dangerous situation.

I run through it all one more time and consider trying Li again. But she dismissed me without much ceremony, and what I have here is still not enough to change Athena's course. And yet, it doesn't feel right to ignore all these new developments. One of those threads could lead to something that would adjust the mission. Someone should be investigating this stuff.

It's seven forty-five, and behind the massive tower that holds Chen Technologies, I wait outside on the street, sipping a double espresso that I've picked up from the Italian café around the corner. My eyes are on the back alleyway, through which I used to be able to enter the building. Adrenaline and caffeine make me feel sharp as I wait for my mark to show up. I take a couple of deep breaths that carry the tangy fumes of city traffic and the smell of coffee.

When Amber appears at the top of the street, I hang back in the shadows. She wears a blue skirt, a delicate shirt, and a summer jacket. The ends of Amber's short, spiky dark hair are streaked with yellow, as if she has dipped them in gold leaf, and her skin glows a pale coffee color in the early sunlight. Amber was top of her class at Imperial College, or somewhere exceptional, took a summer job at Li's company after she graduated, and never left. Li looks after her— not in that nurturing, huggy way that Peggy does with Caitlin, but with fierce, tough love. Maybe when she gets home, Li throws on sweatpants and becomes a softer personality, but I doubt it.

Amber uses her fingerprint to open up, and I'm right there, before the metal gate slams behind her.

She jumps as I touch her shoulder, then takes a breath of relief as she turns and sees me. As usual, there are no pleasantries.

"Lurking in alleyways? You must be up to no good."

"I was just having a coffee," I say. "And enjoying the beauty of the day."

My eyes meet Amber's, and she looks away, a half smile on her face. Then she remembers I don't work here anymore.

"What do you want?" she asks.

"They gave me happy pills a month ago, and I left them behind before the last job. In my locker."

"You're not depressed," Amber responds. It is a statement; no hint of a question about it. Most of Amber's speech is like this. Direct declarations, in a crisp, upper-class accent. She looks like a South Asian artist and she sounds like Mary Poppins.

"How do you know?" I ask.

"I don't. I just wonder if it's your personality that makes people think that."

It actually makes me want to smile, that assessment, but I stifle it, because Amber hasn't moved any farther inside and I feel like she's blocking me.

"Jessie, I can't let you in here," she says. "We'll send you your things by the end of the week."

I nod, a picture of understanding, and then I look away from her, like I'm suddenly emotional and need to get a grip.

"It's been a tough time, to be honest," I say, keeping my voice low. "I don't care about the clothes and stuff—but the pills? I think I might need them sooner than later."

When I look back at her, Amber's eyes hold genuine concern. Which makes me feel crap about pulling this kind of emotional drama. But then, that's what Athena has trained us to do. Lie to almost everyone, at all times, about who we really are. It just feels a bit harder with someone you like, I suppose.

I can see Amber is wavering, and I try to push her over the line.

"Two minutes, and I'll be out of your hair. Forever, probably."

That last bit popped into my head from nowhere, but we both

realize, suddenly, that it's most likely true. And we would miss each other. She likes me, and I like her. I can't describe it. We're not friends—not really—but we get each other. She starts walking and indicates I should follow.

Once we're in the confined space of the elevator, I lean against the side wall to give Amber enough room while the space fills up with the perfume that she always wears—floral and honeyed.

"Enjoying your newfound freedom?" she asks.

"Adore it," I say. "I'm taking up Pilates. And origami."

Amber smiles, and as the elevator doors open, I stick close behind her as she flicks on lights from an app on her phone, straightens a vase of flowers, and drops her bag onto her desk. Then she turns, at last, and looks at me properly. Her gaze is intense, and I step back a bit.

"You do look terrible." She frowns. "Tired."

"Well, you look great," I tell her. Which is true. Amber smiles, though I can see she is trying not to.

She turns away and picks up a record. When I say record, I mean one of those big round pieces of black vinyl that play music. Amber, the technology worshipper, is also a vinyl addict. She has an entire wall of them right here in her tech cave. What she really loves is old music, of all kinds. Now and then, she'll listen to stuff from this century, but nothing much past 2010, which means that Kit is also one of her heroes—not that she would admit to it openly, in case it makes her seem less than professional. I watch her as she slips her chosen record out of its sleeve and places it gently onto the turntable of her prized record player. Then she actually *wipes* it clean with a little microfiber cloth that she keeps just for that purpose, and only then does she actually let the thing play. It's Dinah Washington, singing "What a Difference a Day Makes." Dinah could be right about that. Amber turns back to me.

"What are you smirking at?" she demands.

I wipe the expression from my face and shake my head.

"Nothing."

Irritated, Amber turns and walks behind a long metal counter that separates us from the wall where the box lockers for each agent are kept. She loves that counter; she uses it as an unofficial line, beyond which we agents must not cross. She likes to stand behind it, handing out weapons and gadgetry as if serving us on a shop floor.

She pulls a slim card key from her left jacket pocket and slips it into one of the lockers—*my* locker. The chamber pops open and the box slides out. Casually, as if I can hardly be bothered to look, I move behind the counter to stand next to Amber. We both look down at the contents of the box.

Inside it is everything that I want, nestled into carefully organized compartments. Guns, passports, my stealth phone, earpiece communication devices as thin as slips of silver foil . . .

"No antidepressants in here." Amber's voice interrupts my thoughts. "Funnily enough."

I whip my fingers clear of the edge of the box just as Amber slams it shut.

"Good reflexes," she says dryly.

"Reactions," I say. "Reflexes are involuntary . . ."

But she turns away, removing the key card and slipping it into her pocket. I turn to her, just a little closer than I need to be.

"Actually," I say, as if recalling. "I think I left them in my clothes locker."

Amber's eyes flick up to another door at the end of the tech cave. Beyond that door is a state-of-the-art gym, health-monitoring equipment, showers, and lockers where we keep our body armor, combat trousers, boots, and other work gear, as well as changes of our own clothes.

Amber hesitates. Just to encourage her, I move far away from the counter and her precious lockers and throw myself into a curved white chair. I pull out my phone and start playing a game. As if I'm waiting, bored. Amber turns and touches a series of numbers on an alarm panel, deftly, and without letting me catch a glimpse of them. Great. With a yawn, I kick off my shoes, waiting while she heads toward the door to the lockers.

"I'll have a look," she says. "Don't move. I just alarmed the floor by the boxes."

"You have trust issues."

"Only with some people."

I smile and continue to look at my phone, listening to the suction sound of the door being released, then to Amber's steps and the closing of the door behind her.

The slam is still echoing in the room when I am up. Since I need to avoid the floor, I jump lightly onto Amber's much-loved countertop in my socks, pulling off the belt from my jeans. My heart is pounding, but it feeds my system the right amount of adrenaline to get the job done. I toss the end of my belt over the exposed ventilation pipes that run across the ceiling between the counter and the lock boxes. The buckle sticks between pipes. Wrapping the other end of the belt around my wrist, I leap and grasp hold of the top of the lockers with my other hand. Not bad—though Hala, the parkour champion of the world, could doubtless do much better.

Having got this far, I pause to listen for Amber, but it's only been thirty seconds, and there is no sound except for my own ragged breathing. I inhale deeply to slow it, then improve my grip on the cool metal and lean forward until I'm almost upside down. In my other hand is the key card that I just picked from Amber's jacket pocket. I reach down to insert the card into my own locker. It slips open smoothly, and I move fast, picking out comms units, the phone, two passports, and a sealed bag with some ID cards. My hand hesitates over a gun before I decide to leave it.

"You have a ton of rubbish in here."

Amber's voice issuing from the ceiling speaker right next to my ear startles the hell out of me—enough that I lose my grip on one of the passports. I see it slip toward the alarmed floor. I stretch to bat it upward, and somehow manage to grasp the edge of it before it can fall.

Panting with the effort, I look back at the speaker. Of course, Amber would be on the intercom. There are cameras recording my every move as well—I can even see myself in the feeds lined up on

Amber's computer screen—but by the time she thinks to wind back and check them, I'll be long gone.

"Try the leather jacket," I call back, and there is a sound of acknowledgment in return, a noise that suggests Amber has found the pills. Swiftly, I pick out my last requirement, a small plastic bag containing a single blue pill, then I slam the locker shut, lever myself upward, and jump back across to the counter. I nearly slip over the other side of it in my rush to make it back before Amber does—for she must be nearly at the door by now. I retrieve the belt off the pipework and jump down from the counter just as the door handle moves. There's no time to sit down without looking like I was just in motion, so instead I stand there, scratching my arm and pretending to watch the daft aquarium screensaver on one of the computers on the desk.

Amber walks briskly over to me, holding out a bottle of pills in one hand.

"You never even opened them," she says.

"I don't like drugs."

I smile, but Amber is looking at me closely now, like she suspects something. I swallow, stressed, as she keeps staring. But then her hand comes up to touch my forehead gently. Her palm feels cool against my warm skin, and we are so close that I feel her breath soft on my face for a moment. Close enough that I can slip the key card back into her pocket unnoticed.

"You're sweating," Amber says, her voice full of concern.

I look at her. Leaving aside the teasing, the flirting, the jokes between us—Amber's a kind person. A grain of guilt sticks in my throat for a moment.

"I must be coming down with something," I say. "Thanks for these."

I hold up the pills and slip on my jacket. To my surprise, Amber reaches out and grasps me in a hug, which is kind of awkward, because I wasn't expecting it. I lean in to hug her back and then she pulls away, briskly.

"Take care of yourself, Jessie," she says.

My guilt at what I've done rises so fast that I can't even wish her the same. I just nod and give her a quick smile, and she walks me back to the elevator. As the doors close on me, the remorse seeps away and a sense of opportunity replaces it. I breathe more easily as the lift moves back down, releasing me to the morning air, and to freedom.

5

ONCE I'VE MADE UP MY mind to go, I move fast. Soon enough, Amber will find out that I was snooping around on the Athena servers and she'll figure out that I've broken into my own lockbox. Li will literally spit feathers. It's bad enough when I imagine it; I don't want to be around to see it in person.

Back at home, I gather clothes, a couple of books, and my debit cards. They pay us pretty well to do the work we do, but I need to buy some things on my way to the station and realize I have more in cryptocurrency right now than in real money. Since I'm going undercover in a place like Belgrade with no weapons, that might not be a bad thing, but I still need some regular cash. I hurry downstairs to the home office where Kit keeps her desktop Mac. She changes passwords every month, but she always has me do it for her—I suppose because she's never had a reason not to trust me. I was always good at school, never one of those kids stealing money from their

parents to try drugs or smoking or whatever. No inappropriate boy-
friends who I snuck around to meet. In fact, I remember Kit sitting
down and giving me a talking-to once, about how it would be okay
to rebel a bit.

I don't think this is what she had in mind. I find the little
password-generating device from her bank in a wooden box in the
bottom drawer of her desk. Right before I pull it out of there, I notice
something underneath it. It's familiar, but I can't place it. Pale-blue
paper with a flowery pattern on the back. I bring it out onto the desk
and unfold it.

It's a note that I wrote her ten years ago, right before she left
on a concert tour. I'd printed a date on the top left, like they taught
us to do at school. Holding my breath, I read through it. It tells her
how much I would miss her when she was on tour again for twelve
weeks but that I would look after the house and Jeannette and keep
up my grades at school. I fold it again, but something wet falls onto
it. I brush the droplet away and realize that there are tears in my
eyes, and one of them has fallen onto the paper and another onto the
desk. I wipe my face with my hands and pull myself together. What
on earth am I getting all sappy about? The fact that I was once able
to say such adoring things to my mother, or that she got notes like
that but left me anyway? Carefully, I put the note back. Alongside
it in the box are a whole bunch of trinkets—a ring, ornaments—
things I'd bought her for birthdays or whatever. I'm surprised that
Kit kept them all.

On the screen, the online banking app is flashing at me. I get on with it and transfer a small chunk of Kit's money into my own account. Just enough that I can buy the kind of extras I might need along the way.

As I close the door of the house behind me, I hesitate, just for a moment. Part of me feels reckless. Heading out to Belgrade on the off chance that my hunches about the new Russian company and Paulina Pavlic mean something. *And* after being fired. But the irony is, if I were still part of Athena, I'd be able to keep following these leads till I had something concrete to hand off to Caitlin and Hala. But now, I've got no other way of doing this.

And there's another thing bugging me. Putting my mother in the field is not a great idea. Sure, Caitlin will be there as her pretend bodyguard, and she's trained well enough to protect Kit from a lot. But Caitlin also has to raid Gregory's office while Kit is onstage, which means she'll have to replace his security camera feeds, disable alarms, and all sorts of nonsense—so guarding Kit is not going to be her main priority. What we're hoping, I suppose, is that Gregory himself will be looking after Kit. Because he's clearly paying her a small fortune to join the ranks of singers who perform privately for millionaires and billionaires. These stars—usually *former* stars, I've noticed—earn hundreds of thousands, or even millions for a single night's work, and the birthday boy earns bragging rights to all his friends. I know Kit will put that money into the foundation she runs to help disadvantaged women. But no one else will know that. If word gets out, it will look like she's sold out to a human trafficker for a nice pension because her records don't sell anymore. I don't know how I can help protect my mother—or her reputation—by following her to Eastern Europe, but it somehow feels better that I'm close enough to try.

After thinking about all that, I'm fairly stressed out by the time I make it to the best electronics shop in Tottenham Court Road. On the bus there, I spend five minutes creating a fake profile on an app that finds accommodations from Belgrade locals wanting to rent their apartments. I know the street I want to stay on, and there's only one room available. I book it online.

Then I head into the shop and scope out the best cameras. An older man brings out a midrange SLR and I shake my head.

"What's that?" I ask.

On a raised display is a camera protected by a glass case. I can feel the assistant looking me up and down. Maybe my combat pants, T-shirt, and backpack don't help. He probably thinks I got lost looking for the pink phone cases.

"I'd like to see that camera, please," I say.

"It's two thousand pounds."

"Yes," I agree.

There's a moment of standoff, when he stares me down and I smile back. Then he turns away and takes forever to find a supervisor to get the key to unlock a storage cupboard behind the till. Finally, he brings out the camera, presenting it to me as if it's the Holy Grail.

"Is this the absolute best camera you have?"

"It came in last week. Brand-new model. And the most *expensive.*"

Nice of him to point that out again.

"I'll take it," I say, and I pull out a wad of cash.

That throws him.

"Would you like me to show you some of the features?"

"No, thanks."

"What about a case?"

"Two thousand quid, and there's no case?" I ask.

Turns out he's trying to upsell a fancy one. I refuse all the extras, pay for the camera, and get out of there. I have a train to catch.

St Pancras station. High glass ceilings let in London's late-morning sun at the Eurostar terminal. Lots of passengers mill around, waiting to check in, and I hope it's the kind of place where I can blend in unnoticed.

Among the items I managed to swipe from Amber was an EU identity card for a German called Helga Hess (really, Amber has almost no imagination in some things, like coming up with fake names) and the picture on it was mine.

With the ID card, I figure I can glide through immigration control with less chance of being flagged than if I used one of the other passports that Amber must surely be able to track through airports. Here, at the train station, they don't usually scan the ID into a system, they just check it.

I make it through security with barely enough time to buy a

selection of newspapers, and a sandwich for later. Then I find my seat and settle in for the journey—it's a little over two hours to Paris.

I'm jolted awake as we pull into the Gare du Nord. I have less than half an hour to get over to Gare de l'Est, but it's only one stop, so I opt to walk rather than wait for another train. There's a light summer rain falling onto the streets of Paris, and two things glow out at me as I walk by the beautiful buildings. One is a McDonald's. The other is a small bakery. Ducking in there, I pick up a ham-and-cheese croissant (definitely not on any diet sheet from Li) and actually make it onto the train for Munich with time to spare. Helga Hess, my ID alter ego, is from Munich, so I try to feel good about heading home, even though I've never actually set foot in the city. I'll barely have time to down a bratwurst before taking the sleeper train to Budapest, and then making the final leg south, at last, to Belgrade.

The June sun is shining over Belgrade, but it only highlights the peeling shabbiness of the gray apartment blocks here in the new part of the city. There is some kind of abandoned state hospital that Gregory seems to have adopted as his trafficking base, and I know from my study of a city map that it's in this area somewhere. I'm in the back of an old taxi, and my eyes meet the stares of young men who sit on walls—smoking, texting, scratching arms, laughing.

In the rearview mirror, the driver's hooded eyes flick up to me, and he speaks in a heavy accent.

"No work here. Only gangs."

I look back outside. The high, ugly towers are giving way to older buildings now; still run-down, but with an old-fashioned elegance. We cross a bridge into the old part of the city, and the small side streets give way to bigger ones. Graffiti is still everywhere though. We make our way down an impressive boulevard, and the driver points out city hall, and then the parliament building, which is where I guess Peggy's friend Aleks, the justice minister, must spend his days.

Several minutes later we pull onto a quiet backstreet that feels chilly, where the sun can't find a way down past the old brick buildings. I pay the fare with the Serbian dinars I exchanged in Budapest and knock on the door that matches the address of the place I booked online. The man who opens up looks surprised, and doesn't seem to speak any English—not a great combination. But when I show him the booking on my phone, he nods and grins, revealing a gold crown in the back of his mouth. My grandmother used to have one of those, before they started making them white to match your actual teeth. All I remember of her is a couple of visits to a dingy house in Streatham. Even after Kit was famous and offered to buy her a picture-postcard house near us, my grandmother didn't want to move from her old neighborhood and her friends. We'd sit at her kitchen table, covered in a wipe-clean cloth, and eat homemade cake spread with jam and cream (which Kit only pretended to eat, not being keen on carbs or sugar), and nobody talked very much. All the nice, expensive things Kit bought for her were piled up in the back room, which irritated my mother no end.

My temporary landlord indicates that I should wait out here for a moment, so I kill time strolling up and down, glancing casually into windows while I wait. When I come back to the front door where he left me, I sneak a peek into his grimy side window. Inside the house another man, thin, with slicked hair, is handing my landlord a stack of money. On the table between them is a bag of pistols. The thin guy zips up the bag and, hurriedly, I step back into the street so they won't know that I've seen anything. Nothing like multiple streams of income. Why rely on room rentals when you can trade guns for extra cash?

The landlord reappears a few seconds later with a large bunch of keys. He opens up the door next to his, and I throw my duffel bag over my shoulder and wait for him to lead the way inside.

The stairwell is dingy—even now, in the middle of the afternoon—and it smells of rotting timber. I trudge up the wooden steps in his wake. He sports sagging jogging pants and a tight T-shirt. A small, round head balanced on a large, round body, like a badly dressed snowman. We reach the fourth-floor landing, and he pauses tiredly and barks out a catarrh-laden cough while pointing upward. One more flight to go.

Discreetly, I turn my head away from the stale breath and wait for him to continue up. The last door we pass gives off a smell of lunch, something fishy with a background note of fried onions. I wrinkle my nose as we reach the top landing and wait while the man tackles the lock. The door is heavy and leads into an apartment that has scuffed wooden floors and just enough light from the dirty windows so I can't miss the cockroach scuttling away under the dresser. I feel the hairs on the back of my neck prickle at the sight of it, but I make myself look away. I walk over to the window.

The view brings a smile to my face. Down there, diagonally across the street, is the art gallery belonging to Gregory's daughter, Paulina. Cleanly painted, huge glass windows, and a view directly inside. I can see the photography exhibits from here. Though I don't have plans to sit and watch the place, I like the idea that I can if I want to. In the back of the gallery there's a long, sleek bar and several tables and chairs—a little upmarket café where well-to-do locals can sip cappuccinos amid the artwork, I suppose.

"Good?"

Behind me the landlord sweeps a pudgy hand across the room, as if to make sure that I've not missed any of the attractive features of the apartment. I go over to the bed and sit down. The mattress is firm at least.

"I make spray," says the man, in response to my silence. "For the . . ."

With a wiggle of his fat fingers, he mimics the motion of the cockroach. I nod, get up to take the key, and escort the man back to the door and close it behind him. Then I throw myself down on the bed to stretch. It's quiet up here. No sounds from the neighbors, so far; only some light traffic passing several stories down below. I close my eyes. I'm a bit of a loner, according to my mother, but I rarely feel lonely. Right now though, here in this strange city with only a cockroach for company, it suddenly feels desolate. I miss my team. For eighteen months I've trained and worked alongside Caitlin and Hala; and before that with the other kids in the Program.

Opening my eyes again, I take in the bumpy beige walls, and they remind me of Hala's apartment; not the one she has now, but the tiny London council flat where she was placed after she finally gained asylum. It took months for Hala to get out of detention and nearly two weeks of interrogation to assure the government that she was not a potential terrorist but a survivor of terrorism by the Islamic state in Syria.

Frustrated by Hala's monosyllabic answers, the counterterrorism team had finally called me in. Not that I was trained for any of that, but my commanding officer at the Program was still part of the British Counter Terrorism Security Office, and he thought it was a good idea. I had no clue how to interrogate anyone. At that time, I was spending my days learning about circuits and wiring and explosives and wasn't happy to be pulled off it, but he had thought that another girl—more or less Hala's own age—might encourage her to open up.

So I tried being friendly, doing all that rapport-building stuff they teach you in teamwork classes. That had zero impact. Then I turned to officious questioning, and finally I lost my temper. None of it had the slightest effect on her. Not even her expression changed.

She just sat there in the metal chair, behind the metal desk in the painted-green room, answering in a flat voice, with no detail. Like she couldn't care less what happened to her. And maybe she couldn't. After a couple of days, it had dawned on me that if Hala *was* telling the truth, then she would have watched her parents lose everything in Palestine and become refugees; then build a new life in Syria, only to have a civil war start. She would have watched her town and the villages around her be razed to the ground and the people in them die. And if her story was real—if her parents had been killed by caliphate soldiers in front of her, and she had stabbed one of the men who did it with a kitchen knife—then she wasn't going to be scared by an arrogant young girl barking at her.

So I dropped the techniques. I just sat with her. Made her tea and talked. About myself, a bit about school, what I had liked about it, what bugged me. Filling up the spaces, asking nothing back of Hala at all. And the funny thing was, with the pressure off, she started to speak. A little bit at a time. Her English wasn't great, but it was okay—her parents were doctors and taught her and her brother the language. Eventually, she gave up enough detail of what had happened and when; details that matched the intelligence they had on her. But she was most animated when she talked about her climbing skills. How her nickname was *il bisseh*, the cat. She had used that ability to scale walls to save her own life and escape, even though she had to separate from her brother. It was a heartbreaking story, to be honest, and I listened without saying a word; I was wary of making any sound that might cause her soft voice to stop, but also, I didn't know what to say to someone who'd been through that much pain.

The day after she was released, I went to see her in the council block where she was housed. The apartment with the beige walls.

The place smelled of bleach and was immaculately clean—and so lonely. Hala's a tall, strong girl, but she looked so small and alone inside that room. I don't know why I went. I couldn't stop thinking about her story—especially at night when I was trying to get to sleep. I tried to make friends with her, and she was polite and offered me tea and food. I remember because it was hummus and cucumber sticks. Which made me feel even worse, like she was having to buy grocery-store hummus just to find something that felt familiar. I tried to chat a bit, but Hala kept me at arm's length, and I left feeling I had disturbed her. After that, I didn't go back. Not until after I'd joined Athena and they were looking to build up the team.

That time, visiting Hala was different. I found her up on the roof of the building, where the old man who was her neighbor told me she liked to hang out. When I came through the stairwell door, she jumped up and ran to the edge of the roof and just stood there watching me. Her shoes were halfway over. Inches from a drop into oblivion.

"Get away from me! I have asylum," Hala yelled at me.

I edged closer.

"I'm not a terrorist!"

I stopped where I was and told her I wasn't there to harm her, or take her back to detention. That I was changing jobs and wanted her to work with me.

"I have a job," she said, which made me smile, because I knew she did, and it was washing dishes in a run-down Italian restaurant on the next street.

"Get down from there," I said. "It freaks me out."

She did, landing like a panther, silently, without taking her eyes off me.

And she softened a bit. When she offered me tea, I said yes, so I could hang around. And, finally, she asked me what the work was. I told her, and the idea of it seemed to light something up in her. And so her time with Athena had begun. Since then, though Hala often kept to herself, I'd always felt like that was just her character. That deep down, she cared about me because, as far as I could see, I was the closest friend she had. And other than Caitlin, probably the only friend. But now, it feels like that's all done with. Maybe it was only Athena that pulled us together, two introverts, two people bound by the secrets we had to keep and the need to put our lives in each other's hands every time we ran a mission.

I'm brought back to the present, to my lonely room in Belgrade, by a police siren passing down below. I wait till it passes, keeping my mind blank, just listening. When it's gone, it feels deathly quiet in the room. I take an audible breath, just to break the silence; but it turns into a yawn. I've been traveling for more than twenty-four hours, and the fatigue hits me all at once. I turn on my side and fall hard into sleep—so deeply that I have no idea how long I've been out when I wake up to the sound of someone banging like crazy on the door.

6

ADRENALINE HITS. I GET UP fast, heart pumping, and look for something to grasp hold of, ready to attack. I pick up a metal lamp base from a side table as I fasten the door chain and edge it open.

It's my landlord, holding up a can of insecticide. Hastily, I put down my makeshift weapon and let him in. He keeps chatting away in Serbian, and lies down to spray under the bed, making satisfied grunts as he works. I don't know what he's found down there, but he uses enough chemicals to knock out an entire colony. I throw open the window and signal him that there's been enough fumigating for one day. Then I shower and change and head outside.

In Belgrade it feels like the buildings carry years of smog and soot, and so many walls are marked with graffiti, even here, in the center of town. But the art gallery belonging to Paulina Pavlic is faced in clean, pale granite. The double-height windows are sparkling clean. And inside, the walls are pure white, showcasing some impressive photography pieces. The glossy surface of the floor looks like marble. At the far end of the gallery are the tables, the long wooden bar, and a coffee machine that resembles a piece of art itself. Gregory Pavlic must have spent a fortune on this for his daughter.

I stand on the curb as the traffic passes, watching the gallery for a couple of minutes. Then I weave my way through the constant stream of passing cars and mopeds to cross the street.

Feeling just a bit nervous, I push open the gallery door, walk past the exhibits, choose a small table, and sit down. I'm really not sure whether Paulina Pavlic will even be here. If your dad buys you an art gallery for Christmas, or your birthday, or whatever, I imagine it comes with all the perks, like staff, so that you don't actually need to get out of bed before noon.

I order a drink. This is one of those places that has a little poster of happy Colombian coffee pickers and tells you what kind of fair trade beans they are grinding that day. It's truly great to know that, even while he traffics women around Eastern Europe, Gregory and his family are concerned about the welfare of coffee farmers. When my espresso arrives, the hype does seem worth it though. The steam is fragrant, and the coffee is smooth but bitter at the same time. As I enjoy the warmth of it spreading down into my stomach, I look out of the massive windows and am happily surprised to catch sight of Paulina emerging from a smoke-colored Mercedes. Not a bad set of wheels for someone her age. She's parked on a double yellow line right outside the gallery. Even in jeans and a shirt, she manages to look like a movie star arriving at a premiere. With a sideways glance, I see that a traffic cop is strolling over, probably to protest about her presumptuous parking arrangements—but she greets him like an old friend, with a light, practiced handshake that lasts just a moment too long. The policeman's hand goes directly to his pocket, casually, as he tucks away the money that Paulina has discreetly handed over. He moves on, pausing only to write out a ticket for the car behind hers.

Meanwhile, Paulina enters, gliding through the gallery, casting brief smiles to people leaving and to a man who is looking at one of the photos on display. She makes her way toward the coffee bar, toward the table where I sit. As she gets closer, into my line of vision, I look up from my iPad, as anyone would. She throws me a passing, radiant smile, and, for a moment, I forget to breathe. Paulina is far more beautiful than even her best photos. Flawless skin, almond-shaped green-blue eyes, and caramel-colored hair that glistens with perfect, expensive highlights of honey and gold. I remind myself to smile back, instead of just staring like a goldfish, after which she passes behind me and I force myself to focus back on reading a riveting website about the major historical sites of Belgrade. But, of course, I'm watching her. She seems at ease and in charge. She pauses to throw a comment to a passing waiter, stops to chat with a couple who are clearly regular customers, then takes out her phone and taps on it for a few minutes.

Using my iPad to log into the gallery's free Wi-Fi, I open an app that helps me find the router that powers it. Once I have that, I'm all set. I signal to a bearded waiter in a half apron for the bill, and I pay it in cash. As I stand to leave, I make sure to scrape my chair, and feel Paulina turn to look in the direction of the noise. I glance up and meet her look and nod goodbye before I leave.

I have a bit of a spring in my step as I head into town. Maybe it's the sunshine, maybe the fact that I've locked on to Paulina already. While I'm out, I stop at a car rental office and collect a motorcycle; nothing flashy but with decent power and acceleration.

Once I'm back in my room, I return to the information that I gleaned about the gallery's router. It's nothing fancy. Probably one that the phone company installed as standard when they put in Paulina's phone line. It takes me all of five minutes to find the detailed specs for it and then to access a website that is helpful enough to list out the factory-set passwords for most household routers. I go back to my phone app and tap in the information, and then I'm into the router itself. Basically, I can see what websites and apps Paulina uses all day. Of course, it also deluges me with a ton of nonsense about what her staff and customers do online—but trying to embed a program on her phone directly feels too risky at this point.

I clear a bowl of dusty, dried flowers off the small dining table and set up my computer; then I unfold a map of Belgrade and tack it to the wall. My own little situation room.

The first thing I do is create a strong VPN, which changes my IP address every few minutes. This way, if Amber somehow gets a lead on my laptop in an effort to find me, it will look like I'm in Madrid one minute and Beijing the next.

Second, I've managed to tune in to the Athena communications system. I swiped my thin foil earpiece from Amber's lockbox—but she closed down my frequency, and I've had to find another one to lock into, for which I have the software. Now I can hear about half of what's happening when my team is talking to each other. The other 50 percent gets lost in silence or in static, but it'll be enough to keep me more or less on track with their progress.

Last—I've got that map of the city all neatly marked up. In red, I've noted the position of Gregory Pavlic's abandoned hospital, which seems to be the center of his trafficking activities. It's on the outskirts of the new part of the city, surrounded by boarded-up factories on one side and woodland on the other, with one main road in and out. And then there's a pin in the map for Gregory's home—which is also Paulina's—on this side of the river, in the swanky suburbs near the embassies. From a few exchanges in my earpiece between Caitlin and Amber, I know that Kit is scheduled to be in that house right now, checking the setup for the concert and probably meeting the evil Gregory for the first time. I hope she switches on the charm.

The rented house that Kit, Peggy, and Caitlin are staying in is not far from Gregory's. Only Hala is out on her own, in an apartment somewhere, scoping out the hospital and, I assume, figuring out how to get photographic evidence of what goes on in there.

While I'm trying to find out more about Gregory's Russian companies and the directors of the Victory Clinic, I tune in to the Athena comms every so often, just to keep tabs. I find out that Peggy is meeting Aleks for dinner in a couple of hours. She doesn't say where, but that bit of code that I smuggled onto Aleks's work computer weeks ago is still sitting there and it's easy enough for me to access his calendar and get hold of the name of the restaurant he's booked into. I don't have a specific purpose in mind in keeping an eye on Peggy, but I'd like to see Aleks in person, get a feel for him.

I'm glad that my next bit of sleuthing will be around a meal because I'm hungry. I make myself a dinner reservation and get decently dressed in black jeans and a smart top. The place Aleks is taking Peggy is one of the best restaurants in the city, according to tourist sites. Before I leave, I make a quick trawl through Paulina's online usage. A couple of Instagram posts, some WhatsApp messages to friends, some browsing on a shopping site that sells art books. And then, while I'm watching, she accesses her online banking. She clicks on statements (thank you, Paulina) and once those are downloaded to her phone, it's not hard for me to open them. A quick scan shows a healthy bank balance, a fair number of charges to clothes shops—and then, something more interesting. Two very large deposits from a bank in Moscow, at around the same time she was there. We're talking mid-six-figure sums. So maybe my hunch that Paulina is part of her father's empire is more than wishful thinking.

I'm itching to sit down and look up the bank, work on this some more, but I figure it can wait a couple of hours. So I head off to tail Peggy and Aleks at dinner.

I get to the restaurant a good forty minutes before Peggy is due to arrive. It wouldn't be great to bump into her at the front door.

Outside, the summer light is soft and golden, but inside the place, it's really dark, which is probably a good thing for me, since I want to skulk around unnoticed. As my eyes get accustomed to the low light, what reveals itself is a place made to look like a 1930s speakeasy. It's sort of like I've walked onto the set of *Casablanca*, except in color. There are booths covered in rich green leather, wooden tables, a long zinc bar, waiters in white tuxedo jackets, ornate brass wall lamps, and, basically, every cliché in the book. There's even a guy playing jazz piano on a black baby grand. Next to him is a small round platform and a microphone, where a blond woman in a tight-fitting dress is singing. It's an old American classic—Gershwin—but she sings it with a strong Eastern European accent.

The waiter seems taken aback that I'm eating on my own, but he gets over it and leads me right to the back of the room, past tables where couples and groups are already sitting and drinking, to a small booth in the rear. He hands me a leather-bound menu with more pages than the complete works of Shakespeare. Since I don't have two spare hours to read it end to end, I immediately settle for the set menu that's on the first page.

I've worked my way through a salad mixed with mayonnaise and nuts, and I'm tucking into some grilled fish with lemon, when I notice Aleks Yuchic. He's way across the room, to the left, holding a chair for Peggy. He's tall and lean and Peggy looks great in a deep-blue dress. Instinctively, I shrink back into my seat, but she has her back to me, so there's not much chance she'll notice me. I call my waiter over and tell him that I'll skip dessert and just take the bill.

While I wait, I watch Aleks. I have a better view of him than of Peggy. Animated, warm, smiling a lot. He doesn't speak much; he's just asking Peggy questions, and looking like he cares about the answers, which is actually pretty rare if you think about it. How many conversations have you been in where people are waiting for you to finish talking so they can chip in and tell *their* story of a similar thing that happened to them?

Then, the headwaiter goes over and shakes Aleks's hand like he's his long-lost brother. He talks animatedly, maybe describing all the special dishes he'll have the chef knock out just for them.

The headwaiter disappears, and I notice that Aleks's hand comes up to touch Peggy's, which is resting on the table. I can't tell if it's a romantic thing or a friendly reassurance thing. Peggy squeezes his hand back, then puts her hands down, off the table, back in her lap. I can't get a read on it. Peggy's a widow—her husband died just a few years back, and she can still barely mention him without tears coming to her eyes. But maybe she gets lonely sometimes. I mean, Aleks is still sort of handsome, and Peggy's not *that* old.

Within five minutes, the waiter returns with a wine bottle and goes through the opening and tasting rigmarole, after which he leaves it in an ice bucket near the table. As I'd hoped, Peggy excuses herself and goes off to the bathroom. I swear, there's an etiquette handbook somewhere that Peggy's parents had her inhale, and it says that a lady must always powder her nose ten minutes after arrival at dinner.

Leaving enough cash on the table to cover my meal, I get up to leave while Peggy is away. Aleks's waiter is still scooping ice into the bucket around the wine bottle. As I walk, I pretend to look in my bag for something and bring out a tiny dot microphone on my fingertip. As I pass their table, I touch it to the base of the ice bucket and keep walking. The bucket is wet, but Amber's microphone dots stick to anything.

Once I'm safely outside and on the next side street, I insert a tiny receiver into my ear and instantly I can hear the waiter talking, and a lot of rattling, which I assume is the ice inside the bucket. In a few seconds, it stops, and I can hear Aleks welcome Peggy back to the table. I stand in the quiet doorway of a closed butcher's shop where a lamb's carcass hangs in the window beside me, and listen intently. It's all old friends catching up with each other at the moment.

"How are the children?" Aleks asks her.

"Alice is in college in New York and Joseph's in Seattle now, with my first grandchild." Peggy sounds as pleased as punch.

"It's unbelievable. You don't look nearly old enough to be a grandmother."

What a line. Followed by silence. I wonder if he's trying the hand-holding again.

"And your son?" she asks.

"In the States."

That's true, I checked on young Sasha's whereabouts. He's studying in Minnesota.

"And Maya?" Peggy asks.

"We divorced, finally."

"I heard. I'm sorry."

Aleks makes a dismissive noise. "She's married again. To a so-called businessman who makes his money on the black market. Now she can have the Chanel bags she always wanted."

Another thing that checks out with what I dug up on Aleks. He pursued this thug through the courts only to have the case dismissed by a judge who somehow found the money to retire to Bermuda soon afterward. Then, to add insult to injury, Aleks's wife, who was a former model, up and left him for the same thug.

After this, they get onto the subject of Gregory Pavlic pretty quickly. Aleks's tone drops much lower, almost to a whisper.

"He's repulsive. But he has a lot of people in his pocket with blackmail."

"Aleks, don't feel I'm being impertinent, but does he have anything on you?"

"I'm not into drugs or one-night stands."

"I'm sorry I had to ask."

"Don't be," Aleks said. "Cleaning up this town has been a long road, getting one bastard at a time behind bars. There are one or two judges who care. And a small group of police. I meet with all of them every week, to keep them inspired. But getting Pavlic would send a message to the whole of Serbia. What's your interest in him?"

"I can't really discuss it at this point. But there may be some information coming that can help you."

"Well, with your contacts, nothing would surprise me. But be careful, Peggy," Aleks says. "You know I care about you."

Good God. Is he flirting with her? But Peggy says nothing and moves the conversation on to a charity gala she's organizing at the end of the year. Everything I've heard directly from Aleks's mouth bears out my research and supports Peggy's faith in their friendship. I decide to head back home and follow up on Paulina's Russian money, which looks like a much more promising lead.

7

THE NEXT MORNING, I GO for a long run first thing. It's a good way to get to know a place, and I've been neglecting my usual training regimen. Along the way, I stop at the main state registry building, to see if I can find any information (ideally a home address) on the directors of Lavit, since my online trawling hasn't yielded anything new. I hand over the details of Mikhail Rostov, the Russian guy, and Katarina Volim, the Serbian girl, but apparently, it takes twenty-four hours to lodge a request and have files brought up from storage. Seriously? Hasn't anyone heard of computer records? I fill in the required bits of paper and make an appointment to return the next morning.

On my way back home, I pick up some bread, cheese, eggs, and a few other bits so I can make breakfast. After which, I get dressed in my favorite shirt, a soft blue one, and check myself in the chipped bathroom mirror. I'm not one for makeup or spending ages on my hair, but I want to look halfway decent today.

What I see in the mirror is dark hair, green eyes, and Kit's nose, which she considers to be one of my best features—unlike my mouth, which she describes as "sullen." Maybe that's from my father.

I bring myself back to the task at hand and smile at my reflection. My whole face changes—for the better, I'll admit. I have a big smile, wide enough that it used to make me feel self-conscious, but people are always telling me they like it. By "people," I mean a couple of guys who wanted to go out with me. One at school, one at this programming class I did on weekends. When you're genuinely not interested, it's amazing how people are attracted to you.

I go back to my computer and tune in to listen for any Athena chatter, but nobody's online, it seems. Then I hang around by my window, waiting for Paulina Pavlic to arrive at the gallery, which she does, at about the same time as she did yesterday. I look down onto the street as she goes through the same bribery routine with the traffic cop. Then I head down to the gallery and take my time to settle in at a table in the coffee area, rummaging in my bag. I pull out the expensive camera I bought right before leaving London. Carelessly, I place it on the edge of my table. Then I switch on my iPad, yawn gently, and start to read.

Within a few minutes, a polite guy in a half apron arrives beside me. Irritably, I look up from my reading and snap out a complex coffee order. He has a little trouble with it, but I've already gone back to my tablet and given him little option but to retreat back to the barista and interpret it as best he can.

When he returns, I throw a glance at the cup and shake my head.

"This isn't what I ordered," I say.

"Double shot cappuccino?" the waiter stutters.

"Double macchiato," I say, a little too loudly. I make a show of tasting the coffee before pulling a face. Completely obnoxious. By now, the couple at the next table are watching me, and from the corner of my eye, I am sure that I can see Paulina heading toward me. I just keep my eyes fixed on the waiter as he hastily removes the cup.

Paulina doesn't come all the way to the table though. She gets close enough to beckon to the waiter and then walks with him back to the coffee machine, where she edges out the barista and prepares the coffee herself. Cool as a cucumber.

I pretend to be surprised when the cup touches the table. I look up, and Paulina is looking down at me coolly. Like she's daring me to make another scene.

"Your macchiato," Paulina says.

"Thank you," I say. "Sorry to have troubled you."

"It's my job."

"Trouble?" I ask, and Paulina smiles. It's like her surface composure splits open, allowing a tiny glimpse of a real person to peek through.

"Making sure my guests are happy," she replies.

I take a sip of the coffee. Paulina appears in no hurry to leave.

"It's delicious," I tell her.

"I know."

This time, I smile. At the arrogance, at the impressive self-assurance. I'm a bit out of my depth, to be honest—not half as composed as Paulina herself. But I'd rather she didn't know that. I look around the gallery, giving myself time to get back in control.

"Is this your place?" I ask.

There is a very slight hesitation from Paulina, and then she nods.

"The photography is stunning," I say. Not a genius comment, but I'm working under pressure here.

"I choose it all myself," she says.

"You have good taste."

Paulina smiles. "I know."

I hold her look, and it's exactly what I wanted; without any words passing between us, the moments seem to stretch out into some quiet meaning, until Paulina makes a conscious effort to look away. As I'd hoped, her gaze catches on the camera that sits on the table and her face lights up.

"Is that a Flex 1201?" she asks.

Silently, I thank the universe for making Paulina a real photography geek and not just a rich girl with artistic pretensions. I pass her the camera. Her fingers explore the controls easily, as if they are familiar to her.

"You can't get this model here yet," she says. "You're a photographer?" She looks at me with total interest now.

"It's my passion," I lie. "Not my profession. I'm still at university."

"Where?"

"London," I reply, which is somewhat vague, as the University of London is made up of a ton of different colleges all over the place, but I'd rather avoid specifics for as long as possible.

"I miss London so much," Paulina says, breaking into a genuine smile. "I was at school in England, and I went into the city as much as I could."

I hold out my hand. "Jessie."

"Paulina."

As her hand takes mine, I am surprised by a literal crackle of feeling in the touch between us. For a moment I think it might just be in my head, because, let's face it, I'm more than a bit taken with Paulina's looks. But when I look at her, I can tell that she has felt it too. She stops being so perfect and in control, just for a fraction of a second. But, immediately, she places down the camera and gives me a quick smile.

"Enjoy the coffee. It's on the house."

"There's no need—" I start to say, but I stop, because Paulina is already weaving her way between tables to the back of the room.

Returning to my apartment, I run through that interaction with Paulina again and again in my head. That thing that happened when she took my hand—it's thrilling to think about, but it also freaks me the hell out. This is the daughter of a criminal and a woman who's becoming a major suspect, in *my* investigations at least. I don't want to feel anything at all when I think of her (except, maybe, disgust). I pace about for a few minutes, then sit down to work. But Paulina and her eyes and her smile keep hanging there, where my logic should be.

That line I spun her about being a university student is partly true. I am registered (with a fake last name) on a master's degree course with a really good college in London. I'm sure the fact that their electronic engineering school got a shedload of new equipment from Li must have helped. It gives me some semblance of a life, if anyone were to ask.

Hala is registered as a cleaner with the company that handles Li's office-cleaning contracts, so when the asylum social workers come around, she has a legitimate job. And Caitlin is officially still Peggy's administrative assistant.

I get back to work. I can't find anything strange about the Russian bank that Paulina's payments came from. It's big, well-known, not an obvious money laundry for gangsters. For a break, I scroll some more through Paulina's Instagram feed. It's her main social media presence and is refreshingly free of pouting selfies and heavy on photos of artwork. She follows lots of photographers too.

From my window, I peer down inside the gallery as best I can, but there is no sign of Paulina. I leave my building and walk away from the gallery until I find a small place that serves local food. I order some kind of steak special and watch the world go by outside the window while I eat it. When I'm done, the waitress smiles at my clean plate and asks me if I want to try the homemade plum brandy. I decline, so she brings me a coffee instead and a slice of cake, even though I haven't asked for it. She's kind, and really young, maybe sixteen. Gregory Pavlic would look at her and calculate the profit he could make from selling her.

The thought bothers me. Every day we leave Gregory alone, another lot of girls gets trapped in his system. How many, I'm not sure, because the tentacles of a man like that go on and on. I finish up the coffee; pay the bill in cash, leaving a generous tip; and go back to my place.

I'm deep in tracking a trail on Gregory's Russian connection when my earpiece sputters into life, more clearly than it has in ages. It's Hala's voice that I hear, crisp and loud, and she's speaking in Arabic. All of which is really weird. If she's having a personal call with someone, why would she be connected to her Athena mic? Unless she's flipped it to a different channel and just carried on talking because she's not bothered to take it out of her ear. Whatever it is, her voice sounds warm and happy. My first thought is that she has a secret boyfriend somewhere, but then she says the name Omar, and I realize that it must be her brother she's speaking to. She has one brother who wasn't home when the attack on her parents happened. But he's still in the Middle East as far as I know. I listen, unable to piece together more than a few fragments of the meaning, but Hala's voice has changed now. She feels stressed, under pressure, talking to him. I flick on an app on my computer that records the audio. The conversation goes for another fifteen seconds before Hala hangs up. Immediately, I run the bit I taped through an online audio translator. I get back something like this:

Omar: "What time do you start work?"

Hala: "I have the late shift."

Her brother thinks she's a cleaner, so this makes sense, and I suppose it's even true, except that she will be gathering evidence from deep inside Gregory's illegal trafficking facility while Omar thinks she will be mopping floors in an office building somewhere. But then his tone changes.

"You said you would help me."

"I need time," Hala replies. "To plan things."

The next part doesn't translate well, but Omar's asking her something, insistent, pressuring her. Hala rushes him off the phone and hangs up.

I sit back and stare at the screen for a bit. Then I go and boil the kettle for tea. I don't know what to think about that little exchange. If her voice wasn't so stressed, I'd chalk it up to a million and one meaningless things. Maybe it's all fine. Maybe what's bugging me is that, once, if there was anyone she would have confided in, it was me.

I stand up and stretch and put Hala out of my mind. Keeping the lights off, I glance out of the window as I close the curtains. The gallery is dark now, with only picture lights illuminating one or two dramatic pieces of photography. A few people come and go on the street, and at a café across the way four men sit outside smoking and talking. The summer night air is cool. On a motorcycle, it'll feel colder. So I put on my leather jacket before I go out.

My first stop is one of Belgrade's trendiest bars. My remote snooping around Paulina's phone has yielded the fact that she's meeting some friends there tonight. Since this is a relatively small city, and since the cool places to hang out are mainly in one tiny section of it, I don't think it would be weird for me to bump into her there.

The place is filling up by the time I arrive. I install myself at the impressive bar, featuring a wall of mirrors, which gives me an excellent view of the whole place, including Paulina's table, which is perhaps the largest in the room. She is sitting with three other people—a young couple holding hands and a man who feels a bit older but who I can only see in profile. Since I'd rather engineer this whole meeting to look completely random, it's better not to rush things, so I order a sparkling water and exchange a few words with the two young guys standing next to me. Just to blend in. They speak good English, and are funny and easy to talk to and the conversation flows so well that when I feel a delicate touch on my back—it literally makes me jump.

I turn on my seat to find Paulina standing there.

"It's Jessie, right?"

She looks incredible. A crimson shirt, faded jeans, a slim gold chain around her neck. I nod, and her face lights up in this big smile, like I've made her night by just existing. She reminds me who she is and where we met. I pretend to remember.

"Of course," I say. "Let me buy you a drink."

"Are you on your own?" she asks, with a quick glance at the young men who were talking to me but who are now mostly just staring at her. I assure her I'm alone and we go through this little charade where she asks me to join her table, and I tell her I couldn't possibly intrude, and then she insists.

I follow her over there.

"Jessie, meet Leka and Maria, friends of mine who just got married. . . ." The couple wave at me and kiss each other.

"They're still in that romantic stage," Paulina says, smiling at me.

Both Paulina and I look away from them, to the older man. He is lean, his suit perfectly cut, his hair sprinkled with flecks of gray that bring out crisp blue eyes. I feel my stomach drop. Holy crap, I wasn't expecting this.

"Papa, this is my friend Jessie," Paulina says.

I shake hands because it's an automatic reflex, but I am so surprised I could fall over. I look down at the manicured fingers of Gregory Pavlic, clasping my hand in his own. He looks much better than his photos. He's also smaller than I expected, with a refined appearance. Not the muscle-bound towering hulk that I had imagined, working his way up in the world from those despair-soaked high-rises.

"Good to meet you," he says in heavily accented English.

I smile politely.

"Where are you from?" he asks.

"London."

"Holiday?" His blue eyes never waver from mine. Cold. Of course.

"Yes."

"Why Belgrade?"

Good question, Gregory. Because I want to crush you and your filthy business activities over the course of the next few days.

"I promised myself to visit every capital in Eastern Europe before I turn twenty-one," I lie.

Already bored with me, he moves aside to offer me his seat, and I slide into the booth. Then he nods at all of us and says something in Serbian, taking his leave. The young couple urge him to stay, but he declines. Thank God.

"My father just came to have a drink with me," Paulina explains, for my benefit.

"I never see her," says Gregory.

"Except that we live in the same house," says Paulina dryly.

Gregory says something affectionate to his daughter in reply, and his hand comes up to caress her hair gently. She pulls away, very slightly. Is she repelled by him or just embarrassed? Gregory turns and walks away, preceded by a bodyguard in a black suit. In his wake trails a headwaiter, hurrying to keep up. I watch as Gregory reaches the door. A coat is produced, and cash tips are handed out before he exits into, I assume, a waiting limo. When I look back at Paulina, her eyes are on me.

"Your dad seems great," I say. "What does he do?"

"All sorts of businesses. I don't keep track." She takes a breath in as if tired suddenly.

"What about the gallery?"

"That's mine," she says. "I always wanted to have my own thing."

But using his cash, I think to myself.

"Why?" I ask.

She hesitates. "Parents put pressure on you. And my father is powerful. I want some independence."

"The gallery seems to be busy," I say encouragingly.

"It's mainly coffee. The art sales make the real income. But Belgrade is limited for that. Not like Moscow. Or London." She's trying to bring me into the conversation, but that mention of Moscow has me on edge. I have to try hard not to jump straight onto it. Instead, I leave a small silence, like I'm interested, but not that much.

"What do your parents do?" Paulina asks me.

I take a moment to erase Kit from my mind and replace her with someone imaginary, based on Li.

"My mother made money in technology. She's retired now."

Having seen just a little bit of Paulina's high-end world, I decide she might feel more comfortable knowing I'm used to wealth and privilege, not overwhelmed by it.

The other couple surfaces from their endless kissing, so Paulina turns her attention to them. There are a few minutes during which we all chat together and order more drinks. After that, I steer the conversation again.

"You mentioned Moscow. I'm thinking of visiting . . ."

"It's great," Paulina says, smiling. "I've been there twice this year already. But for work, mainly."

"What work?" I ask, wondering why she's being so open about it.

She looks at me, surprised. "The gallery," she says.

I listen as she continues.

"I've been working with a few art spaces in Moscow, getting them interested in the young Belgrade photographers I show here."

"Good idea," I say. "How is it going?"

"Really well. They already bought a lot of artwork at really high prices. I mean, they are good pieces—but sometimes the Russians have more money than sense."

I smile, and Paulina holds my look, like we're sharing a joke. As I take in her open gaze, part of me is totally relieved. That there is a real, honest explanation for those trips to Moscow and for all that money in her account. And that she's clearly working to earn her own living, away from Gregory's businesses. Paulina is beautiful and self-assured and perfectly turned-out but despite all that, I can't help but like her. Part of me is relieved that she seems to be, as Thomas put it, squeaky-clean. I look around the bar, trying to stop myself from just staring at her. Because she is pretty amazing to look at.

"Popular place," I comment.

She nods. "Belgrade is small. There are maybe two places where anyone who's anyone goes for drinks. And this is one of them."

We talk for a while longer, and as Paulina speaks, she leans in to me, to be sure I can hear her over the loud music that pounds in the background. She's very close, and the warmth and the scent of her are making me forget what I was doing here to begin with.

Maybe a little abruptly, I excuse myself and head to the bathroom, fighting through the ever-growing crowd. I take my time in there, calming down, giving myself a moment to get centered again. Exiting the toilet stall, I wash my hands and check myself in the mirror. Be charming, Jessie. You're in control here. And remember who she is.

The door of the bathroom opens and, just my luck, Paulina comes in. I smile. So does she. I wait for her to go into a stall, but she doesn't. She just stands next to me.

"What is it?" I ask, a bit thrown.

"Are you okay? You got up so fast."

"I'm fine. Are you?"

She's standing a bit too close to me. Not too obvious, but a tiny bit inside my personal space. Not that I mind it. At all.

"You always answer a question with a question," Paulina says, her eyes smiling.

"Do I?" I ask, and we both laugh.

The bathroom door opens again and, it's weird, but we both step away from each other. Like we were up to something, even though we weren't. The woman who comes in walks straight to the stall at the end and closes the door. I look at Paulina. She is touching up her lipstick, now. But her eyes meet mine in the mirror and she smiles.

The breeze is cool, verging on cold, but it feels good to be outside and alone as I get onto my motorbike. I made myself leave the bar after another twenty minutes; I have a task to complete tonight and hanging out over drinks with a girl I can find nothing incriminating on is probably not a good enough reason to skip it.

The bike handles reasonably well, and anyway, I'm not trying to break any speed records. I just want to drive out to where Gregory has his horrible trafficking operation. A few cars come and go through the tower blocks of New Belgrade, but there aren't many people on the street except a couple of women who hang around in short skirts and makeup, looking for passing trade. I'm almost relieved to get past the high-rises, and then a small area of suburb, and onto an open road with nothing on one side but scrubby wasteland that becomes more thickly wooded as I ride.

There's something soothing about the dull roar of an engine. I ride the motorcycle at a steady speed and the noise washes my mind clean. It's a moment of release. For a few moments I forget about Paulina. I forget about Ahmed and what happened in Africa. And I stop worrying about what will happen this week. Then the red line on my phone's map shifts to show an imminent left turn, and I slow the bike so I can find the turnoff. When I see it—a thin trail of gravel—I slide onto it and drive through the woods slowly, weaving past potholes.

At a small break in the woodland, I stop the bike and swing down off it. Ahead of me, a brick wall towers above the trees. A few security lights are perched on top of the bricks, nestled in among barbed wire. From this angle I can only see the top floors of the abandoned hospital rising behind it. Dark windows that you can't see into, and an aura of despair.

On foot, I track back to the main road, from where I came. Behind me, there's a sound and I spin around quickly. But it's nothing. The woods are full of creaking, cracking twigs, and the rustling of small animals. But now I can hear something more—an engine, coming down the road toward me. I stay back, well hidden, and watch it as it passes. White, no markings—standard supply truck. I make a mental note of the make of the vehicle and watch as it goes all the way to the end of the road.

I made sure to wear the zoom contact lens we used in Cameroon, so with just a couple of blinks I can get a much better look at what's happening without having to get too close. The truck stands there, waiting, by a massive metal gate. As it opens, four men come into view, hanging around, watching, cradling automatic weapons in their arms. Just like that, not even trying to hide them.

But then, who would they be trying to hide from? There's nobody out here, and the police probably know enough—or are paid enough by Gregory—to keep well away. I try to get a glimpse of what's behind the gate, but I can't see much except a lit-up loading bay and a greenish light in a corridor. The place looks huge, and I wonder how many women Gregory has in there. And what he releases them to? A life of slavery, to be used in whatever way yields him the biggest profit.

I'm walking back to the bike as quietly as I can when I hear something else. From above, like a bird. But it's nighttime, and it feels weird that there should be a bird rustling up there. I look up and it's too late. Something big and heavy falls onto me, and I crash to the ground.

8

I HAVE A MOUTHFUL OF dirt. Damp earth and pine needles. I fight to twist my way out, but my attacker has legs on either side of me and an arm on my head, and I can't move. Feeling paralyzed sets me off into panic, but somewhere in my head, there's a sense of the familiar. The look of the hands that are grasping mine, the scent of the person on top of me. My brain makes a connection. I stop resisting and wait, suddenly realizing who it is. Slowly, Hala releases the pressure of her arm, so I can move my head to look at her.

"I missed you," I say.

My face hits the dirt again. Okay, maybe there was just a hint of sarcasm in that comment.

"Let go of me," I try, but it comes out a garbled mess with my mouth against the forest floor. But suddenly Hala's grip softens again, and it's almost easy for me to twist and cuff her off me entirely. I sit up.

"What are you doing here?" I ask, spitting a few times to get rid of the dirt in my mouth.

"I just landed a micro drone on that van," she says.

I get it now. She'll get a camera the size of an insect right into the middle of Gregory's facility and get video footage of what's happening inside. And all by remote control from her phone.

But even as I catch a glimpse of Hala's screen, the picture from that drone cuts out. All she has is lines of static, no video at all. She looks at me, alarmed.

"They must have a scrambler," I say.

She nods, and I hurry to follow her, because she's already taken off, heading toward the hospital.

"What are you doing?"

"Is that it?" Hala asks, ignoring the question, and pointing to an antenna that's perched high on top of the wall that surrounds the place.

"Probably." We've dropped our voices to a whisper, because we are close enough now to hear the low sounds of the guards talking on the other side of the wall. I'm thinking about how we can jam the signal on the scrambler or, failing that, try to get the drone out of range, when I see that Hala is already scaling the wall, finding tiny foot- and handholds in the crumbling brick.

"Are you nuts?" I hiss in a whisper that she can't hear, because she's already twenty feet up. It's breathtaking to watch, but I also feel like she's climbing to her death. Those guards are right there, on the other side, decked out with machine guns. A laugh bubbles up as they tease each other about something.

Hala's at the top of the wall, hanging there with ease, like she's relaxing on the beach. But she can't reach up and disable that scrambler without the guards seeing her if they so much as glance up. She looks down at me. I spread my hands. Like, what does she want me to do?

Hala takes a small ball from her jacket and drops it down to me. It's a tiny smoke ball that disintegrates after use. So it leaves no trace, not to mention being environmentally friendly. Okay, not a bad plan. I take a few paces back, then run and fling the ball over the wall as hard and far as I can.

Hala peers over, and I stand below her, waiting. Then—there's some commotion. The guards must have noticed a stream of smoke issuing up out of nowhere and they head toward it, their voices receding from us. Hala shoots me her happy look (almost indistinguishable from a frown on anyone else) and swings herself onto the antenna, hanging off it while she opens a panel holding wires. Using a cutter, she clips them, then rips out the electronic board inside for good measure.

The antenna creaks and buckles from her weight but, lightly, Hala jumps back to the wall and starts to descend, the worn bricks crumbling under her feet. She falls the last few feet and I help her up.

We run back into the trees and crouch together to check the screen on her phone. The signal is back and, for a moment, Hala pilots the drone deeper into the hospital till it reaches a ward. Old metal beds, torn curtains, and women lying there, some on drips.

It's like something out of a horror movie.

But now, I'm getting a weird feeling from Hala herself, like she is watching me as much as the footage. I don't feel good about it.

"Why did you jump on me when I first got here?" I ask her. She doesn't reply. And in my gut, I know the answer.

I take off. Run for it, like crazy. I glance over my shoulder to see where Hala is—and I stop running. Because she has a gun out. And it's pointed at me. I'm speechless. Almost.

"You must be joking," I say.

Hala doesn't answer, but she has enough grace to look a little bit sheepish.

"Put it down," I say. But she doesn't.

"It's only tranquilizer darts," she says.

Like that makes it much better. That I'm staring down the barrel of something that won't kill me, it'll only sedate me as if I'm a mad dog. In a way, I'd like it better if it were a real gun because the chances of Hala shooting me dead are zero. But with this thing, who knows if she's stressed enough to go ahead and pull the trigger?

"Hala?" I ask. "We're friends, right?"

Her dark eyes waver. But she doesn't look friendly, only angry.

"I have orders to bring you in if I find you."

"So you just do what you're told, no matter what?"

"That's what an order is!" Hala snaps in an undertone. "You broke orders and killed Ahmed, and you broke us up as a team."

She's right. I raise my hands and walk slowly toward her, defeated.

"Put it down. I'll come in with you."

Hala looks relieved but doesn't actually drop the dart gun.

"Do you have a car?" I ask her.

"Motorbike."

"Do you really want to haul my drugged body all the way to your bike and drive me unconscious through the streets of Belgrade?"

I reach her and push the gun gently aside and then wait while Hala holsters it. I even offer to carry her backpack for her, because that's what friends do, but she declines. We walk back toward where her bike is, which is very near mine—not surprising, as we both must have taken the same path in. And then I drop back a pace and deliver an almighty chop to the back of her knees. While she's still down, kneeling in the dirt, I come around to her front and deliver a couple more blows. I literally hate doing it, but she hasn't given me much of an option. A one-two punch to her solar plexus and then an upward push from her stomach to her ribs winds her. That's all I want to do—buy some time to escape.

She lies there, gasping for breath and, for a moment, I hesitate. In any other universe, I'd be helping her, not hurting her.

"I'm sorry," I tell her, and I mean it.

I run hard, to my motorcycle, kicking it on and roaring out of there as fast as I can.

As I ride back toward the center of town, something occurs to me. I veer off into the tower blocks and, when I can't see anyone around, I pull up next to one of those big rubbish dumpsters. I take off my beautiful, broken-in jacket, empty the pockets, and toss it inside, just in case Hala has thought to stick a tracking device on me. Amber's team makes everything so transparent and wafer-thin that I don't trust I'll find anything just by patting myself down.

Back at the apartment, I get into bed, but I'm too keyed up to sleep. All I can think about is Hala, out there, gasping in the forest. And the way I lied to her so I could catch an element of surprise against her. It's not doing wonders for my self-esteem, but the alternative is to be waking up in the Athena house a couple of hours from now with a bloodstream full of drugs and zero control over my destiny. I switch on the TV. They're playing an old movie dubbed into Serbian, and finally I drift into sleep.

I wake just after 8:00 a.m., blinking and gritty-eyed. The television is still on. I flick it off and reach for my laptop and my new morning routine of scanning the local newspapers online. The only thing worth translating this morning is a profile piece on Aleks Yuchic. The article is about how many arrests he's managed since becoming justice minister, though there's a snide paragraph about how the gangsters he's rounded up so far are small-timers. But it all bodes well for the job that Peggy has lined up for him—bringing Gregory Pavlic, the biggest gangster of them all, to justice.

When I go into the gallery this time, I don't head straight for the coffee area at the far end. Instead, I move slowly from exhibit to exhibit, pausing before each piece of photography and examining it. The prints are a series of city scenes, highly treated, saturated with color in a way that seems to have sapped the life out of them without replacing it with any other meaning. Maybe it's art, or maybe it's someone trying a bit too hard. While I'm looking, I run through the coming conversation with Paulina in my mind. How she might begin it, how it could end. It's a habit I've had for a long time now. Playing out a situation in my head. I first started to do it when I was nervous to see my mother again after Kit had been away for weeks; when I wanted to seem confident and funny, not nerdy and intense—a daughter who Kit would appreciate and who she might regret not being with more. Sometimes it worked, but after a while I began to resent the fact that Kit was still always away, and I stopped trying so hard to please her.

When I'm done with the exhibit, I swing my bag off my shoulder, drop it onto a chair, and sit down. Finally, I look over at the coffee bar. Paulina is using a remote control to flick through silent TV channels on the big flat-screen above the bar while a waitress ties on a black apron and prepares to come over to serve me.

With her eyes still on the screen, Paulina says something to the waitress, and the girl stops in her tracks. Paulina goes over to the coffee machine and throws me a smile.

While she makes the coffee, I look out the window, counting passersby to focus myself. Soon enough, Paulina's standing before me and I half rise to take the cup she offers.

"Your macchiato."

"Thank you. You didn't have to make it yourself."

"But I don't want you to terrify the staff." Paulina's eyes smile.

"I'm sorry about yesterday," I say.

"You were more relaxed at the bar. It was good to see you."

I nod my agreement, and she sits down at my table, while I take a sip of the coffee.

"I feel like I did all the talking last night," she begins. "I want to know more about you."

It flashes into my mind that Paulina might not just be making conversation. What if she suspected my motives yesterday and spent the past twelve hours using Gregory's highly evolved network of Eastern European tech geniuses to trace my true identity? What if she knows that, far from being a graduate student, I work for a rogue organization that is now dedicating all its resources to taking down her father? I blink and try to focus on Paulina's eyes. Which are smiling at me.

"What's your subject? At university?" Paulina asks kindly. Maybe she's used to people behaving like nervous idiots in front of her.

"Electronic engineering," I say, recovering myself. "I like circuits and wires and computer code."

"Wow, that's impressive," she says, and it feels like she means it.

I reach into my bag and bring out a small gift-wrapped package. She hesitates, confused.

"To say thank you for the coffee yesterday," I say. "And the drinks." Although I originally arranged this "gift" with an ulterior motive, it turns out I'm genuinely happy to be giving it to Paulina.

She lifts up the tape, edging back the wrapping paper as carefully as if she might use it again one day, and lifts out a book of photography. I watch her fingers caress the dust jacket and then open the book gently, as if the pages might be made of glass. She looks up at me.

"It's really beautiful."

"I'm glad you like it."

The moment feels awkward, somehow, and I glance away, to the pictures on the walls.

"Who are your favorite photographers?" I ask.

She names a few people, none of whom I've heard of, and I ask her a little more about how she became so passionate about it. It's clear she knows a lot about photography and art. The conversation comes to a natural pause. Here's my opportunity. I steel myself.

"Why don't we have a drink tonight?" My voice is low, so the waitress can't hear me, nor the older couple who have just strolled in for coffee.

Paulina meets my gaze. "I can't. I would have but . . ."

"It's fine," I say lightly. Funnily enough, I still feel disappointed, even though I know very well that she is busy tonight. Paulina seems anxious to explain.

"I have to be at my father's birthday party."

You don't say.

I try to appear uninterested and take a sip of water.

"Sounds nice and quiet."

There's a bit of teasing in my tone, and Paulina gives me a half smile.

"My father is lacking in a lot of things—but he knows how to throw a party," she says.

I look unconvinced. "That's great."

"Have you heard of Kit Love?" Paulina asks, apparently intent on defending the family honor. "She's pretty good. And loud."

"Who?" I ask.

Paulina shakes her head indulgently at my ignorance.

"Come as my guest tonight."

I look appalled at the idea. "Seriously? No! I wouldn't crash a family birthday!"

"You won't be crashing."

I shake my head again, brushing her off.

"Really, trust me," she says, working hard to convince me. "It's me, my father, and five *hundred* of his closest friends. He won't even notice you. You have to."

Paulina touches my hand gently. As if to stop me from protesting. Does she have *any* idea how I feel when she touches me? I look at her and I realize, yes, she does. She smiles. And I nod, hesitantly, accepting her invitation. Paulina's eyes are clear and direct, and yet I can't read them right now. For a moment, I wonder if I've opened the door to more trouble than I can handle, getting myself invited to Gregory's party, where my mother is the headline act. But the thought flies out of my head as quickly as dust in a breath of wind. I have what I wanted.

I make plans to meet Paulina back here this evening and go with her to her father's house, and then I head out to the state registry, where I'm hoping that they finally found my files.

9

DEALING WITH GOVERNMENT DEPARTMENTS ANYWHERE in the world is a big pain, but the public records office here is something else. It's been over an hour since I went up to a metal counter that looks like a relic from the sixties and communicated my request to the clerk. She's a hundred years old if she's a day, but with hair dyed platinum blond and a cigarette stuck in the side of her mouth.

She keeps me hanging around forever, even though I had an appointment. The place smells like boiled cabbage, and there are a few people in and out, but it's hardly overrun. While I'm sitting there, I start thinking about all the births and deaths and marriages that have been registered here. Millions of them over generations, just for this little city in this tiny country. Babies being born, screaming for air, learning to walk, going through school, falling in love, having more babies, working like mad to pay a mortgage and food bills, and then dying. It makes me wonder if I'd ever want to have children. I'd want to be someone they could look up to and trust. Not like Gregory with Paulina. Though, he probably thinks he's giving her a good life, and on some level, she must love him. Even if she wants to break away.

Thinking about Paulina and Gregory makes me think about my father. Except there's a big vacuum where that thought should be. At first (meaning, for the first fifteen years of my life) Kit told me that he'd died when I was two. I had a whole story about him in my head that I built on when I was a kid. I used to picture him to myself as a long-haired hippie type of guy who played guitar and who'd had a quick fling on the road before dying of an unspecified illness, probably due to him being a sensitive, poetic soul in love with a self-absorbed music star who'd flung him aside.

This definitely made it easier at school when it was time for us to make Father's Day cards. I always made a card for my mother instead and got the silent sympathy vote from my teachers. And that, if you can believe it, was Kit's justification for using that lie my entire life. She lied to make it *easier* for me. What she really meant was, to make it easier for *her*.

When I was fifteen, I got fixated on the idea that I wanted to see his grave. Kit evaded it for a while; tried to avoid the subject. But then, I tracked down my own birth certificate and there it was—a big blank in the space for my father's name. After which, Kit admitted that my father wasn't dead at all. That he had been married at the time (to someone who wasn't Kit, clearly), and that she had never told him about me.

To say I was upset is a bit of an understatement. I didn't talk to her for a week. The deceit drove me crazy. That all my life she had lied to me and only crumbled and told the truth when I pushed it. Not because it was the right thing to do.

I've worked myself up into such a fury about Kit that I miss my name being called by the clerk. She has to practically yell at me to get my attention, and I jump up and take the folders she's handed me. They are files on the two directors of the holding company linked to Gregory Pavlic, the two my research suggested might possibly still be alive. Inside the thin cardboard covers, there is nothing much on the Russian guy, Mikhail Rostov; but there is a birth certificate and social security number and basic information for the woman director, Katarina Volim. From the certificate I calculate that she's twenty-three. So it could actually be the same person I saw on Facebook; but could she really be the third director?

I ask the clerk if there isn't another record under the same name, but she insists that's the only one. I snap a picture of the birth certificate, address, and other information with my phone, hand back the file, and get out of there.

The address is in an old part of the city, in an area of tiny little houses packed together. At least some of them are painted, and a few have flowerpots on the window ledges. It takes me a while to find the right place, because street names around here seem to be hit or miss. Kit's always lecturing me about the law of attraction— visualize something and it will happen over time. So when I knock on the door, I imagine the girl—this mystery director of the Russian shell company—flinging open the door and speaking perfect English. What I actually get is a man who might be around fifty but who looks older just because he's so desperately sick. Pale, ashy skin, and flyaway hair. He stares out at me, and the sound of his every breath hangs between us, a series of painful-sounding wheezes. Before I can say anything, he is pulled away from the door, and a plump, tired-looking woman takes his place. The man shuffles back into a living room with a patterned carpet and a small oxygen tank sitting next to his flowery armchair. He probably has emphysema. Though he still keeps a pack of cigarettes on the side table.

His wife seems pleasant enough, but she rattles off a question in Serbian.

"I'm looking for Katarina," I say in English. "I'm a friend of hers."

I'm not sure she understands, but speaking in English is helping me, I think. At least she must figure I'm not police or the tax authorities.

"Katarina friend?" she repeats.

I nod encouragingly.

"Do you have her address?"

Nothing.

"Where is her house?" I try. The mother (because I'm assuming this is her mother) hesitates.

"You have work for Katarina?" she asks.

I look at her. Her eyes are hopeful.

"Yes," I say.

The woman disappears, leaving the door open. The father turns a bit in his chair and looks at me balefully. I venture a smile, but he just turns back to the TV. The sounds of game show buzzers and applause floats out to me.

Katarina's mother comes back with a piece of paper on which an address is neatly written in scrolled letters, the kind they must have taught in school forty years ago. I smile and thank her. Then she steps back as if to welcome me in and says something else, making a tea-drinking motion with one hand. I thank her, but point at my watch to suggest that I have to hurry. Disappointed, she stands at the door and waves while I get back onto the motorcycle. I wave back and head off before stopping farther down the road to tap the address into my navigation system. Katarina lives quite a way from here, over in New Belgrade.

I haven't been wandering around this section of town for long before I figure out it's where the prostitutes work. Maybe Gregory Pavlic has a setup here, but it certainly doesn't look like the place in which a legitimate company director would be hanging out. But then this is a shell company, an obvious front for something dodgy, something to do with that Russian clinic.

I walk through a warren of urine-scented alleyways that pass between gray blocks of government housing. Empty beer cans decorate the streets here, and even the ever-present graffiti looks less skillfully applied.

The address I want leads into an open doorway where a sheet of paper is taped to the wall with an arrow that points up the staircase ahead. Above the arrow is written a word in Serbian and, below that, the word *SERVICE* in smudged orange marker. I guess they don't want to miss out on the international clientele. As I pause at the foot of the stairs, I hear a clicking sound. Behind me, an old lady is sweeping the steps in the opposite doorway. She wears a head scarf patterned with yellow daisies, a bit of freshness in this depressing place, but she regards me with suspicion, clicking her tongue again, disapproving. Quickly, I head up the concrete steps, taking them two at a time. I'm freaked out, to tell you the truth. I've never been in a place like this before, and I'm not sure what to expect.

Turning left into a tiny hallway, I find the right door. It has a splintered edge that I touch as I knock. I focus on the rough shards of broken wood under my fingertips as, again, I try to picture Katarina coming to the threshold and having a nice chat. The door opens, and there's a huge man standing there. He's not just tall but also wide, shaped like a squat refrigerator. This visualizing thing is not happening for me.

"Is Katarina here?" I ask.

The man just looks at me.

"I'm a friend of hers," I say.

The great thing about being a girl my age is that no one ever sees you as a threat. Or, in this case, as a customer.

He holds out a paw-like hand to indicate that I should stay put. Then he leaves the door ajar and lumbers back into the apartment. When he returns, someone is with him. With a careless flick of her wrist, a young woman draws him back and steps onto the threshold. She's not that much older than me, but it feels like she's seen a lot more of life than I have. She's wrapped in an indigo polyester robe that stops just above the knee. Her dark, tousled hair falls over eyes that are still hazy with sleep.

"Katarina?" I ask.

"Who are you?" she says, having acknowledged her name with a quick nod of her head.

"My name is Daisy," I say, thinking about the flowers on the head scarf of the old lady sweeping down below. "Can I have a few minutes to ask you something?"

"Journalist?" Katarina asks. Her eyes rake over me.

"No. I promise, I'll only take five minutes."

I try to look young and clueless and friendly. I don't have to act the first two. But it's not having much impact.

"I can pay you for your time," I try.

That seems to do the trick. Katarina motions me inside.

I follow her down the thin hallway, past a living room where the bearlike man slumps in an armchair in front of a TV playing cartoons. We veer left and into Katarina's room. The wallpaper is striped maroon and gold and the bedcovers, so recently thrown back, are also maroon, with satin edging. In one corner there's a low armchair, and in another, a floor lamp casts a warm pool of light. Katarina sits down tiredly on the bed. I perch on the chair and try to think of a conversational way in.

"Your mother gave me your address," I say.

"Why?" Katarina asks crisply.

So much for a chat about the parents, then.

"I told her I had work for you."

"Do you?"

"No," I reply. "But I will pay you for your time."

This makes Katarina laugh, and her laugh dissolves into a cough that sounds like the residue of a thousand cheap cigarettes. I'm feeling out of my depth here. I can't gauge her at all. I decide to plow on and see what happens. I take out two fifty-pound notes and reach across to leave them on the table beside the bed.

"You want only to talk?" says Katarina.

"Yes, please."

"Then this money is too much."

I appreciate the honesty, but I leave the cash where it is.

"Do you know a company called Lavit?" I start.

Katarina shakes her head, and I believe her.

"You're listed as a director of the company."

Katarina shifts slightly. "I never hear of it," she says.

"Have you heard of Gregory Pavlic?" I ask.

She shrugs the question off, but this time I know she's lying. She picks up a pack of cigarettes and takes one out. She offers me one, and I refuse. I watch her light up and drag on it and I think about her father dying of emphysema in front of a TV game show. If there's one thing I can't stand, it's smoking. You stink, your clothes reek, your mouth tastes like an ashtray, and then you die an early and painful death. Awesome marketing from tobacco companies though; you have to give them their due.

"You know Gregory Pavlic," I say.

Katarina sighs. "You're stupid," she tells me. "Pavlic will kill you if you write about him."

"I'm not a journalist."

She shrugs again.

"I don't know Pavlic, and I don't *want* to know him," she says, and she turns her head away from me.

I'm beginning to get ticked off. "Everybody here knows him," I say.

Katarina sighs again and looks at her watch. "His guys are always around," she offers.

"Do they give you any trouble?"

"I'm not worth it for them. There are many girls who are young and stupid enough to buy their stories."

"What stories?" I ask.

"The usual. They sell dreams. Money, champagne, rich guys in fancy nightclubs . . ."

As she talks, Katarina uses the nail of her right thumb to chip away at the black varnish on her left hand. It seems like a losing battle to me, but it's probably a nervous habit.

"And they fall for that?"

Katarina looks at me sharply. For the first time, her eyes take me in properly, my clothes, my shoes. Hardly high-end but not cheap either.

"When you're fifteen," she says, "with no job, and a boyfriend who beats you, you fall for anything."

That shuts me up. Katarina looks down and continues picking at her nail polish until tiny black splinters fall onto the sheets. I'm not sure what to do next except try hinting at the half-formed theory that's been bugging me since I found that website with the designer babies on it.

"Pavlic is doing something new," I say. Just from the way she glances up, I feel like I'm on to something. I wait, because Peggy once told me that, given a silence, most people will fill it up. But Katarina apparently hasn't read that page in Peggy's Ivy League etiquette manual. She just gives me a good, long stare, then carries on tormenting her nails.

"He's harvesting eggs from these girls, isn't he?"

She seems almost relieved at that. Why would she be *relieved* to hear that Gregory is taking eggs from these women?

"They like it better," she says. "No sex work. Just take fertility drugs and give the eggs."

"What does he do with the eggs?"

Katarina looks up. "How do I know? Probably sells them."

"To Russia?"

Katarina's eyes catch mine. But she says nothing.

"The company you are a director of is Russian, and it has something to do with the Victory Clinic near Moscow."

Katarina stands up, stubs out her cigarette, and hands me back the cash I left her. I refuse to take it. I stand up too, planting myself in the room. What's she going to do, throw me out? Then I remember the enormous guy in the other room. I change tack.

"Please, Katarina," I say. "A lot of money is going through this company suddenly. What for?"

I am a little taller than her, and stronger, but I try not to intimidate her.

"Do you work for Pavlic?" I ask.

She sticks to a stubborn silence.

"Katarina, there are a lot of girls in trouble. You can help them. And, whatever is going on, when it comes out, you'll be the one in jail. It's your name on that company."

More silence. But I can feel her caving. Whether from the goodness of her heart, or the idea of rotting in a Serbian prison, I don't know and don't care.

"Pavlic let me go," she says. "He liked me. First, I was one of those girls. In the nightclubs. I made friends with big politician. Married guy. For Gregory to take pictures of us together. And I told him what this politician told me. It helped Gregory. So he helped me. He paid for my father's hospital treatment. And he told me he will not use me anymore, only my name. For a business."

"So why are you still working here?" I ask. I'm not trying to offend her, but the idea of this young, fragile girl in this room with a succession of customers stresses me out.

"I am good at this job," she says with a short laugh.

I feel nauseous, suddenly, and oppressed. I look at the window while I think. I can't figure out why she's told me all this. Beyond the net curtain, a thin branch curls past, touching the glass, and a little brown bird lands on it. The living creature feels out of place here, where everything else feels dead. I turn to Katarina again. She leans her head back against the wall and adjusts her robe back over her thigh.

"So the new business in Russia is selling eggs to infertile couples?"

"I don't know what Pavlic is doing." Her voice rises, and it sounds like panic. "But he is the devil. Trafficking is not enough. Eggs, not enough. He wants more."

"Like what?"

But she just stands up and opens the bedroom door.

"You want some service?" she asks, matter-of-fact. "You paid a lot."

That takes me by surprise. "No, thanks," I reply, polite.

I come out to the hallway. Katarina's voice calls out an instruction in Serbian. I assume she's asking meathead to escort me out, but instead he lumbers into Katarina's room. He is gone for maybe twenty seconds before he emerges and moves down the hallway to where I stand. He hands me a business card. A thin, dog-eared scrap with an outline of a naked woman on it, and a phone number.

I step out into the concrete stairwell, confused and a bit depressed by the whole incident. As I reach the bottom of the steps, I'm relieved that the old lady with the daisy scarf and the broom has gone. I look down at Katarina's card and as I turn it, I see black ink scrawled across the back. Quickly, I read. She's written down an address, here in Belgrade, along with a time—3:00 a.m. I look back up at the dingy windows, and they stare back at me blankly. I tuck the card into my pocket and walk away as fast as I can.

10

THE FIRST THING I DO when I'm back in the apartment is locate the address that Katarina scrawled down. It's not all that far from where she lives, just a set of high-rise apartment blocks. So, what is happening there in the early hours of tomorrow?

Then I settle in to try and dig up something more on this Victory Clinic in Moscow. I get as far as page nineteen of an internet search. That's persistence for you, but sometimes it pays off. There's a blog sitting there, in Chinese, with a JPEG attachment. I can't make much sense of the blog, even with a web translator, but the attachment is a photo of part of an article (in English) about the Victory, and, even though one side of the article is missing, it's pretty clear that it's a place where wealthy Chinese and Russians go for fertility treatments, surrogacy, and designing their perfect babies—which are mostly boys, it seems. Clearly the article has been suppressed. But then, Victory Clinic can probably afford to hire a hundred

Russian hackers to bury anything they think is bad press.

In any event, what that piece tells me is that my guess was probably a good one. That Gregory most likely imprisons these girls in the abandoned hospital, pumps them with drugs and harvests their eggs, sending a constant supply to Moscow. That also fits what I saw on Hala's screen from the drone footage. And yet . . . Katarina's words come back to me—that eggs were not enough for Gregory. What did she mean?

My little apartment feels dark and drab suddenly. I divert myself by connecting back in to Athena chatter. Now that Gregory's party is happening, the final piece of the plan is being put into place—the plan to break into Gregory's office and retrieve the drive where he keeps the data that he uses for blackmailing police and politicians. I tune in and listen. Hearing Caitlin's slow drawl makes me smile as she chats to Amber. The truth is, I miss Caitlin and Amber, and even Hala's pessimism. It's like having a family. *Was* like having a family.

"She's had two rehearsals and she sounds great," Caitlin says, obviously discussing Kit.

"Is she nervous?" Amber asks.

"Jumpy as a cat before a thunderstorm."

One day, I plan to spend some time in Kentucky and see if people really do talk like that, or if Caitlin enjoys playing it up.

"How about you?" Amber asks.

"Got everything I need."

"Make sure you plant that dot on the camera feed first," Amber instructs. She loves laying down the law.

"Check."

"And careful how you get his fingerprint. Without a full one, you can't access his office."

Caitlin is supposed to pick up Gregory's print off a glass or whatever and re-create it using a tiny little 3D printer and skin solution, so she ends up with a print to place over her own finger. We've tested the tech before but never used it in the field. Li is super proud of it, the way it reconstitutes skin. It sounds disgusting, and it is, but it's quite incredible how it works.

"I hear you," says Caitlin.

"Good."

Another voice chimes in.

"And you're sure Aleks is all set?" That's Li, of course. If she had a coat of arms, it would be inscribed with the words *Trust No One*. And Peggy answers her. So it's a full-on Athena conference call, minus Kit, who's probably stressing about her performance. Impossible to tell if Hala's on or off the call, because she so rarely speaks unless expressly asked a question.

"Aleks needs a little time to build the case against Pavlic, but he's keen on it," says Peggy.

"And where does he think this evidence is coming from?"

"He thinks I have contacts in the CIA who want to help stabilize Serbia," Peggy replies. "He suspects nothing more."

Now Li starts in on Amber, demanding to know why she hasn't tracked me down yet.

"The dot Hala put on her led to a dumpster," says Amber. I smile.

Good thing I threw my jacket away then. But I can hear the tension in her voice. Li is going nuts that she has a building crammed full of cutting-edge technology and she can't find me.

"She's using a dark web browser—or it's possible she's offline completely," Amber is telling Li, about me. "Sooner or later she'll use a debit card, or her VPN will drop, and I'll find her."

Li makes unhappy noises, but Caitlin cuts in.

"Listen," Caitlin says. "I gotta go. It's two hours till showtime, and I've gotta get into my bodyguard suit."

"Okay, break a leg," Peggy says. "Hala will be outside in an unmarked van as backup for Amber when she replaces the camera feeds, and in case there's any need for an extraction. We're a woman down on this mission. I wish we weren't, but just be extra careful, okay?"

"You bet."

The call ends, and I sit back. A woman down means me, of course. And they won't get Hala in to help tonight, because if something goes wrong, they want her able to lend a hand without being trapped inside Gregory's four walls. Somehow I feel better that they mentioned me. And, also, that I will be there this evening, even though they aren't expecting it.

A few, final streaks of sunlight smear over the late-evening sky, and in the gathering darkness, the light from hundreds of candles in Gregory Pavlic's garden dance and glimmer. I say "garden" but, really, what I see here is more like one of the major London parks.

Seriously, I'll bet the grounds of Buckingham Palace are smaller. But then, if you live in Serbia, maybe you can buy half the country for what Gregory makes.

I get out of the passenger side of Paulina's Mercedes and wait while she hands her keys to one of several valet parking attendants who Gregory seems to have hired for the night. Unless he keeps them on staff every day. As we step forward, a black-suited security guy blocks me, guides me through a metal detector, and asks me to hand in my phone. Paulina looks embarrassed.

"Kit Love doesn't want anyone filming her."

No kidding. That wouldn't get a deluge of likes on social media. I pass my phone across, but I'm not happy about it.

It's the stealth phone that I swiped from Amber's locker. A normal phone has a single, static IMEI number that identifies it no matter if you change the number. But this one can change its IMEI and does so at the slightest sign of intrusion, even if you just download any old app. It's virtually untraceable, and I hate to let it go. But I don't see much option. The phone is tagged, placed into a secure mini locker, to which I choose the combination, and taken over to a guarded, portable cabin that seems to be there only for that purpose.

Once that's over, I take a good look around. Several hundred guests, dressed mainly in black tie and evening dresses, are already mingling on immaculate lawns that look like they've been trimmed with nail scissors. I glance dubiously at my own outfit. Slim black pants and a black top suited for an evening out, but not exactly in the same league as the other women here. Paulina, who's in jeans and a blazer, seems to read my thoughts.

"You look great, Jessie," she says kindly. "But I need to change. Come up with me?"

I follow her up to the house, more than interested to see how she lives. To one side, an Olympic-size swimming pool is lit from inside, like a magical aquarium. Blue, blue water and scarcely a ripple. Maybe I'd have liked it better if Gregory's home was dark and forbidding, but the truth is, with the candles and strings of fairy lights on every tree, the place looks enchanted.

To the right, a long stage has been set up for Kit with a huge white canopy cresting over it like a wave. On each side of the stage are massive posters of my mother, caught in midperformance. These are famous pictures of her, photoshopped and highlighted till they reek of glamour and stardom. My glance drops away, behind the stage, where grimy generator trucks idle, powering a bewildering number of lights and speakers.

"What do you think?" Paulina asks.

"Your home is beautiful."

She leads me along a path that curves away from the guests and toward the house, which is like a mini castle complete with a couple of turrets. The gray stone walls are broken up by long windowpanes that are lit up from within.

"What does your father *do* again?" I ask, as if I am simply awed by the luxury and size of the party. Paulina answers without hesitation.

"He has his own businesses. Clubs, restaurants, things like that."

She sounds so honest, but she can't really believe that to be true. She feels my gaze on her and glances sideways at me with a soft smile.

"He must be very clever," I say.

"He is, but he also likes showing off to his friends."

"That he's wealthy?"

"And that he can afford to buy Kit Love for the night." Paulina smiles. I grin back, a big smile to hide the stab of horror that just hit me at those words.

"She just has to *sing* for him, right?" I ask. I'm a bit panicked, to be honest.

Paulina pauses to look at me, and her blue eyes are laughing.

"Of course. But he's invited all of Belgrade society. And everyone watches everyone else."

"Like a fishbowl?" I ask, recovering my sense of humor, but Paulina shakes her head and leans in to me, close enough that I can feel her breath on my ear when she whispers into it.

"A shark tank."

She moves ahead. I like Paulina; I like her wit. We're at the back door of the house now, where a massive ice sculpture shaped like a mermaid is being carried out into the garden. Paulina waits for it to pass before leading me inside, through a prep kitchen buzzing with caterers and chefs, and up a back staircase.

Glancing across to where the main body of the house is visible through a series of double doors, I wonder where Kit and Caitlin are. The concert is due to start in less than forty minutes, and they will be working to get that fingerprint from Gregory and disable his office security. Caitlin can handle that okay, but, really, I'm concerned about Kit. She hasn't given a concert in a few years, except for a short charity gig with several other bands in Hyde Park two summers ago. She's always lived off her nerves as a performer, which was one of the excuses she had for constantly hydrating herself with vodka on tour. Now that she's sober, I wonder how she'll cope.

Paulina's bedroom suite looks like it's ready for a photo shoot for *Architectural Digest* or something. There are no clothes tossed onto the backs of chairs and no magazines lying about. No sign of a computer or laptop—and certainly no embarrassing posters left over from teenage obsessions. Only tasteful, muted colors, a wide bed with cotton sheets that just *look* as soft as silk, expensive furniture, glass shelves stacked with pricey coffee-table books, and some incredible framed prints. The first thing she does is slip off her shoulder bag, pull out the photography book I gave her, and place it on a table in front of the sofa. There's another book already there, considerably bigger and more expensive, which she removes and places onto a shelf, leaving only mine displayed.

"Look how beautiful it is," she says.

I smile. It's thoughtful of her to make such a big deal out of a small gift. Promising to be quick, Paulina disappears into a small hallway running off the bedroom from which two farther doors open out on each side. She's taken the right-hand door, clearly the bathroom; I can hear water running and cabinets opening.

While she showers, I stand about, taking in the room in detail. The place is immaculate. Even her bedside table is free of clutter. Then, out of the corner of my eye, I feel something move, and I turn. Behind me, the most impressive photography print takes up an entire wall, and it's changed. I swear it was a bare, desert landscape when I walked in, all sky and low mountains. And now, there's a black-and-white shot of umbrellas in the rain, and New York defocused in the background. I go up to the wall. The image sits in a sort of slim box. It must be ten feet tall. Up close, I can just about make out the pixels. It's a massive digital frame.

Within five minutes, Paulina emerges, trailing with her a scent of freshness. She's in a thick toweling robe, the kind you get in five-star hotels, and she's heading for the other door across the hallway but pauses to glance back into the bedroom where I'm standing, sort of marooned awkwardly in the center of the floor. She laughs.

"Sit down! Make yourself at home."

Obediently, I take a place on the sofa. I glance behind me, and the photography on the wall has changed again. Now there's a dusty village in India, with a bus arriving in the distance. I turn back, disconcerted.

"I'll just be a minute," Paulina says. Behind her, I catch a glimpse of a walk-in wardrobe with rows of perfectly aligned clothes. I think briefly of my own duffel bag in the apartment. I've hardly bothered to unpack it. I just pick out the clothes I need whenever I need them. Paulina leaves the door ajar, so she can speak to me while she dresses.

"Why did you come to the gallery?" she asks.

I feel a jolt of tension at the question, but I've become so used to being economical with the truth that I barely hesitate before giving her a half-honest answer.

"I read about it online."

That part, at least, is true. In a small city with not very many major landmarks, the photography and the gourmet coffee of the gallery made it onto several tourist websites that I found while surfing around.

"Well, I'm glad you did," Paulina says. That feels really honest, and for a moment I feel a pang of guilt. That I'm using her. Lying to build our relationship, while she's being open with me, inviting me into her home, her life—her room.

Restless, I stand up and wander over to the window. Down below in the garden, the party is growing in guests and volume. A jazz band plays on a smaller platform, away from the main stage. Teams of white-jacketed waiters offer trays of champagne and canapés to guests. The ice sculpture has been placed next to an enormous bar area, and people are laughing and holding glasses under the mouth of the mermaid, where clear liquid pours out in a thin, steady stream.

"What's in the ice sculpture?" I ask.

"Vodka," Paulina says. "By the end of the night, they won't be using glasses. They'll just stand under it with their mouths open." Her voice holds an edge of distaste.

I keep looking out the window, at the guests. Diamonds glitter at the throats of most of the women; the men are stuffed into tuxedos and shined shoes; but I can't see Gregory anywhere.

"I feel a bit weird being here," I tell her. "I mean, we only just met."

"I know," she replies. "But I feel like I've known you for a long time."

Paulina appears, closing the dressing-room door behind her, and for a moment I find myself just staring. At her slim-fitting red dress, which drapes elegantly to skim the floor, and just at the way she stands—relaxed, not self-conscious at all—as if she was born to have people admire her. Paulina holds out her arms as if inviting comment.

"You look stunning," I say, and then I catch myself. "I mean, it's a beautiful dress."

Very cool, Jessie. Well done. *Try* to remember what you're actually doing here.

Paulina comes over to where I'm standing, and her amused look makes it clear that she knows I was referring to her and not the dress. As she reaches me, she turns so that her back is to me. I don't even get what she's doing until, with one hand, she lifts the light-brown hair away from her neck, revealing the back of her dress, which lies open.

"Zip me up?"

Now I'm nervous. As gently as I can, I reach for the zipper, which sits way down at the base of Paulina's spine, and I slide it upward. By accident, my fingers brush Paulina's neck as she turns around again. For a fraction of a moment we are standing too close together. I feel her eyes drop to my mouth; I can smell the perfume on her neck—and then I step back.

Just a little, just enough to clear my head. I can't look at Paulina directly, so I look away, at the photography installation thing on the wall.

"That's amazing," I say, and my voice sounds weird, all thick—heavy with the effort of trying to ignore the moment of intimacy.

The wall frame displays another black-and-white photo there, replacing the Indian landscape. But this one lacks the artistry of the other pictures. It seems like a family photo. A woman in a plain, printed dress, in a small living room, hugging a little girl.

"Who is that?" I ask.

"My mother. For my last birthday, my father gave me a memory card with every picture of her that he could find." Her voice has changed, and so has her mood. As she speaks, the image of her mother fades away and is replaced by a winter scene.

"It's too much to look at them all the time," she continues, her voice so low I have to strain to hear it, "so I mixed them up with other photos."

The whole thing feels sad, but also a bit bizarre. Paulina moves to her bedside table and opens a drawer, picking out a pair of diamond earrings.

"What happened to your mother?"

Paulina puts on the earrings, using a mirror to guide her.

"Her kidneys failed. She needed medicine and equipment that

you could only get in England or America at that time," she says, "or on the black market. And my father couldn't afford it. Not then." Her tone is flat—the way people speak when they are trying to hide how emotional they are.

Paulina turns. The earrings are in place, but her eyes look haunted and, in the lamplight, a darker shade of blue.

"I'm sorry."

Thousands of years of language and literature and we haven't come up with something better than these two, tired words—*I'm sorry*—to express sympathy for a loss. Maybe because deep down, we know that nothing we say can help someone who's suffering. I clear my throat, feeling all inadequate, while Paulina picks up a ring from a heavy crystal bowl on her desk and slips it on.

"My father watched her die," she continues quietly. "And he promised himself he would never be without money again."

Well, it's certainly a touching story, and as Paulina comes to stand next to me at the window, I have to remind myself that while Gregory Pavlic might possibly be human somewhere in the black abyss of his rotten heart, there are too many layers of criminal ruthlessness on top to make me feel remotely sorry for him. But Paulina—I do feel badly for her.

"It's strange," she says softly, looking sideways at me. "I can hardly remember my mother. But I know nothing can ever replace her."

She moves away from me, to the digital frame, which displays a photo now of the three of them. Paulina as a child, her mother, and

Gregory, with his arms around both of them. Using a remote control that sits in a clear glass holder on the desk, she switches it off. The photo disappears, and the screen drops into blackness. I blink. It's like that click of a button drained all the emotion out of the room.

"I can't sleep if I leave it on," she says.

From the window, all I notice now are those enormous posters of Kit. Stylized images that bear a resemblance to the mother I adored as a child, when I was completely in awe of Kit's stardom, and style, and grace.

But through the past several years—as a teenager, I suppose—I haven't seen this side of Kit. Maybe I've chosen not to. I've spent my time being resentful of the time she spent away on tour and in the studio, being disgusted by the drinking, and being pretty relentless in picking at the scabs of Kit's emotional scars. I just wanted her to be different, and maybe I also knew, deep down, that she wanted me to be different. Cooler, more artistic, less judgmental of her, maybe. Less of a nerd who loved computers and circuits and who always wanted her attention. When we fought at home, Kit told me that she was tired of trying to please me, which I always dismissed, because I never noticed that she cared for anyone but herself. But maybe she just got tired of being judged the whole time. Would I rather have grown up without a mother at all, like Paulina? I know the answer, so as I look at Kit's pictures out there, I try to be grateful. For once.

On the way down to the party we take the main staircase in the center of the house. I express my admiration at how beautiful her home is, and, encouraged by my enthusiasm, Paulina gives me a quick tour. We don't go into every room—there are just too many for that—but she points out the main living rooms, the dining room, the home cinema (complete with monogrammed blankets and a bar). Finally, as we exit into the garden, she points out the top floor of the house—at the front is a gym and sauna; at the back, Gregory's office. I make a note of that, the geography of where it sits.

It's easy for me to see spaces and locations in my mind. Like, if I look at a house plan once, I can visit that house and find my way around it easily. Same with directions. It's just logical to me, and it drives me mad when Kit can't find her way back to where her car's parked half the time. Anyway, I'm not planning to go roaming around Gregory's home, especially since we've passed at least seven guards in black suits stationed at every corridor. Caitlin will have her work cut out for her, breaking into the office, even with Amber taking over the CCTV feeds, and even with Gregory's fingerprint. Those men in black look like they just retired from some Eastern European Olympic wrestling team.

As soon as we are strolling through the party, Paulina is stopped every few steps by one or another of Gregory's guests. She attracts stares as she moves through little pockets of partygoers, the way celebrities do. At a party where everyone seems obsessed with air-kissing each other, Paulina keeps guests at arm's length with a delicate handshake. A few people cast interested glances in my direction, but Paulina ignores the looks. Finally, we emerge onto a quieter patch of patio, and Paulina turns to me.

"I'm sorry I haven't introduced you."

"Don't be."

"They're not worth knowing anyway."

As she speaks, we're interrupted by Gregory himself. He grasps Paulina in a warm hug, then he pulls back to take in her outfit. A couple of looks play between them; the quick, silent communications of two people accustomed to each other. The closeness makes me tense, suddenly. Somehow, until now, I've liked the idea that Paulina is emotionally distant from her father. They exchange a few words in Serbian, probably telling each other how great they look, because Paulina casts a critical eye over Gregory, picks a nonexistent speck of lint off his white tuxedo jacket, and gives him a smile of approval. Then she consciously switches to English.

"Father, you remember Jessie?"

Gregory couldn't care less. He shakes hands with me briefly, and I resist the urge to wipe my palms on my clothes afterward.

"I invited Markus for you," he says to Paulina pointedly. On cue, an expensively dressed young man appears, greeting Paulina with a dazzling smile and a courtly bow, which is, if you ask me, a bit over-the-top. He gives me a quick glance, and this time, Paulina introduces me.

"This is my friend Jessie," she tells Markus. He looks me over, trying to figure out whether I matter, but extends a hand to me eventually. Then he smiles and says something to Paulina in Serbian—some greasy flattery about her dress by the feel of it.

"Maybe you can practice your English, Markus," Paulina says

haughtily. "So that Jessie can understand the conversation."

I appreciate her manners and that she's looking out for me, but neither Markus nor Gregory look thrilled at her words. Since you can cut the atmosphere with a knife, I turn away and pretend to admire the pool, where a leaf has just settled on the perfect surface, creating a slight ripple. I watch the water shiver outward from the disturbance. Meanwhile, Markus struggles to articulate himself in English. It's all getting a bit fraught.

"I'm going to find a drink," I say. "Please excuse me."

I smile at Paulina as if to assure her things are fine and move away quickly. Not only am I happy to step out of that little attempt at matchmaking, but also meeting Gregory twice has stressed me out. I worry about being recognized. Despite Amber's best efforts, there are still a few photos of me lurking around online when I was a lot younger, with Kit. Paparazzi shots of us leaving West End restaurants, that kind of nonsense. Obviously, I don't share a surname with my mother. "Kit Love" was a stage name that Kit dreamed up because she didn't think "Kathy Archer" was exotic enough. She was probably right too. And my first name has changed from Jennifer, which was the name I was given, till I was nine or ten, when I insisted on Jessie. But it's still on all my legal documentation, from my passport to my birth certificate. And for most everyday purposes, like university or car rentals, I use a completely fictional name and one of Amber's fake IDs.

I keep walking to a quieter spot, where I take a tiny piece of gold foil out of my jacket pocket and place it deep into my ear. Any minute now, Caitlin should be breaking into Gregory's office while Kit takes the stage.

There's a tiny receiver in my bag, tucked inside a tampon, which is rarely something even the most zealous security people want to mess with. With a bit of fiddling, I can pick up the signal I want, and—I hope—avoid being picked up in return. Within a few seconds I hear Amber's voice speaking to Caitlin. Her clipped vowels sound like home, and I feel more relaxed. But it's not long before I realize that something is wrong. Very wrong.

11

IN MY HEAD, I CAN hear Amber going nuts.

"You haven't planted the dot correctly," she's saying to Caitlin. "I can't access the camera feeds. Can you, Hala?"

"No," is Hala's curt reply.

Caitlin doesn't answer them, probably because she's with someone.

"Get back in the camera room," Amber pushes.

Christ, Amber, I think. Give Caitlin a minute to *think*.

"Dammit," Caitlin says to whomever she's with. "Kit wants a new camera system, and I meant to ask your guys about the panel they use."

A pause. "You want to go back to the camera room?"

An accented male voice. Probably some security guy escorting her around.

"Just for a minute. Kit may *kill* me otherwise . . ."

It's a bit of a lame excuse, but I can imagine Caitlin smiling that big, Southern, cheerleader smile, giving it everything she's got.

I find myself circling around to the back of the house. In my bag I have a dynamic rope that's perfect for climbing walls. Thin, black, discreet. My hand is already clasped around it as I reach the back wall of Gregory's home, where his office is, an area that is not lit at all. I mean, I'm not sure what on earth I could do to help Caitlin from here, but on instinct I want to be there, ready to try.

I hear Caitlin walk back into the camera room and greet the security guards who must be watching the camera feeds. She spins her line about wanting to know how their CCTV works.

"Is that a magnum panel?" she asks.

"Yes, Chinese technology."

"Facial recognition?"

That gets the guard excited, that she seems knowledgeable.

"Yes, and heat mapping, here—"

Someone barks something in Serbian. The guard shuts up and stops flirting with Caitlin over the CCTV box.

"I'm sorry," Caitlin drawls apologetically. "I love this stuff, I get carried away. . . ."

She must have fixed the dot access because I hear Amber come in again.

"Okay, got it. Thanks."

Caitlin wraps up the chitchat, and I stop where I am, because everything seems back on track now. And because I've just seen one of Gregory's security goons—another muscleman in a black suit—walk around the corner of the house toward me. So far, I estimate at least twenty of these hulks. I counted seven in the house, and there are probably one or two more I didn't see. And, including this guy, I've got twelve outside; a couple at the entrance, three around the stage, one always with eyes on Gregory, and the others sprinkled around the house entrances. This one is far enough away that I can slip around the other side, unnoticed, and head back toward the party.

I'm so absorbed in my own thoughts that a whoosh of sound and the thumping of bass drums makes me jump. The stage is flashing, lights strobing in rainbow colors. The drums are joined by electric guitars and a keyboard. Kit's band is already onstage, warming up the crowd, who start moving forward now, a wave of tuxedos and colorful dresses, taking seats on the rows and rows of padded chairs in front of the stage.

I look around at the house because, if the band's on, Kit must be close behind. Sure enough, there's a tight knot of people walking briskly down a side path and toward the stage. In the middle of that small group, somewhere, is Kit. Being moved along in a protective shell of bodies. I recognize a couple of women who have sung backup for Kit before, but the others are all entourage I don't know. Probably hair, makeup, and a costume person, if Kit is doing an outfit change midperformance. Caitlin is walking right next to Kit. And encircling them both are three of Gregory's black suits. Looking around as if they're expecting an assassination attempt, for goodness' sake. The irony. That the most feared, ruthless man in the country is protecting my mother. I catch only a brief glimpse of Kit as they round the path to the back of the stage. She's looking down, serious. Probably nervous as anything. And then she's gone.

Onstage, the band has moved into the opening bars of Kit's most famous song, a house-rocking number that she usually leaves for her last encore, but I guess she wants a big opening for this party. They play the intro again and again, teasing the audience, and I watch, intrigued, as the crowd gets louder and louder, more and more excited, until they are literally chanting Kit's name.

I move closer, a little, but staying in the shadows, until I see Paulina's red dress. She's sitting in the front row next to her father, along with the eager Markus. There's an empty seat on Paulina's other side, and I feel guilty that she must have left it for me. Another young man approaches, shaking hands with Gregory. He's angling for the seat beside her, but Paulina fends him off and keeps it clear. I feel a quick rush of gratitude toward her. Being so loyal to someone she just met.

In my earpiece, I hear Caitlin talking to Amber.

"I'm back in the house. I need you ready in ten seconds."

"As my boyfriend told me last night," is Amber's crisp reply, and I smile. Caitlin doesn't answer though. She must be busy laying the print onto the security pad.

"Print's not working," she says, her voice stressed.

"Is it moist?" Amber asks.

"What?"

"A tiny bit damp. Try a little saliva."

That seems to work, because Caitlin makes a happier sound.

"I'm in."

Now that I know she's made it inside Gregory's office, I relax. I head toward Paulina, ready to reconnect with her—but Kit's appearance onstage makes me stop in my tracks. My mother is no more than five-foot-four, a good three inches shorter than me. But right now, appearing in a haze of backlit smoke, she looks a hundred feet tall.

Gregory's guests go insane. They're all on their feet, clapping, whistling, cheering—and she hasn't even sung a note yet. She just stands there, letting them all adore her. Then she hums the opening of the song. They go even more crazy. She hums a little more. Then, with a beautifully timed nod back to the band, she starts singing. The applause dies down and everyone is listening, entranced. Not a single set of eyes is off the stage. I watch my mother, and I have to say, it's astounding. The *power* she has over these people she's never met. One long low note, and she'll make them go quiet. A command to dance, and they'll all jump to their feet. I look at the faces in the crowd. Excitement, joy, smiles everywhere.

Before I can get anywhere near Paulina though, I hear more stress in Caitlin's voice.

"This isn't right, Amber."

"Are you in the safe?"

"Yup."

"Tell me what you see."

"A tiny black box. Doesn't look like a hard drive. There's a digital panel on it. Letters and numbers running over it. Changing all the time."

That's not the drive, I realize, it's a decoder. Immediately, I turn and stride back toward the house, stopping to pick up a glass of champagne at the bar, so it looks like I just want a drink. As I round the corner to the rear of the house, I toss it away. The black suit is there, but he's walking back the other way. I wait for him to be out of my range.

"Sounds like a decoder," Amber's telling Caitlin.

"For what?"

"Probably for reading encrypted files on the hard drive. . . ."

While they try to figure this out, I toss my line up and start scaling the wall. The edge of the roof has those little baby turret things along them, like Cinderella's castle. Bizarre design, unless you're aiming for that Disneyland look, or you're expecting a medieval army to attack, but it's easy for me to catch the metal at the end of my climbing line onto them. It takes me eleven seconds to scale that wall. I know, because I am running on pure adrenaline now, and everything is focused. I can count every second that passes without thinking about it; I can move easily; I can hear and see everything much better than in normal life. Sometimes I think it would be great to have these heightened senses all the time—except when you tried to stop moving, all those stress hormones would probably kill you.

The top of the roof is mostly flat. As I run toward the air-conditioning vent, the stage blurs past my vision. Kit's rocking it. I open up the vent and drop inside. There's dust and crap everywhere, accumulated from the air being sucked in and out. I deal with it and struggle through.

"I can't see it," Caitlin is saying, still looking for the sodding hard drive, I imagine. "So do you need the decoder?" Caitlin asks, impatient.

"Can't hurt," Amber replies.

Caitlin acknowledges. Then she swears—and it's so rare for her that I know something's wrong.

"I just pulled out the decoder," Caitlin tells Amber. "But there's a timer under it. Dammit, it's counting down . . ."

I've reached the end of the air-conditioner tube. The room below is completely dark, but I think I can see a flicker of light and the top of Caitlin's head. I push on the grate. Caitlin doesn't respond to the noise because she is utterly freaked.

"I have two minutes," she's saying. "Shit! Two minutes to what?" Amber sounds like death.

"Best case, an alarm trigger. Worst case, the safe explodes and takes you with it. What can you see?"

"What can I see?! I see a minute and fifty seconds left."

Caitlin is almost panting with fear. I bang on the grate.

Now she hears me.

"What the hell?" she says to Amber.

I drag the grate aside at last and look down. I can't see Caitlin till she steps out, her gun trained on me. I push my legs through, and Caitlin takes me onto her shoulders to help me down into the room.

"Where'd you come from?" she says, breathless.

I ignore the question as we're a bit short on time for a catch-up right now. She leads me straight to the safe. The timer reads 1:23. I look at it. It *is* an explosive. Not a massive one, but enough to blow us sky-high if we stand here looking at it. If we run, the explosion will give us all away, and that's if we're not just gunned down by the plainclothes army patrolling Gregory's house. Gregory would know that Caitlin was planted, and that would mean he'd suspect Kit. . . .

Meanwhile, my hand is probing under the timer to see what I can find. The safe floor seems solid, but as I tap around it, there's a hollow sound in one corner. The clock is at 1:04.

"You've defused these before, right?" Caitlin asks me.

"Yeah."

"What was your fastest time?"

I hesitate. "Eight minutes."

She gives a little groan of despair.

"Knife," I say.

Like lightning, Caitlin whips a knife out of her boot. I use it to probe at the hollow edge.

We both look at the clock. Forty-five seconds left. But now the safe floor gives way under the pressure from the blade. It feels like progress, and I can feel Caitlin's eagerness—but, really, there's still an awful lot to do, and I don't know that I can pull it off.

"Flashlight. And cutters," I say.

She hands me both, and I peer down into the gloom, assessing the wire situation. It's funny, but if you rush, time goes faster. I learned that in training. You start panicking and making mistakes.

So I force myself to concentrate on doing the job. My face feels painful, contorted under the pressure. Sweat trickles down my nose. I touch the wires. Tracing them back. Not that it's a guarantee of anything. Bombs don't follow safety guidelines. They have creators, and those people delight in mucking around with the conventions.

Thirty seconds to go.

"What are you thinking?" Caitlin says.

"That I should have stayed in my sodding room. In London."

I squeeze the wire cutter into the gap, and it hovers between the three wires.

"Twenty-three seconds," Caitlin says.

"What are you, the speaking clock?" I'm pissed now.

"Isn't it usually the red wire?"

Seriously?

"Thanks, genius, they're all black," I snap.

I've eliminated one. Of the other two, one is much more likely to be the detonator. I move the cutters away to the other wire. But what if I'm wrong?

"Caitlin?" I say. "I'm sorry I snapped at you. I've always appreciated your friendship."

"Shit," she says. "We're gonna die."

I squeeze the wire cutter, hard, and the wire snaps in two.

The clock has stopped.

Two seconds left.

Neither of us is breathing.

But we're still alive.

12

I'M LOOKING AT THE SOLES of Caitlin's shoes as she crawls ahead of me, back through the air-conditioning vent. The decoder is in her jacket pocket. It's a lot harder getting back up than it was coming down, and dust is everywhere. We're both coughing from the dirty air, but as quietly as we can.

"Come on, Cait, nearly there," I say, trying to push her along.

I'm calming down now. We spent the past few minutes tidying up the safe and office till there was no trace of us, and we're hoping that cutting those wires hasn't alerted anyone, or someone would have shown up by now. And without a security override, no one can get into that office except Gregory (or Caitlin with her fake fingerprint), and he is busy watching Kit's concert, so it feels like we have a little time at least.

Emerging onto the roof and into the cool night air feels good. Caitlin reaches down to help me up. We can see the top of the stage and hear Kit singing. Neither of us says anything. We both feel rough, to be honest. All that stress and planning, and we nearly died, with nothing to even show for it. Gregory's hard drive wasn't there, and so we can't prove how he blackmails the most powerful people in the region to keep himself out of trouble. Basically, we've failed.

Our earpieces come to life. It's Amber.

"I've got a match on that decoder. It's generally used to unscramble coded information attached to JPEG files."

"You mean like photos?" Caitlin asks.

"Yes, or scans. Meaning Gregory probably keeps the information coded into files that look utterly innocuous."

Caitlin pats the pocket holding the decoder, like she's making sure it's still there.

"And we have no intel on where those JPEGs are?" she asks Amber.

"No."

Caitlin sighs. She's pissed off that Amber sent her in and nothing was there, but she won't say anything.

Amber's voice comes back through our earpieces: "Caitlin?"

"Yeah?"

A pause. Amber hesitates, then stumbles over the next part:

"Jessie stole equipment and IDs. Li's orders are to bring her in."

Caitlin looks at me, and I stare back. I can't believe this. I just saved her life. Caitlin jerks her head at me. Telling me to get out of here.

"What does Li want me to do?" Caitlin asks Amber dryly. "Knock her out and throw her over my shoulder while I go back to being Kit's bodyguard?"

As she speaks, I take hold of my bag, which I left hidden before I jumped into the vent, and pass my head and shoulder through the strap, so it's held tight against me. Checking over the wall between turrets for guards, I see a black suit almost directly below me, patrolling away. I wait for him to pass. In my earpiece, Amber is conferring with Li, and Caitlin turns to give me a look—*Hurry up*. I indicate the guard situation, and Caitlin nods. Her hand goes to her pocket, and I know she's popping a couple of her anxiety pills out of the foil. I turn away, looking over the wall again to give her some privacy. The guard rounds the corner, and I'm clear.

"Anyway, it's too late," Caitlin is saying. "She's gone. And I have to get back to Kit."

I start to lower myself down the wall.

"The bigger question," Caitlin says, turning angry to deflect attention from the subject of me, "is why you sent me in and there's no hard drive?"

Amber's flustered. "It doesn't make sense. Right until tonight, data shadows were coming from that section of the house. From his office."

Amber's words make me pause halfway down the wall. Above me, on the top floor, is Gregory's office. Below it, *right* below it, is Paulina's bedroom. In the exact same part of the house as the office. Could the data packets be coming from there? I'm hanging off the building, and I'm right next to one of the windows. Not the one I looked out of with Paulina earlier, at the front of the house, but one on the other side of her suite, at the back, where the walk-in wardrobe is. But she had no computers in that place. Maybe she has a laptop neatly placed in a drawer somewhere. Where else could there be files, or JPEGs? And then it hits me.

I look back up to the roof to see if Caitlin's watching, if I can give her a sign, but there's nothing to see above the top of the house except an inky sky and a new moon, sitting there like a perfect sliver of fingernail. Below me, the guard is due back within a minute. I press the soles of my feet against the wall to walk myself over to Paulina's window, which is open a little. Why wouldn't it be? It's a warm summer night and the place is gated and alarmed with security cameras everywhere and guards on patrol. It doesn't take me long to crack the window wider and slide in.

The first thing I do is slip off my shoes. They've sunk into about two inches of deep, soft carpet, and I don't want to track dust from the air-conditioning vent all over her immaculate suite. Luckily, the lights are all off. I had noticed a tiny security camera in one corner of the bedroom, placed facing away from the bed (even traffickers' families need privacy, I suppose), but I can't see any surveillance equipment in the wardrobe. If anything does pick me up, I'm counting on the fact that Amber's still in control of the internal house cameras and has replaced all live footage with tape from earlier. Quickly, I make my way into the main bedroom area. It's really dark inside, but glimmering light from the concert gives me enough to work with. The whole place smells like Paulina, a sort of warm, citrus scent that only belongs to her.

I run my fingers along the base of the digital picture frame—and there it is. A little door that slips open. Inside is the memory card. I grasp it with my fingertips and pull it out. But now what? I don't want to swipe the card and have Paulina find it missing as soon as she tries switching on the frame.

I pad over to Paulina's en suite bathroom. No one with eyebrows that perfect could fail to have tweezers. I find them, then use them to separate the edges of the SD card. Once that's done, I can tug the plastic casing of the card apart and pull out the metal chip, which is where the photos are kept. I pocket the chip and sandwich the card back together so that it slides perfectly into the frame again. If you didn't take it out and examine it, you'd never know there was anything wrong with it. Then I use the same tweezers to tease out one of the wires in the cable casing that runs up the rear of the frame. That should kill the power so the frame won't switch on at all. That way, they'll waste time fixing the wiring before they even think to check the SD card. As quick as I can, I put everything back where it was and get out the way I came in.

Outside, I navigate a quiet route to the portable toilets that Gregory has set up for his guests. Since everyone's enjoying the concert, the toilet stalls are completely empty, which is great for me. My outfit is a mess—dust and dirt from the vent covering my legs and arms. My hair is all over the place, and my face looks like I've sweated through the most stressful few minutes of my life, which I have, but it's not a stylish way to reappear at the party.

The bathrooms smell like flowery disinfectant. The walls are pink, the sinks are pink, the stall doors have pink flowers on them. And in the background there's putrid piped elevator music coming in. Which *sounds* pink.

On my earpiece, Caitlin and Li have exchanged words, and Caitlin has gone back to be ready for when Kit gets offstage. Amber is busy trying to figure out why the files we needed weren't in Gregory's office.

I pull out the earpiece. If they think they can manage without me, let them. I don't see them making an outstanding success of this plan on their own, and, frankly, I'm hacked off that I'm still being treated like a leper by Li. If I hadn't been here, Caitlin would most likely have been blown to bits or shot by one of Gregory's thugs.

I spend a good few minutes brushing off my trousers till they look halfway decent. Then I take off my shirt and use the hand soap to wash my face, neck, underarms, and arms. By the time I've rinsed it all off, I feel a lot better. Cooler, and definitely cleaner. In my bag is another shirt. I always carry a spare top in case of spills. Juice, tea, blood—you never know. This top is the same as the last one. If there's one thing I hate, it's shopping, so when I find something I like, I buy lots of them. The upside tonight is that Paulina won't notice that I've changed.

When I come back toward the stage, I try to position myself off to the side, behind the first rows of chairs. I'm hoping that if Paulina looks around from her front-row seat with Gregory, she'll think I've been watching quietly, not wanting to impose. I glance over the crowd. They're all thrilled with the concert.

I recognize the song that Kit starts next. As a reflex, I step back just a bit more into the shadows. She stands alone at the mic. The backup singers are gone, and there's nothing but an acoustic guitar and a soft drum-brush accompanying her. A series of familiar, repeated chords start to play "Baby Mine"—a song that Kit wrote for me. The chords slow down, ready for her to join in, and when she starts the opening notes, I can feel everyone in the crowd stop breathing for a moment. She has an amazing voice at times. People tend not to realize, when there's a lot of beat and noise around it, but just with a guitar, on her own, she hits every note, and she has that cool rasp in her throat, like she's been gargling with razorblades. I listen to her singing, and she's right in the song; it feels like she means every word.

> It took too long for me to understand
> But like a tree that just won't bend
> I will be here till the end
> Baby of mine . . .

I close my eyes for a second because I feel it coming back, that memory I get only in dreams, because I was so young. Five, six, maybe. In the early days, before I was at school, when she sometimes took me with her. We're on the tour bus, in the back, and

I'm cradled in Kit's arms, and she's singing this song to me. Just her voice, and the comforting roar of the road beneath the bus wheels. She's holding me really close, her long hair hanging down over my face, shielding me from the highway lights speeding by outside.

"Jessie, where did you go to?"

I open my eyes—a hard snap back from the past—and Paulina is there, in front of me, looking concerned. Behind her, Kit is singing her heart out.

"I met a few people," I say. "Then the concert started, and I didn't want to intrude . . . you know, with you and your dad."

"I thought something happened," Paulina says.

Well, I did break into your father's office and defuse the bomb he uses to protect his decoder. And then I prowled around your bedroom in the dark.

I laugh. "No, what could have happened?"

"She's amazing, isn't she?" Paulina glances at Kit, onstage.

"Better than I expected," I agree.

"She's old." Paulina nods. "But she's still got it."

I imagine how Kit, in her midforties, would feel if she heard that. She'd probably want to throttle Paulina. I stifle a smile.

"Come back and sit with us."

"Listen, I don't want to impose—it's your dad's birthday."

"But I want you there," she says, earnest.

That kind of just spilled out, and she looks down, like she's embarrassed.

Again, she's a little bit in my space—a little too close—but this time I don't step back. Then, as Kit finishes the song and the crowd breaks into applause, Paulina reaches down for my hand and guides me back with her toward the front row. Somewhere along the way, casually, she releases her hold on me and we arrive back at our seats as Kit is getting ready to pound the stage for her big finish. I'm nervous. At Paulina's touch, at Gregory's curt nod when he turns to see me, and at the fact that Kit will surely see me from here, because even with the stage lights glaring at her I'm just too close for her to miss.

You know the way little kids playing hide-and-seek close their eyes, because they think if they can't see you, you can't see them? I try a bit of that with Kit. I focus off behind her, beyond the wings of the stage, where the trucks are, but the only people I can see there in the shadows are technicians—and Caitlin, back on duty as Kit's bodyguard. Which reminds me that I need to get this SD card chip to her so she can check it later using the decoder.

But now Kit starts into her final song, and everyone's up and dancing, and she's looking at Gregory, giving a bit of attention to the birthday boy. Her smile is big, and I know her well enough to know that it's also fake. But Gregory's lapping it up, smiling, nodding to the excited friends who surround him. When Kit's eyes meet mine, I'm impressed. There's not the tiniest flicker of anything from her; she's so intent on entertaining everyone that for a moment I wonder if she actually did register that it's me sitting next to Gregory and his daughter. But her eyes come back to mine eventually, and I know that she knows.

The concert ends in a blaze of lights and music, and the stage goes dark, the blackness somehow heightening the sound of the clapping, cheering crowd. For a few moments the lights come back up, and Kit takes a couple of bows, but that's it. She doesn't look at me again. Even though the crowd is yelling for more, the lights go off for a final time, and I can see my mother's outline heading back-stage. It's funny, but when you've lived with someone all your life, you can tell how they feel, even at a distance, even in the dark. And as Kit disappears from sight, I know that she's angry. Already irri-tated by having to sing for Gregory, the sight of me sitting two seats away from him has probably sent her into a complete meltdown.

Instinctively, as the crowd begins to disperse, I move away from the stage, but Paulina pulls me back. While Gregory is accepting all sorts of congratulations for a fantastic concert—as if *he* were the one doing the singing—Paulina is lingering near her father.

"We're taking some pictures," she says. "With Kit. Backstage."

Well. I guess when you're spending that much on a forty-five-minute set, you can expect the performer to stand still and grin through a few snapshots for the family album.

"I'll wait here," I say. The last thing I want is to get too close to Kit at this point, or to make myself more of a thorn in Gregory's side. Paulina hesitates, then nods. But she gives me a look. Like, make sure you don't run off.

"I won't move," I tell her.

I watch them troop backstage, where they all pose for pictures while I hang around near Caitlin. She's overseeing everything, pushing a few stray guests off to the side, acting the bodyguard, and giving the photographer the occasional order.

I sidle a bit closer as she guides two teenage girls out of the way. "Ms. Love is not giving autographs right now," she tells them.

Caitlin completely ignores me. But my fingers have already dropped the metal chip into her jacket pocket.

"Check it with the decoder," I murmur before moving back to the sidelines.

The photo call is over, and Kit is chatting with Paulina, who is being super charming and flattering about the concert. I see Caitlin's hand casually check her jacket pocket, but she doesn't give me another glance. And then Paulina turns and comes back toward me.

We walk together, away from the stage area. To our right, a DJ is turning up a thumping bass that shakes the dance floor beneath us. A big crowd is dancing already, still on a high from the concert. When you watch someone like Kit move to music, it looks easy, but most people just can't get it right.

Paulina follows my gaze. "You want to join them?"

"I'm not much of a dancer," I tell her.

"Me neither."

Which leaves the question of what happens now. It's midnight. There's some time before the 3:00 a.m. appointment that Katarina scrawled down for me. Really, I should get out of here, away from Paulina, and Gregory, and his fortress full of armed guards. But I don't feel like leaving her just yet.

"Come," she says, and I follow her to a small patio area by the side of the pool. Clusters of garden furniture are dotted everywhere, and she chooses one of the quietest tables. We move some cushions and sit down on the same sofa. In front of us are silver ice buckets stocked with bottles of vodka, vintage champagne, and expensive mineral water. Every table in sight has a similar setup. Paulina pours us both some water.

"That's better," she says. "It's hard to talk in that much noise. They're all getting more and more drunk. And less and less amusing."

I glance over to all the guests. At the edge of the dance floor, Gregory is laughing hard with a group of men that includes Markus. Another guy with a huge belly is spraying a magnum of champagne over a group of young women who are dancing nearby. They are laughing hysterically while people around them applaud. I look away, disgusted, and before I can wipe the judgment from my face, Paulina catches my gaze and holds it, as if she understands how I feel. She shrugs.

"This is what people do when they have a lot of money."

Maybe that's true in Paulina's world. But Li's company is worth billions. I'm willing to bet she has a lot more money than this entire group combined, but I don't recall seeing her partying drunkenly and trying to hook up with men young enough to be her child. And Peggy and Kit have found a more useful way to spend their spare cash too. But, to Paulina, I just nod.

She kicks off her heels and pulls her legs onto the sofa. Her perfume is the same as the citrus essence in her room. Tired suddenly, I feel as if I could close my eyes and drift off, enveloped in that scent. Instead, I make myself sit up and focus.

"What about your father? Doesn't he think you should be hanging out with Markus?"

"I don't care what he thinks," Paulina says sharply, and she turns her head so she's even closer to me. "I don't want you to be part of his world. Just mine."

Her voice lowers and I feel myself blushing at that last part. I actually do. Paulina's embarrassed too, because she sits up, a little bit away from me, and takes a sip of water. Her other hand is on the sofa next to mine, but I don't have the courage to touch it.

"I'd like that," I say.

The laughter of Gregory's group draws nearer. We watch as about ten of the men walk back to the house. Lots of orders are shouted at the domestic staff as they settle inside.

"Now they'll stay up till dawn playing poker," says Paulina, disconsolate.

"I think I should go," I tell her.

"Please stay," Paulina says.

She looks at me, hopeful. On the sofa, curled up, she looks young and lonely. I know that she wants me with her right now, but nothing good can come of me spending any more time here. Suddenly it feels depressing to me. This party, full of people dancing and drinking, just to feel something, anything at all. The echo of Kit's song is still in my mind. And then there is the horrible fact of Gregory, right there, a hundred meters from me. And his daughter, inches away, an intimacy that I am getting too relaxed about.

I stand—a touch abruptly—and Paulina glances up.

"You were very kind to invite me," I say. It comes out a bit more formally than I'd wanted.

"When do you leave?" she asks.

"In a couple of days."

"To London?"

I nod.

"Back to university."

"Yes. After the summer."

She is so completely trusting of me and my phantom degree course. She looks at me for a long moment, with a quiet smile.

"Maybe one day soon I will come to London and see you," Paulina says.

I imagine it. On the one hand—a disaster, a web of lies that would have to be maintained. On the other, I really like the idea of seeing her more. Of us being together, beyond the few hours and days that this mission involves.

"I'd like that," I say.

It's true, and I'm afraid of my own feelings. It's time for me to leave the party, and Paulina, as fast as I can.

13

ONCE I'VE PICKED UP MY phone from the entrance where I'd left it with the security goons, Paulina has one of Gregory's drivers chauffeur me back into town. I give him the name of the Metropol Palace hotel as the place to drop me, as I'd rather no one around Gregory has a clue where I'm actually staying. The ride back, alone in the luxurious back seat, is a quiet relief after the intensity of the past few hours. It's weird but, in the grand scheme of things, reliving that minute watching the countdown of the timer on the bomb is the thing that bothers me the least—for now, anyway. I'm sure it'll come back to haunt me in a night sweat at some point.

What I can't shake off is the tangle of emotions that has come from being around Paulina. The touch of her hand on mine. Her eyes smiling at me. And that song of Kit's—*my* song—and my mother's sandpaper voice taking me back to memories that are so real I wonder if they ever really happened, or if I've just made them up.

It's nearly one thirty in the morning and I have around an hour before I need to get to the address that Katarina scrawled on that business card. At the Metropol, I make my way into the lobby. A clerk looks at me, but I walk with purpose directly to the ladies' room, and then come back out and into the bar, which opens onto the street by way of a side entrance. From here, it's a ten-minute walk to my place.

Once I'm inside my apartment, I empty my shoulder bag and put away the earpiece and climbing rope. Back there on the roof, it crossed my mind to slide Caitlin's gun out from the holster on her back while she was arguing with Li. I would have felt safer heading to this unknown place in the dead of night with a bit of protection. But I didn't want to put one over on Caitlin, and I especially didn't want to leave her and Kit in Gregory's world without protection. Still, right about now, I wish I had a weapon. I don't know what's about to happen in the worst part of town at 3:00 a.m., but I'm pretty sure it's not going to be a church social.

I change into jeans, light running shoes, and a T-shirt. A jacket seems like a good idea, just to carry stuff in and in case it gets colder while I'm hanging around. I'm starving now. I picked up a couple of canapés at the party, but, frankly, a bit of seared tuna with sesame seeds, and quail eggs dipped in whatever will only take you so far. I glance out the window just to confirm that everything is shut—and only dark glass reflects back at me. Even the greasy burger place at the very end of the street. What is it about late-night hunger that makes you want to devour the kind of food you'd never consider putting in your mouth in broad daylight? But I find some bread from yesterday and a few slices of cheese, so I put them together and wash it all down with a cup of tea. Then I head out.

So I had expected to be in among the depressing, towering apartment blocks once more, and I am, but in this little patch of town, something is different. Just plain wrong. I park a fair distance away from the address I need; I don't want to attract attention coming in with the engine noise from the bike. It's starting to rain a little bit after a beautiful clear evening. How nice for Gregory that the weather gods have played ball, keeping away the clouds till his party ends.

The place that Katarina has sent me to isn't a specific apartment but a small street running in between a couple of huge high-rises. There are few streetlights around, and where I'm heading, it looks like the lamps have been deliberately broken or turned off. That's the first thing that's odd—it's miserably dark on the streets, at least, in this particular patch. But there are a number of windows that are lit, so even as I track a winding path to get to the place, I have something to guide me.

The second strange thing is those lit-up windows. Each tower block must have about eight small windows per floor, and they are maybe twenty stories high. And a large number of them—especially on the lower six or seven floors—have lights on inside. There are a number of other blocks some distance away and, at this time of night, they are all dark; everyone's asleep.

As I get closer, I move slowly, quietly, listening hard—and there's a sudden sound behind a dumpster. My hand closes into a fist. More noise, a bottle clinking as it hits the ground—and a stray dog slinks out. Its eyes are luminous in the dark, slanted like a fox's, eerie. I watch it till it passes me and is well out of range.

I continue on. Sticking to the shadows isn't hard, as the street-lights are now entirely gone. I'm almost at the first tower block. Inside the main entrance hall there's a dull, greenish light—one of those depressing emergency fluorescent things—but no one's around. I look up at the lit windows again. Another odd thing—not a single window is open. It's not like there are air-conditioning units on the outside of the building. Usually, people leave windows open in summer. And though I can catch the odd shadow, the sense of people inside, there's no real sign of everyday, normal life. You know—mail on the entrance floor, a TV flickering in a dark room; even rubbish bags that people have dumped. In Katarina's building and the others around, there was that feeling that people were liv-ing there. No matter how downtrodden a place is, *someone* wants to stick a plant on a window ledge or hang their laundry out on a balcony line. There's nothing here. The building feels occupied but not lived in.

The sound of an engine startles me. Then two engines. I look around, but I'm in a warren of small streets between blocks, so I can't see the vehicles, but they're definitely coming closer. I get off the street and into a little stairwell on the side of the building.

My original plan had been to find a way onto a roof some

distance away and watch the area using Amber's zoomed contact lenses. A safe, smart, intelligent plan. I try to remember why on earth I didn't stick with it as I stand pressed into the stairwell, which smells like a hundred people recently used it for a bathroom.

Something soft and warm touches my ankle, then runs over my feet. A rat slips by in the dark. I literally feel the hair on the back of my neck prickling. I'm not squeamish, but if there's one thing I can't stand, it's rats. Luckily, I'm immediately distracted from the disgusting rodent situation by the swish of tires over the wet street to the side of me. Two large white vans—unmarked of course—pull up outside the other tower block across the street.

I lean out of the stairwell just a bit, to see what's happening. The summer rain touches my head and trickles onto my face. I don't dare move, even to brush it away. A couple of guys jump down from the vans, and four more come out of the block. They do some fist-bumping and macho-handshake stuff. One of them makes a call on his cell. Another moves off to the side, a little closer to me, to take a leak against the wall. They're all armed—shoulder holsters and pistols.

My attention moves higher up the building where a few of the lights are going out. And now, down into the greenish, miserable lobby come two more armed guys, followed by a long line of women. I say women, but they are girls, a lot of them—my age, maybe younger even. I had thought, going in, that this must be where most of the women trafficked by Gregory do their work. But these girls don't look like they're up to speed with that line of business. Not yet. They look scared and tired. I catch glimpses of faces as they trudge through the lobby, and then out into the rain. What really throws me is that there are also a few boys—young men, maybe eighteen, nineteen—small, quiet-looking. Along with the girls, they are pushed to get into the first white van. Once that fills up, the men direct them over to the other. No one tries to resist. In fact, the armed thugs sound positively encouraging, like they're herding up reluctant kids and heading out for a lovely trip to the seaside.

Behind me, I can hear something—another animal probably—shuffling through the dirt in the stairwell, but I make myself ignore it and focus on what's happening ahead of me. I'm working out how fast I can get back to my motorcycle to follow the vans when I feel it. I wish it were a rat, or anything but this: the cold touch of a silencer against the back of my head.

It must be the guy who just peed against the wall. He's the one who's missing from the group across the road at the other block. I put my hands up and start to turn, but he tells me to stay still. He says it in Serbian, but I'm not in much doubt about the meaning.

A hard push of the gun against my head urges me forward. My eyes look for escape, for something to hit him with—but the truth is, I can't do anything. I'm faster than most people, and I know martial arts techniques that give a girl my height and weight a good chance against a man twice my size, but they all need a moment, just one, to surprise, turn, hit—and I don't have that. Not with a bullet inches from my brain. It's funny, but what I think about now is Ahmed. How he looked after I shot him. How I would look the same way if this trigger got pulled.

As we approach through the spitting rain, one of the other guys looks up. He asks my captor what's happening, and they have an exchange, from which I gather that the guy who's escorting me at gunpoint assumes I was in the building and tried to run and hide. I am the same age as the others and dressed in a similar way. They shake their heads at me, disapproving, and I swallow down panic. What if they make an example of me by shooting me in front of the others?

The doors of the first van are slammed shut, and the second is almost full. I am shoved forward, and before I can do anything about it, I'm in the second van. Two more girls are hustled in behind me, and the doors crash shut, dropping us into complete darkness. Outside, I hear a lock being turned, a solid metal clang that feels very final. Ten seconds later, the engine starts and the van pulls away. I'm trapped inside with thirty other people, and no idea of where I'm going.

14

THE BEST WAY TO DEAL with fear is to channel the adrenaline into something that can help you, like an ingenious plan. The thing is, I'm not finding it easy to do that at the moment. In fact, I have to work hard just to slow my shallow breathing. As the van bounces over potholes, we are thrown about a bit, but we're so tightly packed in that no one can move that much. It's a press of bodies, and a smell of stress, of sweat, of unwashed clothes.

As my eyes get more accustomed to the darkness of the van, I look around. The whites of my fellow prisoners' eyes gleam in the blackness, though most of them stare ahead and don't meet my glance. But one girl does. I reckon she's sixteen, maybe seventeen. She still has a baby face and short, spiky dark hair. I give her a quick smile, and she smiles back. But then her eyes start to fill—tears glint in the tiny bit of light. I shake my head, and she actually listens and holds herself. I try to look encouraging. Don't worry, I tell her silently, in my head. I'm a trained operative, fast-moving and quick-thinking. I could beat everyone in this van at chess and at least two martial arts.

But that won't get us out of here. And the men escorting us look pretty fit. And they have weapons. Even if I managed to take out two of them, I'll be lying in a pool of my own blood within three paces. And no one else knows where I am. And the police are in Gregory's pocket anyway. . . .

I make myself stop. Or maybe the van lurching to a halt makes me pay attention. There's some chatter outside between our escorts, and the sound of gates opening. Then the vehicles start to move again, more slowly this time, and within a few seconds we have pulled up to another stop.

The doors at the back of the van open, and I have to adjust to the glare of white light. Blinking, I am pulled out with the others into some kind of loading bay or receiving area. There are big swing doors ahead of us. I glance back over my shoulder, trying to see where we are; up high, at a distance, is a perimeter fence with barbed wire on top. Pine trees beyond.

Please, no.

We are herded through a series of corridors. The walls were once white but are now yellowed and stained, and on them are old, peeling signs. Medical signs: X-ray symbols, first aid crosses, and other stuff that transcends language barriers. In the back of my mind, this is where I was dreading we would end up. The place I had seen from the woods with Hala. Gregory's abandoned hospital.

Hospitals are never my favorite place to hang out, and this particular building is like central casting for a Victorian mental asylum. The other captives and I are moved like lines of cattle through another door, and down dark corridors punctuated with pockets of fluorescent light. I glance into every open door we pass. Some of them look like old labs, others open onto wards. It feels as if every bed is occupied by girls like us, except they seem even more tired and drained of hope than we do. So my egg-harvesting theory is likely correct. But I look back at the few boys who are also mixed in with the group. What are they here for?

The girl I connected with on the truck has started crying, and one of the guys barks at her to stop. She tries, but she still gets a whack on the back that sends her stumbling into me. I keep walking and reach for the girl's hand. The guy who shoved her has moved ahead of us now, to keep the front of the column moving. I touch my chest and say my name. That is, my new Serbian alter-ego name:

"Daisy."

"Dasha," whispers the girl.

I squeeze her hand encouragingly and muster a smile. I release my fingers to let her hand go, but she's having none of it, gripping onto me for dear life. And then she smiles. In fact, she's looking positively optimistic now, and I start to get worried. We're waiting in a small corridor, but behind us is an emergency exit, and Dasha keeps looking at it, and then at me. Like, We can do this. I shake my head at her. It's twenty paces to that door if we run, and we'll be gunned down faster than Butch and Sundance. There's no question I need to find a way out of here, but this isn't it. But Dasha doesn't get that; all she sees is a dream of escape. She's giddy with panic—skittish—and when I grasp her hand harder to calm her down, she lets me go. And then she runs for the exit.

I can't believe it. She's fast, but those guys are faster. It takes them a second to realize what's happening, and then they are on her. They grasp her by her jacket just as she is pushing open the door, and she is swung back into the corridor toward us with such force that she ends up sprawled in a heap on the floor. I go to give her a hand up, but one of the men pushes me back roughly. On instinct, I go for him, and he swipes at me. I dodge, surprising him, but a quick whack from a guy behind me is enough to keep me in check. My ears ring from the blow, but my hands are still up, ready to fight, when I hear laughing. The other men are watching, chuckling at me, daring to go up against one of them. The other girls spread back into a terrified ring around me. The men all have pistols, relaxed in their hands, and I have just enough sense left in me to realize I've no chance here. I drop back and submit. Dasha is hauled up by her collar, and her gaze catches mine. She looks at me like I betrayed her, and I look away.

We are pushed into an elevator where the most interesting thing is that all of us, even the guards, do that thing that happens in elevators the world over—we say nothing and stare at the display as we move up three floors. Exiting into a dark, empty corridor, we are herded into the stairwell. Then up two flights of stairs, and into a longer, lit hallway with doors leading off it.

I am up near the head of the group again and—along with the other front-runners—I am pulled aside by one of the armed men, separated out. He marches me down the hallway a few paces, knocks on a door, and thrusts me into a room.

The door slams behind me as I look around. It's a doctor's office. The first thing I notice is there's a radio playing—a really old song. Dusty Springfield is belting out "You Don't Own Me," which I can't help but think is somewhat ironic considering where we all are.

The second thing I see is an examination chair. One of those reclining jobs. And on the end of it is a set of stirrups like you get in a gynecologist's office for internal examinations. I can't tell you how much that makes me want to just scream for help.

The room also contains a doctor. Or, at least, a man in a green smock. He must be around sixty, with a kind face. He smiles at me and says something in Serbian. I turn and go for the door handle. It opens, no problem, and I edge out into the hallway, but there are two wrestling champions on patrol. One of them starts toward me, so I get back into the room quickly. The doctor hurries to the door, says something reassuring to the guard, and closes the door behind us. And locks it.

He points to the examination table. I just look at him. What kind of person *does* this for a living? There's not much private health care in Serbia, so doctors probably earn a pittance from the state. He must have gotten tired of running out of money every month and taken up Gregory's offer of a retirement fund. He's asking me something but, clearly, I'm lost as to his meaning and, finally, he realizes I can't understand a thing.

"Me no Roma," he says, pointing to himself. "You have English?"

I nod. So he thinks I'm Roma. One of the itinerant people who used to be called gypsies. They never seem to be welcome anywhere in Europe, and I'll bet the kind of documents or ID that most people have are nonexistent for them. Making them an easy target for pigs like Gregory.

"Take off." He motions undressing.

Now I really wish I'd taken Caitlin's gun. Slowly, I unbutton my jeans and slip them down over my hips. I do all this turned away from him, as if modesty is my main concern, but it gives me a moment to assess the escape routes. It doesn't look promising. There are no windows; only an internal door into a bathroom. A snap of latex makes me look round, and he's busy pulling on gloves. Now I feel sick. The doctor—sensitive soul that he is—figures out that I'm one of the nervous ones. He reaches for a syringe and prepares some kind of injection.

"To relax," he says, dropping back into his chair as if he's fainted, just to demonstrate that soon I'll be sedated and won't feel a thing.

"Make happy." He smiles.

I doubt that. But it gives me an idea. Tentatively, I climb onto the table and wait while he tests the injection. A thin squirt of relaxing happiness drug sprays into the air. He smiles at me and reaches for my arm. Obediently, I hold it out. I even make a fist with my hand to help him find a vein. He leans over my inner elbow. He taps the thin veins. And I smack my fist straight up and into his nose, as hard as I can.

Blood spatters, but I don't pay any attention. My hand is on that needle. I grab the syringe, and while the doctor is gasping and grasping his bleeding nose I inject it into his neck.

He's right. It *is* relaxing. He drops, and I am quick to catch him and lower him quietly onto the floor. The door into the corridor is still locked from the inside. Quickly, I pull my jeans back on and head for the bathroom. There are no windows here, just a small skylight forming a glass pyramid above me. But no latch or anything to open it with.

I grab some tired, gray towels from a stack under the sink and drape one over my head. Then I wrap my hands in two more towels and step onto the toilet seat. With a fist I smash the glass as quietly as I can and clean out the shards that remain. Then I channel my inner Hala and lever my foot up the wall, so I can just about pull myself up and through.

On the roof the air is cool, and fresher than the stale stench inside. It's still spitting with rain though, making it hard to see very well. I'm on a thin ledge five stories above the ground, and I can hear guards talking below me somewhere. I creep along the edge of the roof in a sort of crouch-walk. The first couple of skylights I pass look down into bathrooms.

I keep going till I get to some dark windows that look into bigger wards. I lie flat on my stomach to try to see in. The rain is seeping into my clothes now, and I shiver, wiping my face to clear my vision as much as I can.

Below me is a ward, bigger than the one I passed earlier, with rows of women crammed together. Several are hooked up to IV stands, bags of who-knows-what fluid dripping into them. Most of them look to be asleep, or sedated. A guard patrols up and down inside the ward.

There's a small fire escape ladder ahead of me. I shuffle on, trying to keep my footing on the ledge. I test the ladder with one foot and it feels shaky, rusted in most places, but I can't see a better option, so I venture onto it and start to make my way down the side of the building. It's pitch-dark where I am, which can only help me stay undetected by any guards below. As I pass the darkened window of the ward, I can see that one or two of the women are awake but staring off into space, defeated.

I've made it down to the third floor when I pass a lit window. The top of it is open and, inside, people are talking. I pause. The ladder creaks. I can feel pieces of the rusted metal literally flaking away under my fingers, but I hang on. Not that I have any other option.

Straining hard, I can just about make out the conversation, but it does me no good because it's mostly in Serbian. And then it stops. I wait a moment, then risk craning my neck so I can get a look inside. Two people are leaving the room. One in a doctor's coat, the other in jeans sporting a shoulder holster. The room itself is a really old laboratory. Deep porcelain sinks, dark wooden shelves, and high, old lab benches. On one of the benches sits a stack of paperwork and a new desktop computer. Which is switched on. Just waiting for me to find out what's going on here—because the more I see, the more I'm convinced I haven't scratched the surface with my theory about harvesting eggs.

Except that getting in is not going to be a walk in the park. I glance down. If the ladder gives way, I'll drop three floors, and there's only concrete beneath me. Hard not to break an arm or ankle from this height. But I might as well go for it.

I use my shoulder to wipe some rain off my face and then launch myself at the open window. My hand grasps it but slips off almost immediately, leaving me hanging off the creaking fire escape. The ladder groans and lurches. Desperately, I reach up again, clawing with my foot for some leverage off the wall. I get a few fingers onto the window's edge—and then I push off with my foot and thrust as much of my arm inside the window as possible. If anyone comes back into the lab now, I'll be done for, but I can't think about that. I pull my feet onto the window ledge and reach in to undo the latch on the larger window. That's a struggle because it probably hasn't been opened since 1974, but it's amazing how determined you can be when you're hanging off the side of a building surrounded by armed men.

I get a cramp in my hand just from grasping the handle hard enough to force it open—but it does creak ajar. And I'm into the lab, crouched on top of the counter. Before I jump off, I take a moment to orient myself. It worked for me back when Gregory's safe was ticking down—that one or two seconds' wait feels like a lifetime, but it really isn't. I take a breath and listen, adjusting to the level of sound in the room. It's a different world from outside, where the rain and muffled wind created a big sound buffer that made even the persistent squeak of the ladder hard for anyone to pick up.

I jump down from the counter noiselessly and tiptoe to the computer. It's password protected but with no other encryption—I almost relish getting in. It takes just over thirty seconds, not my best time, but close.

With my other hand I search my inside jacket pocket and find a USB drive. I always keep three things in every jacket—a thumb drive, an army knife, and the blue pill that Amber usually gives us when we start a mission, and which I stole from my own lockbox this time around.

I slip the drive into the computer and drag the documents folder onto it. As the files move across, I click over to the open documents I find. They are in Russian and English, with a logo on some of the paperwork, and a name in the Russian Cyrillic alphabet. It's a logo I recognize from the website of the Victory Clinic. Seriously, the arrogance is something else. I mean, if I was going to do something illegal, the last thing I'd do is emblazon my company logo all over it. But maybe the Victory doesn't care. Maybe it's above any law. I turn away. If I make it out of here, there'll be plenty of time to look through the electronic files, so I focus my attention on the papers on the desk now, which are in English with Russian translations.

Full donations—estimated 7-hour procedure:
heart

lungs

kidneys

liver

corneas

ovaries

Remains of subjects to be incinerated within two hours
of organ extraction . . .

My blood runs cold. I rifle the papers underneath for anything more, and it's hard to focus on so much information so fast, but what I do get is that these "donations" are scheduled to begin tonight.

I fold up the papers that seem the most obviously helpful and thrust them into my jeans pocket. Then I jiggle the computer mouse to see how long the file transfer is going to take. There's another ninety seconds, but now I can hear footsteps in the corridor right outside. I pray for the steps to pass by. But they don't. And the door to the lab opens.

15

SOMEONE HAS COME BACK INSIDE. I can't see whether it's a doctor or an armed goon because I've dropped like a stone behind the counter. The problem is, I'm sure the shift of my clothes moving has made a noise. In fact, I know it has, because the person who comes in doesn't move about with purpose. He sort of pauses by the door, like he feels something's wrong. Then solid, heavy footsteps start moving toward the computer, and the place that I'm hiding.

Please let it be a doctor, I think—but no, it's one of Gregory's armed guards. He stares at me. I'm lying on the floor, eyelids drooping, like I'm drugged-out. It's an Oscar-worthy performance, if I say so myself, nice and subtle, and it stops him in his tracks. He pulls out his gun and points it at me, but I don't react at all. My hands are limp by my sides, splayed open, nothing concealed. He hesitates, then reaches a hand down to pull me up. I stagger to my feet, swaying a little.

He asks me something, disapprovingly. Probably wanting to know how I got in here. I answer him with a hard chop to the throat from the side of my hand. Then I push my fingers into his eyes and knee him in the solar plexus. Not that different from what they teach you in school self-defense classes, but with surprise on your side it works like a treat. While he's doubled-over and gasping for breath, I grasp the gun from his hand and give him a solid whack on the head, and then one more, till he's knocked out.

I tuck the gun into the back of my jeans, drag him out of sight behind the counter, then retrieve my USB drive from the computer. From the window, I can see my fire escape ladder almost within reach—except that it really is hanging by a bit of rust now. If I throw myself onto it, chances are I'll be plummeting to the ground in a second. Plus, I can hear guards talking outside. I turn and head for the door of the lab.

In the corridor, a doctor is walking away from me, having just passed by. I pull back and wait, and then go straight for a fire-exit door farther down the hallway. It's open, and the stairwell is dark and free of guards; but then I hear a scuffle and screaming coming from another room off the hallway I just left. I picture Dasha, in trouble. But they're all in trouble, all these women; I can't start meddling now. I push on through the fire door, and it slams behind me. But even through the thick metal barrier, the wails come again— and they're heartbreaking.

Somehow I'm back through that door and striding toward the screaming. It's coming from a doorway to the right and, no surprise, it *is* Dasha who's in trouble—but clearly still determined to get out of there.

Three girls cower in one corner watching, terrified, but, to her credit, Dasha is giving it her all. Kicking, screaming, even biting the guy, but she can't last forever, and he's almost subdued her. Even though he has a gun, he's not using it. I guess all these organs are worth too much for them to be allowed to shoot dissenters. But he's angry, red-faced and grim-mouthed, and he pushes Dasha against the wall and leans on her, yelling. I don't want to know what kind of lesson he's planning to teach her, so I take advantage of the chaos and slip up behind him. Releasing the safety on my stolen gun makes a small click, but, combined with the metal barrel touching his head, it's enough to shut him up. He stops moving.

"Laissez-la partir."

Why I'm telling him to let her go in French, I'm not sure, except that I'd prefer they don't know I'm British. In any event, he steps back from Dasha, and with my free hand I pull her toward me. She's crying but trying to stop, clinging to my arm. I get him to drop his gun, but I also want to take a shot at this guy, just his leg, just enough to stop him from following us—but I don't want the gunshot to alert a hundred of his friends. It seems that Dasha's screaming has already done that though, because heavy steps come pounding down the corridor and a new guard hurtles into the room.

I pivot and shoot, and I get the new guy in the shoulder, and then the leg. His gun drops, and I kick it out of his reach. When I spin back, the first guard is already on me. I'm angry with myself. If

I'd just shot him when I had the chance, we'd be halfway out of here by now. He's trying to get the gun from me and, with his massive fingers, he squeezes it out of my hand, but all his focus is on that, giving me a split second to swing my leg around and kick him hard in the chest. The gun scatters across the floor.

Then I go for him, and we're hand-to-hand fighting. He's not much taller than me, but he's squat and wide. When I punch his neck, it's pure muscle, like punching a wall. But I'm faster than him. I go lower, feinting, turning, kicking, so fast that he's getting confused, lashing out and missing. I get a good blow to his groin area. He feels that, and crumples just briefly enough for me to chop at his windpipe. I'm definitely on top now, but his flailing fist connects with my chest hard enough to knock some of the wind out of me. I stagger back onto the floor and scramble up, but Dasha's jumped on his back now, her fingers in his eyes.

Picking up the gun, I give him a heavy whack between the legs and, as he crumples, another on the head. Then I grab Dasha's hand and run. The corridor is empty for less than a second before double doors at the far end crash open. Two more men run toward us. I push Dasha through the fire-escape door and we pound down the stairs. I'm switching off lights as we go, and as soon as I hear the door open on the floor above us, I pull her out into another doorway. Shots fire into the stairwell behind us, whining as they ricochet off the metal handrails.

The floor we emerge onto is pitch-dark, unused. With Dasha at my heels, I turn right and run. There's an operating room with a sink halfway down the hall. I turn on the water, and it creaks to life. Then I grab Dasha and run hard, back in the opposite direction.

Skidding on the floor, we head into an empty ward. Only a little moonlight penetrates the darkness, and the shadows of old equipment and drip stands make us both jump because in our terror we mistake them for guards. I take Dasha by the shoulders and try to calm her down because they'll find us just from the sound of her breathing. She manages it, and fast. If I have to drag along a sidekick, I'm glad it's her, because she certainly has guts.

We hurry to the window. I do my best to find an opening, but it's sealed shut. Up high there's another small window with a latch. I motion for Dasha to cup her hands together, and she gives me a leg up so I can reach it. The latch is stuck tight.

Behind us, in the corridor, we hear the fire door open out from the stairwell. One of the guards is creeping in quietly, trying to find us. Listening. He hears the running water from the tap and he's heading that way, in the opposite direction from us. Pleased, Dasha gives me a smile, but I'm too tense to return it. I'm trying to decide what to do. Escape and make a noise. Or play hide-and-seek in the hospital from hell. I don't think we can ever win that game, not with this many guards around.

I turn back to the window, cover the butt of the gun in an old sheet from one of the gurneys, and bash at the glass as quietly as I can. The glass and frame start to give. With a big push, I get the thing open, then drop back down to the floor. Now I boost Dasha up, and she wiggles through it while I drag a gurney over to the window. The metallic screech could wake the dead, and immediately I hear the guard's footsteps moving toward me, faster now. I jump onto the gurney and hoist myself up. Outside, Dasha drops down onto some shrubbery. My legs are halfway out the window when the guard rounds into the doorway. In the dark, it's hard to see what's going on, but this time, I can *feel* him. I twist and shoot, low. He drops.

I fall well, and Dasha is waiting for me. I grasp her arm, and we run for the perimeter wall. Around us we can hear walkie-talkies crackling, men shouting. It's a full-scale hunt for the two of us. Ahead of me a guard pounds into view around the corner of the building. We run harder, but he's too close to us to outpace. Turning, I raise my gun and aim for his leg. He goes down, but I feel Dasha's hand jerked out of mine. When I turn, another guard has her in a choke hold, and is dragging her back toward the hospital. It's dark, and I can't get a shot on him without risking her.

She's screaming now, but as they drag her farther and farther back, I realize she's not begging for help. She's telling me to run. I shake my head and move toward her.

"No!" she screams. "Run! *Cours!*"

Jesus, she's even trying to tell me in French, since she heard me talk to the guard who was attacking her inside. I can hear the men from the perimeter sprinting toward me. I turn away from the hospital—away from Dasha—and run. I can't stand leaving her there, but if they get me, all these women are going to start dying tonight because no one has a clue what depths of depravity

Gregory has sunk to in his quest for money.

My feet fly over scrubby grass and concrete, heading diagonally toward the wall. It's dark and still raining, which helps obscure me from view, but the wall has large security lights on it, and when I glance behind, there's a wide semicircle of flashlights closing in on me from all sides.

I veer right and keep running, toward the darkest section of the wall. I really wish I had that climbing rope with me now because—no surprise—they don't make it easy to climb walls that are designed to keep people in. My best hope is a tree that grows next to it. I start up it, struggling for foot- and handholds in the darkness on the rough bark. The flashlights move closer, forming a long line that will be able to check most of the wall in about thirty seconds. Behind them, that wretched hospital looms like a massive tomb.

Once I'm at the top of the trunk, I sit astride the branch that grows out toward the wall and drag myself along it. Not far from me, two guards below are already sweeping the wall with their flashlights. I lie still on the branch for a moment, and when they talk to each other, I move to the end, take off my jacket, wrap it over my arms, and leap.

Barbed wire rips through my jacket and makes a jagged cut on my arm, but I'm hardly aware of it. I've made it to the top of the wall. Using the jacket as protection from the wire, I lower myself onto the other side. Now my legs are dangling on the side of freedom, and I make the drop onto grass and pine needles. Hitting the ground hurts, but I don't care. I'm out of there, and I run, hard, away from the gate, which is opening to let more men out to find me. I head into the forest and run and run. Only once I'm far in, maybe two or three miles away, and deep among the trees, do I stop to catch my breath, and to think. I can't figure out which way the road is. I'm suddenly aware that my arm is throbbing from the cut from the barbed wire, and my hip is aching from the drop down from the wall.

The sound coming out of my mouth is like crying, and for a few seconds I can't make it stop. Maybe it's relief, or just the accumulated horror of that awful place, and the image of Dasha being dragged back in, begging me to leave her and run. And the idea of what they might do to her now. For a moment my stomach turns so badly that I lean over and wait to throw up, but nothing comes, only a few spits of saliva. I drop down onto my knees and rest my forehead on the ground, because just for this moment, I can't move, and even if I could, I don't know where to go.

16

IT'S BEEN ONLY A COUPLE of minutes, but I've pulled myself together, helped by the realization that the longer I knelt in the dirt feeling sorry for myself, the more likely it was that I'd get dragged back to that hospital by Gregory's thugs. A pale dawn is beginning to wash across the edge of the sky. Just the promise of light makes everything better, as if it can brush away all the shadows, all the nightmares that choke you when the world is drenched in blackness. I've stopped to check several times, but there's no one following me now. Exhausted, I hoist myself up into a tree yet again, just to get a sense of where I am. My arms feel like lead. Hala's biceps must be strong as steel to make climbing that much look so easy. This time, I'm rewarded with a line of roofs, red-tiled against the gray-blue dawn sky. I clamber down from the tree and walk toward them.

My mind is a mess, replaying everything that's happened. Already, Gregory's party feels like it happened a lifetime ago. My thoughts are with Dasha and the other girls I left behind. I need to get to the Athena team with everything I know.

The roofs belong to a little row of houses sitting on their own in a ramshackle mess. Curtains are still drawn, and each house has a small car in front of it. One of the cars is missing a tire, but the others look decent. I make my choice before I emerge out of the trees opposite and hurry over the road. First, I go for the chain-link fence that sits to the side of the last house in the row. I rip off a small section of loose chain and force it into a straight line with a curve at the end. Then I move quietly back to the cars.

The oldest car is a pale-blue job, some local brand that I've never heard of, and it's so old that it locks with a key in the door, not a remote. Which makes it relatively easy for me to pull away the rubber seal on the window, slide the fence metal between the window and the door, and pull up the lock. Once I'm in, I get to play with wires again, but hot-wiring a car of this age is much easier than defusing a bomb, and it takes me no time. And I'm away. In the rear-view mirror I glance back, but no one seems to have noticed that it's gone yet. I don't feel great about it, because they probably need it to get to work, and I'm pretty sure they don't have money to sort out a replacement; but for now, I can't see another way to get clear of here.

The car handles like a bad shopping trolley, but I do my best, and stop at a tired roadside convenience store, where I buy some antiseptic and bandages to stick around my wound. The place is manned by a guy who hardly bothers to look up from a movie playing on an old TV. As I'm leaving, I notice an old pay phone on the wall. Using the coins I just got as change, I call Peggy on her personal mobile. It rings just once before she answers.

"I'm coming to see you, right now."

"What's happened? Are you all right?"

Her voice is thick with sleep. I must have woken her up.

"There's a lot I need to tell you."

I won't say more on an unsecured line, and Peggy gets that.

"I'll tell our security guys to look out for you."

I hang up. The car takes two tries to start, but it coughs to life finally, and I'm off again, heading toward the house where Peggy, Kit, and Caitlin are staying. My head is pounding. While I drive, I worry about the girls in the hospital, but I also think about Paulina. Earlier tonight, I started to forget that she was a means to an end, and what I felt when I thought about her was excitement. But now, it's uneasiness that rises to the surface. What does she know? What does she choose not to think about? But I'm pretty sure that *no one* knows about Gregory's new plan to send people off to be slaughtered for their organs. I imagine a conversation where I open Paulina's eyes to the true business that her father is running. Would she do anything to stop it? Would she even believe me? And if she tried to stop it, would Gregory ever listen to her?

It's embarrassing how bizarre your thoughts get when you've had no sleep. It's a relief when I pull up outside the gated house. A slim guy in a black suit approaches. In this town, almost anyone in a large home has security, so it doesn't look unusual, and if you're up to what Athena is up to, you certainly don't want any uninvited guests strolling in. I spend five seconds looking for the button to open the driver's window before I realize I have to *wind* it down with a handle. How retro.

Impatient, I wait as the guard consults his phone, then looks back at me and waves me through. Peggy must have sent him a photo. Another thin guy patrols the other side of the gate. Neither of them looks very strong, but at least they're armed. Maybe Gregory has first pick of all the wrestlers, boxers, and weight lifters around here. I pull up and notice Hala's bike parked in front of the door. I touch the engine as I pass it. Still warm. Maybe Peggy called her in just now.

As soon as I'm shown into the kitchen of the house, I feel like crying. After a night spent with criminals, being chased by armed men, and trapped in that hellish hospital, the sight of this big, clean kitchen, and Peggy standing over a coffeepot by the stove, makes me feel grateful. For what, I'm not sure. Just that I get to be here, I suppose, when Dasha and the other girls I left behind don't.

Peggy turns the instant she hears me. Her eyes look tired, but her hair and clothes are immaculate, like she woke up hours ago. We look at each other for a moment, then she comes toward me quickly and grasps me in a hug. She smells like shower gel and that perfume she always wears. I don't know why, but I feel tears rise up, and I force them back down, staying in the hug a bit too long till I've pulled myself together.

When Peggy moves back, she examines my face, then my arm, which is seeping a bit of blood through the bandages.

"What happened?" she asks. She pours coffee and puts on some toast. I sit at the high counter, hesitating. There's so much to tell her that I don't really know where to start. And yet I do.

"Gregory's not trafficking these girls to work the streets, or even for eggs. He's planning to take all of their organs at once."

Peggy stares at me blankly as if I just rattled off an explanation in Japanese.

"How do you know that?"

My mother's voice behind me is a surprise. I turn around. Kit doesn't sound angry or accusing, just worried. Her hair is pulled back in a loose ponytail, and she's wearing sweatpants and a fitted souvenir T-shirt from one of her own past concert tours. Behind her, Caitlin appears. She's also in sweats, but she looks like someone who just woke up, while Kit looks like an off-duty superstar.

"I was there a couple of hours ago. In his abandoned hospital." There's a general gasp from everyone in the room, and again, I feel tears coming up. Maybe it's just too fresh, or maybe it's because I haven't slept.

It's Peggy who moves first, coming over and putting an arm around me. Kit moves into the room, closer to us. Caitlin still lingers near the door, and, behind her, the outline of Hala hangs back farther still.

"It's okay," Peggy says. "Take a minute."

But I don't feel there is a minute to waste. At a nod from Kit, Caitlin uses an iPad to dial Li into the conversation. Then, taking a breath, I explain about Katarina's tip-off; what happened in the tower blocks, how I got caught and driven in with the other girls and the boys, and most important, what I found in the lab about the plans to take all the organs from all the captives and send them to Victory Clinic. As I finish, I hand over the papers I found, and the flash drive with the downloaded information.

A moment of silence fills the kitchen while the horror of this sinks in.

"Slaughtering innocent people to cut wait times for organs? Who's buying them?" Peggy asks, appalled.

"He must make at least a million a girl," says Caitlin quietly.

Kit just stares at me, reaching for my hand. She holds it so tightly that, for a moment, she scares me.

"You could have been one of them." Her voice is a whisper.

"I'm not," I remind her. I have to say it again, just to calm her down. "But those 'donations' are due to start tonight. We have to do something quickly."

"Can we break in?" Kit asks Caitlin.

To her credit, Caitlin looks to me for clarification. It was me in there, not her.

"There are a lot of armed guards. Fourteen, fifteen at least. They'll be on high alert after I escaped."

"Security cameras?" Caitlin asks.

"No. They probably don't want any record of what goes on in there."

"Then, maybe . . . ," Caitlin starts, but Peggy shakes her head.

"It's too dangerous. Three of you against Gregory's whole army.

And even if you found a way to pull it off, it won't stop Gregory from starting over somewhere else, with a new headquarters and new victims." Peggy turns this over in her mind. "I need to see Aleks this morning." She picks up the flash drive and documents. "This should help him," she says.

"Can Aleks move that fast?" Kit asks.

Peggy nods. "If he doesn't, and it goes public or these girls die, it would be disastrous for the Serbian government. As justice minister, it would probably end his career."

A moment of quiet descends while we all think. Now I can smell that toast, and I realize how hungry I am. Helping myself to a piece, I slather it with some jam that's sitting on the counter and wolf it down.

"What about the SD card?" I ask while I chew.

Caitlin nods. "You hit the jackpot. It has the info we need. Lots of dirt on lots of politicians, police, judges . . . I'll show you." She nods toward the living room, and I'm getting up to join her when Kit's voice interrupts us.

"Jess—where did you find it? The SD card?"

"In Paulina Pavlic's room." I look away from my mother's keen gaze as I explain. "Amber's tip about the decoder working on picture files made me realize."

"But how did you know it would be there?"

I hesitate. To be honest, I don't know how to explain how I knew, or what I was ever doing in Paulina's room. But I feel like Kit's judging me anyway.

"That SD card was a birthday present from Gregory, and—as far as Paulina knows—they're just pictures of her mother."

Kit moves toward me. Into my space, in fact.

"What?" I ask, defensive.

"*Paulina Pavlic?*" she says. "How do you even *know* her? How did you get into the party? How *reckless* are you?"

I'm guessing these are all rhetorical questions, so I keep my mouth shut. I see Peggy give Kit a look to ease off, and my mother takes a breath and drops her voice.

"Jess, Paulina is *Gregory's* daughter. You can't trust her. You can't get close to her."

That last bit feels like it carries a double meaning. Certainly, the way Kit says it makes both Caitlin and Peggy look down. And Hala moves away from the doorway, where she's been standing, listening. All of which makes me furious with Kit.

"It doesn't matter if I trust her or not," I say. "I managed to steal that card from her because she trusted *me.*"

I look at my mother defiantly, but she only seems to be waiting for me to justify some more. But there's no way to explain why my gut tells me that Paulina is not the same kind of person as Gregory. Why I like her—and yes, even trust her—enough to feel guilty about using her. So I don't try.

"Great concert," I say instead. That throws her off.

"Thanks. I sang 'Baby Mine' for you."

"Except you didn't know I'd be there."

Awkward silence. But I don't regret it. It bugs me, the way she pretends she sang it for me, and the way she's so sure that Paulina is tainted by association with her father. I turn away and follow Caitlin into the living room.

It's a vast space, with very modern, white furniture everywhere. A step up from my own pest-infested quarters. Caitlin settles into a chair in front of a massive flat-screen, and Hala paces around in jeans, a shirt, and a scowl. Her biker jacket is thrown onto one of the white armchairs. Her eyes meet mine, and her face lightens a bit.

"Are you okay?" she asks.

"Yeah, thanks."

We both look away from each other. Back in the kitchen, there's an undertone of murmuring that must be Kit and Peggy (and Li, connected in by video) deciding what to do next.

Meanwhile, on the screen, Amber and Thomas gaze at us from the Athena office in London. It's 5:00 a.m. there. And he is *still* in a suit. They must have pulled an all-nighter decoding that SD chip.

"It's here," Caitlin says, glancing across at me. "The information that Gregory has on all his blackmailed friends. Embedded in the corners of each photo."

"I've run a number of copies of the files here, remotely," says Amber. In case we forget how efficient she is.

Caitlin taps the screen where a distortion is clear on the lower edge of a photo. A small window opens off the distortion revealing the information, and more images attached to it. Dates, times, tiny thumbnails of a chubby older man, presumably some judge or politician, with a young woman. Both Hala and I lean in to look.

But, for a moment, despite myself, my eyes are drawn to the main image. The color is faded, and it shows a little girl—a beautiful kid, maybe six years old—sitting on her mother's lap, arms flung around her neck. Paulina as a child. She looks at the camera but peers over her mother's arms shyly, clinging to her for dear life. The woman's eyes are closed, enjoying the hug, and her mouth is curved in a gentle smile. I make myself look away, and my eyes catch on Caitlin. She's watching me as I take in the photo. I turn aside, ignoring the next photo that Caitlin brings up. Instead, I look at Amber, and I decide to start off on the right note—by saying sorry for breaking into my lockbox.

"Not interested in your fake apologies," she says, crisply cutting me off.

That opens up a gap in the conversation.

Meanwhile, Thomas's glance shifts to Hala. "*Marhabah*," he says. Which is *hello* in Arabic. Very smooth.

Hala looks surprised but returns the greeting. Thomas is smiling like an idiot.

At the doorway, Peggy calls out to me and I trudge back to the kitchen. Peggy closes the door behind me and pours me a fresh cup of coffee. Kit is sitting by the counter. Li is on video, her face filling the screen on the tablet that Peggy has propped beside her.

"We owe you a great debt," Peggy says, which sounds good. "But at the same time," she continues, "Athena can't run like this."

That sounds bad. And Kit's still not looking at me. I take a sip of scalding coffee and wait for Peggy to continue.

"You could have gotten yourself killed earlier. Trapped in that place with armed men, ready to murder on a whim . . ."

"The girls are too precious. They're trained not to shoot them."

"That's beside the point," Peggy says sharply. "And getting into Gregory's home under false pretenses? Did you think about what he would do to you if he figured it out?"

"Peggy, everything we do could end badly," I point out. "If we worry about every little detail, we'll be paralyzed."

Now Kit pipes up. "We *have* to worry about details, Jessie. We have to agree on a plan. There has to be some consensus, some government of this organization. Can't you see that?"

"If I hadn't ended up in that abandoned hospital last night, hundreds of girls would be dead by tonight."

Kit looks away. Because I'm right, and she can't argue it. Peggy pours her coffee down the sink, carefully. Then she spends a minute putting the cup into a dishwasher. Calming down.

"You should have come to us with the information, when you got it from Katarina," Li says, from the screen.

"I didn't know if this lead was any good or if Katarina could be trusted. And you dismissed me when I came to you the first time with what I had on Victory Clinic and Lavit. You thought it was too thin."

Peggy sighs gently, a slight raising of her eyebrows serving as a small acknowledgment of my predicament.

"Jessie, the issue is we're trying to bring to justice people who get away with terrible things, like trafficking, that no one else does anything about. But nobody polices *us*," Peggy continues. "We have to be sure we don't abuse that power. And sticking together as a team—making group decisions—is one way to avoid that."

I take a turn at the dishwasher. Putting my plate and cup away; keeping my mouth shut. But not for long. Because I can see where this is going.

"You needed me to finish this mission," I said. "I got you Gregory's blackmail files and I found out what he's really up to. I'm part of this team, and I want to know I'm back permanently."

Peggy looks at me seriously, then her eyes move to Li on the screen.

"I'm against it," Li continues. "For the reasons Peggy just outlined. We're already a rogue agency. We can't have a rogue agent. It's chaos."

That's a blow. I turn to Peggy.

"You agree?" I ask.

Peggy shakes her head. "No. I want you back. With the caveat that you agree to stick to orders, or you're out."

I nod. I get it; I can try harder, I'm not an idiot. And the truth is, I don't like being that person, the one who could kill a handcuffed man. It's not a place inside me that I ever want to go back to.

But there's still tension in the room. My gaze moves to Kit in the corner. The deciding vote.

Her eyes flicker down, away from me, as she shakes her head.

"I don't think you're ready, Jess. People don't change overnight."

My shoulders slump and my eyes close for a moment. Behind

the lids, they feel gritty and exhausted. My own mother—the woman who asked me to come and work with Athena—is the one pushing me out now. Talk about betrayal. The frustration that rises is strong and fills me with sudden energy. But I don't want to prove them right; to show them that I'm out of control. And I *definitely* don't want Kit to know how much she's hurt me by turning against me. And after everything I've just done.

In the silence, a text pings on Peggy's phone. She glances at it.

"Aleks will see me in an hour," Peggy says. "Jessie, why don't you take a few days' rest? Goodness knows, you need it."

But her voice sounds distant. My head is throbbing from the effort of pushing back the anger, the exhaustion, the worry about Dasha and the others.

I turn to go. Behind me, Kit says something, but I can't hear it, and I don't really want to. I'm dimly aware that Peggy is advising her, holding her back from following me. The front door lies across a double-height hallway that is an expanse of polished granite flooring, and it takes forever to cross it.

Outside, I take a breath. The clouds are giving way to some morning sun that filters through onto my face. I close my eyes for a few minutes and just feel the warmth and softness on me.

And then I hear Hala's voice carrying out into the morning air from a window to my right. I wish she would've stood up for me just now, when Kit was hassling me about Paulina, instead of staying on the sidelines. She's obviously on the phone, and she's speaking too quietly for me to make out much of what she's saying, but again, there's that feeling of stress in her voice, like she had when I overheard her talking to her brother. I take a couple of steps toward the window; silent, silent steps.

"I know, you have to be careful. . . ." Then something longer in Arabic. I'm sure Hala becomes aware of me moving out here, because she hangs up really quickly. Whatever is going on with her is a mystery. And with things the way they are between us, I can't even talk to her about it.

What could her brother want? Is she in trouble? Is he? I walk back to the driveway, toward my stolen blue car. As I open the door, I glance back and see Hala's eyes watching me from her window. We look at each other for a long moment and, on an impulse, I raise my hand in a half wave. Hoping for a smile, a look, even just a nod. But she turns away and draws the curtains, blocking me out.

17

I DRIVE THE BLUE CAR back to where I parked the motorcycle last night. Even though it's in the center of the most crime-ridden part of the city, it is still there, so I park the car on the side of the road and switch over to the motorcycle. I don't want the local police tracking that stolen vehicle right to my door.

I go back to my apartment. It's funny how quickly you can adapt to a routine, to the same place, and get attached to it. Even though I've come from a magnificent house that's clean and light and airy, it's a relief to be back here in a room that's crummy, but is just mine, where I don't have to answer to anyone.

In the apartment, I take a long, hot shower, then lie down. I'm asleep before my head touches the pillow, and it's like being drugged. No dreams, no memories, only black, solid sleep.

I wake up hard, with a gasp for air as I sit up, confused. My hand grasps for my phone to check the time. Only half an hour has passed. The first thing I remember is what happened at the house, just now; that Kit refused to let me back on the team. Then I remember Dasha and the hospital. And then Gregory's party. And Paulina.

While I dress, I look through the net curtains at my window. The gallery door is propped open, and someone's moving inside. On the street, Paulina's Mercedes is parked. It's not quite 9:00 a.m. I would have expected her to be sleeping till noon after her father's celebrations, which didn't seem to be slowing down at all by the time I left. Just knowing there is someone around to talk to lifts my spirits. But first, I head to the pharmacy two blocks away and pick up some antiseptic cream and some big Band-Aids. Back in my room, I clean up that cut on my arm. Then I roll down the sleeves of my shirt, buttoning the cuffs so none of it can be seen.

When I walk into the gallery, music is playing. There's the aroma of fresh coffee, and a wash of sunlight over the walls. And Paulina is alone, sitting at a table, typing on an iPad. She's more casually dressed than I've ever seen her—faded jeans, a slim white T-shirt—and it's a relief. I can relate to her more like this than in her party gear, surrounded by her father's fake friends.

Of course, she sees me the moment I am at the door, and she doesn't move at first, except to look up from the screen. She just sits there, watching me, with a slight smile, and her calm gaze makes me self-conscious. I glance away to the flat-screen TV on the wall, playing a muted loop of local news coverage.

"Jessie," she says at last. "I'm so happy to see you."

That feels pretty amazing. I can't remember the last time anyone used my name except as a preface to telling me off or giving me advice. Such easy words to say—*I'm happy to see you*—but how often do we actually say them to each other? She walks up to me, pulls me toward her, and kisses my cheek, and it feels kind and welcoming and everything bad seems to fade away. For a moment, at least.

Paulina motions me to sit down while she moves behind the counter and makes a coffee for me. I look around, at the photographs on the walls, at the morning light gleaming off the polished glass of the windows, at the smooth, clean, marble floor. All I can think about is how different it is to the abandoned hospital. And that her father's "businesses" have paid for this place.

"Your macchiato."

A cup of expertly foamed coffee is placed in front of me. I watch Paulina's manicured fingers on the saucer; I look up to her perfect mouth and her eyes, eyes that shift easily between blue and green. She is so beautiful. And I wonder who she really is.

"What is it?" she asks me.

I shake my head. "Nothing."

"You look tired."

"I had nightmares," I say.

She doesn't need to know I was awake through all of them.

"I couldn't sleep for a long time after you left," she says.

I wait for her to explain, and she smiles briefly and looks down, away from my gaze.

"I kept looking at everyone at the party through your eyes. Like an outsider. Even my father and his friends. They were still playing cards this morning. I couldn't stand the noise, the vulgar jokes. They're so . . ." She doesn't complete the sentence, but a flick of her head suggests her dissatisfaction.

I don't imagine it's my job to join in the critique of Gregory or his guests, so I stay quiet and just watch Paulina, but her eyes are still cast down, and she's frowning. Like she's struggling for words. When she does speak, her voice is so quiet I have to lean in to catch the words.

"I know we only just met," she says. "But you feel like the most real thing in my life right now."

I smile; I can't help it. There's a touch of red at the tops of her cheekbones that makes me think she might actually mean what she says.

"My life is so complicated, Jessie. I wish I could explain it to you."

Her hand is on the table, really close to mine, and her fingers move just slightly, enough to touch mine gently. At that touch, it's like everything else in the world stops existing. Slowly, she leans in to me, a little nearer, and then her eyes are on my mouth, her lips moving closer, till she brushes my mouth with her own—

And someone arrives at the door. One of her waiters, I think. My heart is already pounding so hard that I'm startled by the sight of another person standing there. But Paulina is unfazed. Smoothly, without any stiffness or sense of being caught in a moment, she turns and walks over to the door. She has a whole exchange with the guy—laughing, joking—and he comes in and goes to the back to start work. Meanwhile, I look up at the TV screen, blinking, trying to recover, trying to regain my balance.

Aleks Yuchic is on the screen. It's not a live broadcast, clearly, but a recent report. Shots of Aleks passionately addressing an adoring crowd, intercut with images of men being arrested and police cars outside a run-down address.

Paulina comes back to the table.

"I didn't realize the time," she says apologetically. "Sorry we were interrupted."

As I think about what we were doing when we were interrupted, I feel embarrassed, and I look up at the TV again as a way to break the spell. Paulina follows my glance to the screen.

"Who's this guy?" I ask, trying to make conversation, struggling to find a space in my head where I can think more clearly.

"Yuchic?" she says. "He's a fraud."

"Looks like he's cleaning up Belgrade," I say.

Paulina gives a short laugh. "Are you kidding?"

I look at her, keeping my tone as relaxed as possible, but my heart has plunged to my shoes.

"What do you mean?"

"Yuchic cares about only one thing."

"What?" Panic rises.

"Money. The guys he arrests are the ones who won't pay him enough. He's the worst kind. Pretending to care about corruption."

Paulina gets up again and walks behind the counter, because

now her mobile phone is ringing inside her bag. I follow her because she can't be right about Aleks, but I need to make sure.

"How do you know?"

"He's always trying to squeeze my father for money in his night-clubs," she says, matter-of-fact. "And he always gets paid in crypto currency. One of the smaller coins—Alexa." She rummages in her bag for the phone. "I remember the name because it's so close to his name."

I know about Alexa. It's used a lot on the dark web. Never has to show up in the usual online crypto "wallets," and is only usable with a printed key. Even PDF keys self-destruct after a set time. Could I have missed something when trawling Aleks's computer? I remember finding crypto trades, but nothing huge, and I thought he was just speculating . . . Please, Jessie—don't have messed this up. Fear sticks in a congealed lump in the base of my stomach, as I think about Peggy. Please don't let Peggy be in trouble.

Meanwhile, Paulina has answered her phone, and something is clearly wrong. She speaks very quickly in Serbian. The agitated voice at the other end undoubtedly belongs to Gregory.

While she speaks, I take out my mobile and text Peggy.

Careful with Aleks. Danger. J

I add my initial to the end because the stealth phone won't show up as mine. I don't know what to think, or what danger I expect her to actually be in. But this whole thing has a bad feel to it. When I think about Aleks and Peggy having dinner together the other night, the way she trusts him . . .

Maybe Paulina is wrong—maybe Gregory's spun her a line about how terrible Aleks is.

But I need to find a way to leave so I can look into this. Luckily for me, it looks as if Paulina's heading out in a hurry. She hangs up the phone, switches off the TV, and puts her bag over her shoulder. Her face is filled with stress.

"What's wrong?"

"My father found something missing in his office," she says. "I need to go back to the house."

"What's missing? Money?" I say. Like I have no idea.

She shakes her head. And then she stops in her tracks. "I don't want to leave you," she says.

I glance at my phone, where there has been no response from Peggy to my text. I'm itching to get out of there.

We both head to the door.

"Let's meet later?" I say. "Back here?"

She nods eagerly, touching my hand with her own, briefly. I watch her get into her car, then I head for my motorcycle. On the way, I text Peggy again, then call her, but there's no answer. As I sit astride the bike, I try Amber.

"I was just going home to sleep," she answers. "Is it urgent?"

"I need Aleks's address."

"I'm not authorized to give you anything—"

"Peggy's in danger."

"Then I'll alert Caitlin. . . ."

"Amber, there's no *time*." Hesitation. I try again. "Will you forgive yourself if something happens?"

I hear her tapping a keyboard.

"Where are you?"

"Paulina's gallery."

"Link me to the GPS on your other phone and head north," she says. "I'll get you there."

18

WHY IS IT THAT IN such a small city, the one route I want to take is now thick with commuter traffic? I weave, scrape, and curse my way in between cars as best I can, but I'm heading to a bottleneck where they are all crammed tightly together. Desperate, I look to the pavement. It's more or less clear, if you don't count a couple of outdoor café tables. Since Kit's always telling me that obstacles are just there to be overcome, I take her advice and swerve off the road and onto the sidewalk, alarming a couple of passersby, and I roar through, past the traffic. Horns blare at my back, and irate drivers curse at me out their windows, but I use the stress to spur me on. Once I'm past the traffic jam, Amber has me zooming along much quieter residential streets.

"Don't kill yourself in the process," she says into my phone's bluetooth earbud.

I don't answer.

"You can't help Peggy if you're dead."

Boy, she doesn't let up.

"Thanks, I hadn't thought of that."

She guides me to turn right at the next junction, and then I'm on the road where Aleks lives. I can see the gates from where I am, in front of which a couple of armed soldiers stand, protecting the so-called hero of anti-corruption.

I swerve into the road and find myself head-on with a speeding ambulance, bearing down on me. I lean and skid to the right, low to the ground, swerving so sharply that I come off the bike—but I make it out of the way, just. I pick myself up, then the bike. Aleks's front gates are wide-open. The ambulance came from there. The top lights are flashing, and the siren begins to wail as it disappears up the road. Through the gates I can see Aleks standing in the drive-way. A woman in a housekeeper's uniform is beside him, wringing her hands. I feel my stomach drop. Because if he's out there watch-ing, it has to be Peggy in the ambulance. Aleks looks up and sees me—a strange girl in a helmet, on a motorcycle, in the road outside his house. I hesitate for a second as the gates start to close. Then I turn around and follow the ambulance.

It takes six agonizingly long minutes to arrive at the hospital emergency room, and I drop the bike right behind the ambulance and run alongside as the paramedics push the gurney, holding Peggy, through the corridor.

Someone talks to me in Serbian, trying to get me to drop back, but I'm sticking to my place, and short of stopping the gurney, there's not much they can do about it until they lift Peggy onto a bed and pull curtains around her. Then the doctor on duty starts listening to Peggy's chest and looks up at me. She says something in Serbian and I ask her if she speaks English.

"Do you know her?" she asks.

"Yes."

"You need to give us space to work."

I nod again. My hand is holding Peggy's, but there is no grip or flicker of movement under my touch. Her eyes are closed, and her breathing is so light and shallow that I can hardly see it.

"Please," the doctor says, and she's kind about it. I know she's right. Reluctantly, I let Peggy's hand go and step back as more medics come in. With one more sweep of a green curtain, she is lost to my sight.

The others have arrived, and we are waiting in the hospital chapel because Kit was too distraught to stay in the antiseptic-smelling corridor while sick people were wheeled back and forth.

The downside is that here in the chapel, the smell of incense is overpowering, and the wooden painted eyes on a statue of a weeping Virgin Mary are staring at me. If it's supposed to inspire comfort and peace, it's really not working that well.

"Jess, please don't."

Sitting on the chair next to me, Kit turns and puts a hand over my own. Her eyes are teary. My fingers have been drumming up and down, tapping out a nervous pattern. But I feel my mother's hand is not just there to stop me from moving. It's comforting me, and maybe looking for comfort too. I guess we both need something to hang on to while we wait for news of Peggy. The first diagnosis is sketchy—they're checking for a stroke—because Peggy is alive, barely, but not responsive.

On the row of chairs in front of me Caitlin sits alone, her strong frame slumped, head down. I lean forward and put out a hand to grasp one of her shoulders, and she turns her head a little to acknowledge, but she doesn't look at me.

The chapel door opens, and Hala stands there, outlined in the harsh light from the hospital corridor. She beckons, and the three of us rise like one body and follow her outside.

"The doctor's back," she says, walking ahead of us.

The specialist is a tall, slim man with thick hair streaked with silver. He's in green scrubs and he doesn't look that different from the doctor who tried to examine me in Gregory's nightmare hospital. I wonder if he'll ever get an offer to work there, and what he'd do if he did.

"Who is the next of kin?" he asks.

"We all are," says Kit, with authority.

The doctor hesitates as he looks us over. We must look like a motley bunch. One dark-haired Brit, one blond Southerner, an Arab, and a music star. None of which fits remotely well with Peggy's African American heritage. I can see that he recognizes Kit, dimly, even if he can't place her right now. As for Kit, she's probably thinking it's better not to mention that Peggy has two grown children in the

States—not if we want to get any answers. She starts firing questions, before the doctor can think up any to ask us. And, no match for Kit's crossed arms and attitude, he starts talking.

"She's not showing the usual symptoms of a stroke," he says. "Her heart results are weak but not consistent with a heart attack."

"Could she have been attacked?" I ask.

He stares at me, uncomprehendingly.

"Could she have been given something?" Kit clarifies.

"Blood tests are due back very soon."

"How soon?" snaps Hala.

The doctor's taken aback by all of us on him like a ton of bricks.

"In twenty minutes, maybe," he says. "For now, we're keeping her comfortable. She's in a private room, as you asked."

He ushers us to the right, to a smaller corridor that leads into a room with a glass door. Through it, we can see Peggy lying there unconscious. She's so imposing in real life, but she looks *tiny* on that awful, metal-framed bed. The sight makes me want to cry, but I do my best to hold it together. From the side of my eye I see Kit's hand go to her mouth. I move inside quickly and find a seat next to Peggy's bed. Caitlin sits beside me. Kit and Hala go around the other side.

There's a choking sound next to me, and I glance sideways. Maybe it's the sight of Peggy laid out like a corpse right here in front of us, but Caitlin has lost it; she can't stop crying. One of my hands is on Peggy's, which is warm but lifeless, and the other goes to Caitlin, just rubbing the top of her back, soothing her as best I can. She's been closer to Peggy than any of us. Peggy is like the mother Caitlin never had. Warm, caring, always a kind word and a smile. And Caitlin is as loyal to Peggy as Amber is to Li. And like Amber, when she was asked to join Athena and sworn to secrecy for the rest of her life, she didn't hesitate.

We sit there, helpless, listening to the steady bleep of the machine that's monitoring Peggy's vital signs. Caitlin calms down a bit, and I look across the bed at Kit.

"Aleks has something to do with this," I say. I swallow, because it's hard for me to put into words my growing fear that I messed up somewhere in the preparation for this mission. I was the lead on researching Aleks. If I missed something, it's my fault that Peggy is lying here, barely alive.

Downcast, I start to explain, but Kit puts a finger to her lips for me to stop talking. On cue, Hala reaches into her compact backpack, pulling out what looks like a normal USB stick, but inside, there's a switch that she flicks on. It's an audio blocker that takes the feed from any listening device and turns it into white noise. It's not likely the hospital is bugged, but we're always aware that our cell phones are possible targets for eavesdropping through an app or virus.

Once Hala nods that it's safe, Kit turns to me.

"Why are you saying that about Aleks?"

"Paulina said he's dirty. And why isn't he here, worried about her?"

Hala shoots me a look. "We're believing *Gregory's* daughter now?"

I ignore the sarcasm and relay what Paulina told me. Kit gives me a searching look.

"Jess, she might be telling the truth, but we need more . . ."

I don't answer. Because the audio blocker made me think of phones and now I'm busy looking for Peggy's bag. It's in a little alcove at the base of her bed.

"What are you doing?" Kit asks.

"I want to know if Peggy got my texts."

Peggy's phone is in the bottom of her bag, neatly placed on top of a makeup bag, wet wipes, and pens. It's her "social" phone, the one she uses for daily life. She wouldn't have brought her stealth phone to a meeting with Aleks. Like Li and Kit, she only uses that rarely to discuss Athena business if our private network isn't usable for some reason. On the home screen is a recording app, flashing that the maximum limit has been reached. That's odd. On instinct, I rewind it back and press play. Sounds of low voices in Serbian, shuffling, movement—and an ambulance siren. This must have been as they were bringing her here to the hospital. I run it back farther and get Aleks, his voice sounding bored and monotone.

"*Monaco, maybe. Somewhere that's not here.*"

Then a Spanish accent. "*Mr. Yuchic, what happened?*"

Aleks's voice changes completely.

"*Elena! I thought you were at church! Thank God you're here. Mrs. Delaney collapsed.*"

Then Elena on the phone, calling the ambulance, panicked.

I pause the recording, and we all exchange breathless glances while I run it back a minute earlier than before, right to the beginning. This part is painful to listen to. Peggy is clearly finding it hard to breathe. She must have turned this on when she started to feel bad.

Aleks: *"You don't feel well?"*

Peggy: *"What was in this?"*

No answer. A sound, maybe Peggy collapsing. Breathing hard.

Peggy: *"Why?"*

Aleks: *"My son needs cancer treatment, Peggy. Do you know what that costs at the Mayo? With this drive, I can blackmail Gregory and partner with him for a while. Then retire. Switzerland, Monaco, maybe. Somewhere that's not here."*

We're back to the same point, and I switch it off. It's just too terrible to listen to Peggy suffering in the background. I can feel the others looking at each other, stunned. But I can't meet anyone's eyes. I feel terrible. Aleks's son is supposedly enrolled at university in Rochester, Minnesota. Which is exactly where the Mayo Clinic is—widely considered to be one of the best in the world for cancer treatment. How did I fail to find any link?

"We have to find out what he gave her."

Caitlin's voice is hoarse, and her face is taut and white. Instinctively, I know it shouldn't be her who goes to find Aleks. Hala feels that too, because she nods to me and gets up. Kit comes around to Caitlin and makes her sit down.

"You and I will stay here with Peggy," she says to her. "In case she wakes up."

Caitlin hesitates, enough to let Hala and me get out of the room together. Kit follows us into the corridor.

"What's the plan?" she asks us.

"Make him talk."

"Then kill him," says Hala.

"Works for me," I tell her.

"Stop it!" says Kit. She glares at both of us ferociously. "Enough with the stupid bravado! You have to stop acting like kids running around with guns and *think*," she hisses.

We shut up and watch her and wait.

"Aleks is still our best hope of getting those girls out of Gregory's hospital alive," she says.

"He's going to work with Gregory . . . ," I start, but I pipe down under Kit's stare.

"And you're going to make sure he doesn't," she says.

19

I TAKE HALA ON THE back of the motorbike with me. It's by far the fastest way to Aleks's home, and I only hope he's still there and not off opening a new Swiss bank account or buying a first-class flight to some tax haven. We have to make a quick stop at the Athena house to pick up some things, giving me plenty of time to go over this whole Aleks thing in my head.

Just the fact that his son was studying in the States was a red flag, because American colleges cost such a fortune. But Aleks had some savings, and a couple of investments that gave him regular dividends, so it passed through the Athena net. *My* net. But private cancer treatment would be a whole other level of cost. Potentially hundreds of thousands of dollars, and who knows for how long? I'm beyond angry with myself for not finding this information about his son's health. It's a huge miss. I feel guilty and, to be honest, it feels like I've taken Peggy to the brink of death as much as Aleks has.

The thought makes me push the motorbike to go even faster. Hala responds by wrapping her arms more tightly around my waist, leaning into curves with me. In her jacket she has tucked the drugged dart pistol that she threatened me with in the woods the other night. And in mine, I have a small syringe.

As we approach Aleks's house, Hala gives my clothes a sharp tug—an indication to stop. We are still about a hundred feet back. I obey and slide the bike off into a side alleyway behind someone else's house so that we can proceed on foot. We're both wearing baseball caps and scarves around our necks that we pull up over our faces.

As soon as we reach the edge of Aleks's home, Hala drops to one knee and boosts me up to go over the wall into his garden. It's about twelve feet high, and without that leg up I'd have no chance of making it. I drop to the other side, using the branch of a small apple tree to help me down. It doesn't take Hala long to follow, and I'm only sorry that from this side I didn't get to watch her scale that wall with no help. Even her descent to meet me almost defies physics. She doesn't use the tree like I did—she just moves like she's suctioned to the wall, and about five feet from the ground she finally jumps and lands without making a sound.

With a couple of strides, Hala's already moved ahead of me. Through the shrubs, we can see a short driveway, and two guards in suits hanging around. Hala pulls out a small ball from her pocket and rolls it beneath Aleks's car, which is parked close to the house. A stream of smoke starts pouring from it, and eventually the guards notice.

As they turn and run toward the car, guns out, Hala stalks silently behind them, lifts the pistol, and dispatches both of them into unconsciousness. They crumple to the ground unceremoniously in the middle of the driveway. Hala pats their pockets and finds the car key. She opens the car and leans in to plant a couple of tiny listening devices, wafer-thin dots that they'll never find. Then she locks the car and replaces the key.

Meanwhile, I'm heading for the back door of the house. Hala catches up and trots behind me. The wooden door has four small panes of glass in it, through which I can see Aleks's housekeeper at the stove. This must be Elena, the one who called the ambulance, probably too early for Aleks's liking. She is facing away from me, watching some kind of TV show streaming on a laptop while she cooks. Quietly, I try the handle, and the door is locked. I glance at Hala, and she nods. Knocking out the lowest pane of glass, I put my hand in, and open the door from the inside.

We're quick, and by Elena's side before she's barely had time to turn around at the sound of the breaking glass. I give her a small shot in the arm. She passes out pretty quickly, and Hala catches her, lowering her gently to the ground. Then she reaches back for a cushion from the nearest kitchen chair and places it under her head.

Meanwhile, I pad into Aleks's study, which is the usual cliché of wood paneling and rows of political books. I dot a couple of listening devices around—one under the desk, another under the chair. Then I lift all the paintings, looking for a safe. It turns out to be in the bottom drawer of the desk. Very basic, and easily accessible with an explosive gel tab that leaves a blackened ring on the base of the drawer. And provides enough space for me to slip a hand into the safe and pull out a bunch of papers. Some of that paper is cash—US dollars, which I leave on the floor. The others are the documents I am looking for—printed keys, or long strings of letters, symbols, and numbers. These will be the only way Aleks's stash of cryptocurrency can be retrieved. I tuck them into my jacket and hurry back to the kitchen, because I can hear Aleks calling Elena from upstairs.

When she doesn't come running, his footsteps descend toward the kitchen.

"Elena?" he calls. "Where are you?"

He speaks English, not Serbian, and so I guess Elena is South or Central American—hardly a genius deduction considering the video stream she was watching on the laptop is in Spanish. Even as Aleks walks in, Hala takes a moment to walk over to the computer and pause the soap opera. Presumably so Elena won't have missed anything when she comes round. Then she looks up at Aleks, cool as anything.

"What— Who are you?" he asks, looking from Hala to me. "I have security."

His eyes go to the window, hoping for rescue.

"They're taking a nap," I say.

Aleks begins to panic. On the counter beside him, a large kitchen knife lies right next to his hand. I move closer to stop him from even thinking about it, but he snatches up the blade, using it to wave me away. He doesn't even know how to hold it properly.

Meanwhile, Hala flicks on the recording from Peggy's phone: *I can blackmail Gregory and partner with him for a while. Then retire.* . . .

We don't have time for the full rerun, so Hala switches it off and I take a step toward Aleks.

"What did you give Peggy?" I ask.

Aleks refuses to answer. I step closer still, and he waves the blade around like crazy, like he's chopping imaginary vegetables in midair. It's the work of a moment to grasp his wrist midwave. Then I cuff the side of his head, punch him right in the solar plexus, and twist the knife out of his hand. He leans forward to recover from the punch, both palms spread on the counter, gasping for breath.

"What did you give her?" I ask again, losing patience.

Still, he hesitates. His breathing is ragged, and it reminds me of Peggy, desperate for air while Aleks watched her suffer. The thought of it, of his lying face, pretending to be Peggy's friend while he slipped her poison, makes my blood boil. I look down at his fingers on the counter. The fingers that were so quick to touch Peggy's that night in the restaurant . . . How *could* he? I raise the knife and slam the tip down into the countertop. Through Aleks's hand.

He stares at it for a moment, at his hand pinned to the counter, then he screams like a baby. Swiftly, Hala whips another knife out of the wooden block by the stove and holds down Aleks's free hand like she's ready to skewer that one too. He freaks.

"The cupboard behind me, at the top. Taped to the side."

Hala drops the knife, grabs a tea towel, and reaches up to check. She brings down a small bottle of fluid that she drops into a plastic bag. I'm close enough to watch the sweat beading on Aleks's forehead before it slides down his mottled cheeks. He's panting with fear and, I suppose, the pain from the knife.

"Antidote?" I ask.

He directs us to another cupboard; another bottle, more tape. A regular pharmacy. While Hala is finding this one, I lay out the plan for Aleks.

"You're going to arrest Gregory Pavlic immediately. As in, this morning," I tell him. "And you're not taking over his business. You're releasing those girls and closing that hospital."

"It won't be easy."

"Nothing worth having is."

Hala's got everything we need, and she jerks her head at me to say we should go. I give Aleks one more look.

"If you fail, you'll be extradited for attempted murder but, most likely, we'll kill you first. Got it?"

"Yes." He looks fearfully at the blade in his hand. I pull the knife out and toss it on the counter while he lifts his bleeding palm and pants with pain.

"We'll be watching to see what happens," I tell him as we get to the door.

"Who are you?"

Seriously? What does he expect me to do? Whip out a business card? I can't stand to look at him anymore. I walk out ahead of Hala and listen with satisfaction as she slams the door behind us.

■ ■ ■

As soon as we've delivered the vials to Peggy's doctor, Hala and I check in with Amber to make sure she has all she needs to take over surveillance of Aleks. The audio feeds we planted in his home and car, combined with her existing access to his work computer, are all up and live. She'll be able to make sure he's following through on the promise we extracted. But now, it's like Hala and I don't know what to do with ourselves. There's an energy you get from this kind of work—from the adrenaline, I suppose—and having subdued Aleks's guards, turned him to our side, and then driven at high speed to the hospital, it's hard to just switch it off.

Hala manages, of course. She retreats back into her own private world as we sit down in the waiting room. Half the time, being with Hala is like being alone. She doesn't show much emotion and demands no energy from anyone around her. She's enclosed and contained, and, most times, I'm grateful for it. Working with her again, to get the poison and antidote from Aleks, felt good—like rebuilding something that had broken between us. While I'm thinking about all this, I'm pacing, which is a habit Kit can't stand, so she sends me downstairs to fetch some tea for her, and I motion to Hala to come along to keep me company.

We're on the ground floor when her phone pings. Pulling it out of a pocket deep inside her leather jacket, she glances at it and then tells me she needs to go to the bathroom.

"Is it your brother?" I ask. I feel like this whole secret-phone-call thing has dragged on for long enough, always pushed aside for something more urgent.

"None of your business," she says. This has to be one of her favorite phrases, but her eyes shift away from mine, and it feels more like an excuse than the usual brush-off.

I turn and walk off toward the cafeteria, and behind me, Hala goes the opposite way into the restroom. I collect a paper cup and select a bag of green tea for Kit, but then I stop. Maybe it's the remains of the power rush I felt when dealing with Aleks, but I feel like it's time to sort this out. I leave the tea on the counter and follow Hala.

20

WHEN I WALK INTO THE restroom, I'm really hoping to overhear more of the conversation between Hala and her brother or whomever. But she's just leaning against the sinks, texting. Everything around us is very white, from the tiles to the doors—well scrubbed and antiseptic. Another woman comes out of a stall and washes her hands. Hala and I stand around, looking at each other, until the woman leaves.

"Stop hounding me," Hala says.

"Feels like it's Omar who's hounding you."

So maybe that wasn't the best move. Don't criticize anyone's parents, siblings, spouse, or children—*even* if they do. It's a good rule of thumb, but I can never seem to remember it in the moment. Hala slams her hand against the mirror, making it rattle.

"Can't I have a private life?" she demands.

"I just want to know what's going on. I heard you. Twice. Talking about plans. Is your brother pressuring you about something?"

"How dare you listen to my calls," she says. "You don't respect anyone's privacy."

Hala pushes past me to leave. But I stop her, grabbing her arm. She's surprised that I did that, and so am I. But, really, what's racing through my mind now is the terrible thought that maybe I missed something when I vetted Hala. The way I did with Aleks. Her brother is still in Syria. For all I know, he became an Islamic militant, or maybe he's blackmailing her for money, or maybe—

Hala wrenches free of my grip, and suddenly it becomes a struggle. I feel stupid, fighting with her yet again, but we're in it now, and both too arrogant to give in to the other.

But then it's like a switch flips in my mind, and I realize it doesn't have to be this way. I drop my arms and stand still, just raising a hand in peace; to calm her. And she steps back, breathing hard, still defensive.

"What?" she asks.

"You're not someone I'm ever supposed to fight with."

I turn away and wash my hands. And Hala doesn't try to leave. There's a long pause, as if she's looking for words. Whether to decide what lie to tell me or just to get over the stress of sharing her thoughts with anyone, I'm not sure. Then she speaks, her voice low.

"I'm trying to get my brother to London. To live with me."

"What?"

"He made it out of Syria and into Pakistan. But UK immigration is a mess. Here."

She taps a few buttons on her phone and hands it to me. It's a series of scanned letters from the UK Home Office, spanning the past few months and, ultimately, declining Omar's application for asylum.

If ever I felt like an idiot, this is the moment. All that bravado and pushing her around when all she wants is to see the brother she hasn't seen in years.

"Why won't they let him in?" I ask quietly, stepping back, giving her more space.

Hala glares at me accusingly.

"Same reason they block most young men from the Middle East. Because they worry he's a terrorist. Even you thought it. Just now."

She's right, of course, and I can't even look at her. And then, to try to make her feel better, I start to deny it. Which is truly lame, I'll admit.

Hala just turns and walks out, leaving only the echo of the door slam bouncing around the cold white tiles.

Leaning over a sink and splashing water on my face gives me something to do while I come to terms with doubting her and, worse, letting her know that I doubted her. Surely there's something Peggy could do to help Hala's brother—she knows everyone. But then I remember that Peggy is upstairs in a coma. Li could sponsor Omar maybe, offer him a job . . . but I'm clutching at straws. I look at myself in the mirror.

"You *idiot*," I say. I kick at the base of the sink, but my heart's not in it. I'm tired of myself, and my big mouth. I'm tired of being wrong about everything. I want to do better, to be the person everyone knows they can trust to do the right thing. And follow orders. Because maybe, just maybe, I don't know it all.

I dry my hands and take a breath. A lot of what I've done this morning looks courageous from the outside, but to me, going back upstairs to that waiting room and facing Hala again takes the most guts, and it's a few minutes before I can gather the will to do it.

We're still in the gray-walled waiting room. Of course, the substances we brought in from Aleks's needed to be tested in the lab before anyone could consider giving them to Peggy. Now that she's been given the antidote, results are still pending. And we are all in agony, nerves stretched tight as wires, waiting.

For entertainment, there's a TV running BBC World News and a Serbian women's magazine with a picture of steaming meat and potatoes on the cover. Caitlin stands a little removed from us, staring out of the inner glass wall at patients being wheeled through the corridor outside. Kit's leg is jiggling up and down nervously. Hala hasn't met my glance even once.

Though I'm trying to stay out of the way—out of Hala's way particularly—I just can't sit still that long. Standing and pacing feels better than sprawling in a chair. Kit looks up as I trudge from one side of the room to the other.

"Please, God, let that antidote work," she says to no one in particular.

"You think there's a God?" Hala suddenly snarls, her eyes on the floor.

Of all the careers that Hala wouldn't be suited to, grief counseling has to be in the top three, along with talk show host and cheerleader. I'm about to say something when Caitlin rounds on her.

"Shut up, Hala," she says. I don't think I've ever heard Caitlin speak to anyone like that before. But she stares Hala down, her face white and drawn. The stress in the room feels like it's at a boiling point.

"Can we all just stop?" Kit says. "I really can't deal with this right now."

That sends me into a tailspin.

"Of course," I say. "Let's make this all about you. Not Peggy, who's fighting for her life. We're *all* close to her, you know, not just you. She's been there for all of us whenever we needed her."

I don't know what's gotten into me, but it feels good to let something out, even if it's blame at the wrong person.

Kit stares. "Meaning what? That I haven't?"

Kit's voice is raised enough that the room is silenced. That is, Caitlin and Hala look over at her, and I think twice about talking back. Kit stands up, meeting me eye to eye.

"I've had enough," she says. "Enough of your accusations and your whining. So I wasn't there when you were growing up. Do you think I don't regret it every day? I've tried to make it up to you, but nothing I do is ever good enough. Well, you know what? You can blame me for the rest of your life, or you can grow the hell up!"

I'm stunned. That was out of left field, all that stuff about us, when I was talking about Peggy. But I feel the color rush to my face. Because I wasn't really talking about Peggy. I was using her as an excuse to have a dig at my mother. And I'm mortified that she said all that in front of Hala and Caitlin. And right at this moment, Peggy's doctor comes to the door. He looks so wrecked that, for a moment, I'm sure that Peggy is dead. My heart stops, and we all stare at him.

"What happened?" Caitlin breathes.

The doctor looks down. "She's taken a turn for the worse. She's still breathing, but now we're having to aid her mechanically. I'm sorry."

Silence in the room.

"Has the specialist from London arrived?" Kit asks the doctor at last.

Li's sending out her private plane with someone who's a whiz with this kind of toxic ingestion.

"As soon as he gets here, I will tell you."

As one, we move out of the waiting room and follow him down the corridors that lead to Peggy's room. In the tension over Peggy, our blowup is forgotten. I look in through the window, past the smeared marks where we—and perhaps other families before us— have pressed their palms desperately against the glass. Peggy lies there, her mouth hanging slightly open, her skin dry and papery. Her hair, which is never out of place, is splayed against the pillow. She doesn't *look* alive, even though the monitor beeping next to her tells us that she still is.

We go in and gather around Peggy's bed. We all just stand there, in shock, unable to look at each other. To my right, I feel Kit take some deep breaths and wipe her eyes.

"I need to tell you all something," she says. "Li and I are talking about closing down Athena."

"What?"

I pull my gaze away from Peggy and toward Kit.

"This was never how it was supposed to be." She gestures to Peggy.

"Peggy would want us to see this through," I say. "Athena is her legacy!" I look to Caitlin for support, but she seems overwhelmed.

"Jessie, you got our last mission plastered all over the news. And then you went off by yourself . . . you could have been *killed*. So easily. And now Peggy is . . ." She can't say the word. *Dying*. "It's enough," Kit adds decisively. "It has to end here."

I look away from Kit, shell-shocked. Slowly, I step forward, and touch my lips to Peggy's forehead. Suddenly, I feel I can't be there anymore, packed into this oppressive room, looking at Peggy like she's an exhibit. Waiting for her to die. The walls are closing in on me. I walk out, on autopilot, and get into the lift. It smells like it always does, of disinfectant and fried food. I don't know where to go, so I head down to the cafeteria, where they are laying out some plastic-wrapped ham sandwiches that look like the most miserable meal on earth. I buy a watery coffee and a chocolate bar. But I don't touch either of them. Instead, I leave them on one of the Formica tables by the window.

Outside, the trees are shifting in a breath of wind, a bird takes off from a branch, a young couple walks by on the street, holding hands. Nothing changes. We have our dramas and stresses, and whether Peggy lives or dies, the world just goes on the same way. It feels unfair and so *random*. That everything Peggy did, every person whose day she made better with her kindness, every girl she rescued from a life of imprisonment—it will all be forgotten when she's not here anymore, and everything will carry on exactly like it did before.

Except that Athena won't be there to help anyone or anything. I leave the depressing cafeteria and go out into the street and start walking, fast. It makes me furious, but not with some higher power—with Gregory, for his disgusting "business"—and also with Aleks. I can't help but feel he's getting off too lightly. Even if he's able to throw Gregory into jail, where's the justice for Peggy in all of this? That's who Athena is—the goddess of justice. But Athena, our organization, is dying. And, the truth is, I'm terrified that Peggy is dying too.

I keep moving. The sky is overcast and gloomy. No longer does all the colorful graffiti look cool and exciting; now it just makes the city feel dirty and out of control. I walk past a wall spray-painted with taglines and pictures of snarling dogs and turn into the street that has started to feel disturbingly like home.

Up in my own apartment, there's a sour stench coming from the kitchen. I flick on the TV and go to investigate. A carton of milk has gone off, left out on the counter. I must have forgotten to put it away last night when I made tea. I get rid of it and boil the kettle. I don't even want tea, but maybe it's force of habit. Growing up in England, that's what you do in times of stress. Put the kettle on. In the background an excited commentary spews from the TV, none of which I can follow until I hear the word *Pavlic*.

Quickly, I walk back into the living room, and there it is on the screen—the hellish hospital. The pictures seem to be playing live, and behind the reporter talking into the camera I can see a news broadcast van, several police cars, and a couple of SWAT trucks. At least Aleks has had the presence of mind to call in the media to make sure we can see what he's doing. I perch on the edge of the bed to watch more. Eventually, a stream of men, Gregory's men, are marched out in a long column, hands behind their heads, and thrust into the police vans.

With much excited commentary from the reporter, the broadcast switches locations, changing over to a view of a private estate taken from a helicopter. From the swimming pool and those turrets, I immediately recognize Gregory's home. Again, the place is swarming with police. The reporter is going ballistic, almost shouting, a fast stream of Serbian that I can't catch anything of. But then a picture of Gregory Pavlic comes up on the screen with a caption underneath that reads:

Pavlic je ubijen

I sit up straighter. There is a cut to some audio, police radio back and forth. All of this plays over the live pictures of Gregory's home, so I'm assuming it's audio from the raid. And then gunfire cracks into the audio. Voices are shouting, more gunfire pops. Then quiet. I tap *je ubijen* into my phone translator—it means *Pavlic has been killed.*

What the hell is going on? And if Gregory is really dead, where is Paulina? Could she have been caught in this cross fire? What if she's shot? I turn up the TV, listening for any mention of her name, but there's nothing that I can make out. Stressed, I run to the window, hoping to see Paulina's car down there on the road outside the gallery—but the street is empty.

This wasn't the deal we made with Aleks. But then, maybe Gregory and his crew were never going down without a fight, or maybe Aleks provoked it knowing that it would be safer to have Gregory finished off than plotting his way out of prison. Gregory's death can only be a relief to his victims and their families, but he was still Paulina's father, and she must be devastated.

On the TV, the live picture cuts out to be replaced with a portrait of Gregory Pavlic in sunglasses on one side of the screen and Aleks Yuchic on the other, positioned like prizefighters pitted against each other. The excitement over what Aleks has achieved by taking down Pavlic is insane. Probably no one believed in a million years that someone like Gregory could actually be stopped. There's another cut to the parliament building where, it seems, Aleks will hold a press conference late this afternoon.

The report goes back to the abandoned hospital, where the girls I was imprisoned with are now being taken out of the building and helped into buses. Their faces are blurred out by the news station, so I can't tell if Dasha is among them. I let the TV run on in the background and go to the window to see if there's any movement in the gallery, but there's still nothing. Paulina must have been at home when they came for her father, and she would be completely freaked out right about now. I hope to God she didn't get hurt—or worse—trying to protect him.

I turn away from the window. On the screen, the news piece moves back to the studio, and in the background, behind the news-caster, a series of clips of Aleks Yuchic play in slow motion. The conquering hero. And would-be murderer of Peggy. It makes me sick. Literally. I feel my stomach turn, and I run to the bathroom.

Leaning over the cracked, stained porcelain of the toilet bowl, waiting for the spasm to pass, I glance through to the living room and the TV. The report cuts to ecstatic reactions from people on the streets. A crowd is already gathering outside the parliament building.

We brought down Gregory. So why does it feel like nothing is right? Peggy is dying. Hala will never get to see her brother. Good people suffer. We work like mad, risking everything to save other women, but we don't see justice done for the people closest to us.

I've had an idea in the back of my mind since I listened to that horrible recording of Peggy's last moments of consciousness. And I've been trying to push it away—but the truth is we didn't choose to fight evil men like Gregory by giving power to slightly less evil people like Aleks. That's not what I signed up for with Athena. But now, Athena is over. And Peggy's not here, and she may never be here again. So there's no one to tell me what to do or how to do it. Anger and adrenaline start to pulse through me, and I feel impelled to move, to act, to finish this the way it should be ended. I throw on a jacket, tuck my hair under a small beanie, and head outside.

21

I PAUSE ON THE STREET outside my apartment, thinking, and then go down a couple of doors to my landlord's place. There's not much sign of life, but I bang on the door anyway. It takes a minute for him to open up. He's in shorts and a torn tank top—not a great look— and he peers at me sleepily. Then he reaches across to a table behind him and thrusts a can of insect killer at me. He thinks I'm here to complain about the roaches.

"I want a gun."

He rubs his eyes, then stares at me. Maybe being a teenage girl isn't helping me in my quest for a weapon. Or maybe he thinks I'm going to blow the heads off the vermin.

"I need a gun," I repeat.

He sniffs and shakes his head like he has no idea what I'm talking about.

"I saw you, the first day." I point inside the room, to the place where his visitor had picked a bag full of pistols off the table like he was doing his weekly grocery shopping.

His eyes open wider. So does the door. I step inside, and the door slams behind us, echoing in the room, leaving a residual rattle shaking the windows. On the table is a beer bottle, a glass, and a small tin containing something he'd rather keep secret because he picks it up and places it in a drawer.

"Gun?" he sniffs. Finally, we're getting somewhere.

"A sniper rifle," I clarify.

He frowns. I'm not sure whether he doesn't understand, or whether he just thinks it's a tall order. I bring out my phone and hold it out to him, showing him a picture of the kind of thing I'm looking for. He sighs.

"Yes or no?" I ask him.

He rubs his chubby fingers together, indicating cash.

"No easy. Big price."

No surprise there.

"How big?" I ask.

He names a price.

"Pounds?" I say in disbelief. I turn for the door.

"Dollars," he says hastily.

I walk back to where he's standing, careful not to get too close because I remember his bad breath from before.

"I need it today. In one hour."

He balks a bit, then agrees, but of course, like with dry cleaning, express gun services cost more. We set a time for me to return, and I head out to the hospital.

■ ■ ■

There's been no change in Peggy's condition. The only surprise for me is that Li herself is here. While her medical expert is busy getting up to speed with the doctors outside, Li stands by Peggy's bedside, arms crossed. She turns to glance at me when I arrive but says nothing. The others are back in the waiting room, but I sit down here, next to Peggy, for a moment. Li's presence makes me even more depressed because it feels like she might have come to say her last goodbye. I watch Peggy closely, wishing and willing that this might be the moment when her hand moves, or her eyes flutter open, and she miraculously comes back to us. But nothing happens. The sound of the respirator grates on my nerves.

I stand up to leave, to carry on with my plan. But Li's voice stops me.

"Athena got out of control," she says.

I'm not sure what that means exactly, but I'm pretty sure I can detect a strong note of blame directed at me.

"You mean I did?" I reply. I mean, let's just cut to the chase here.

"Control is essential. Of an organization and each person in it."

Li's way of talking—in little sound bites of wisdom—drives me a bit nuts at the best of times. But she's looking at me, and there's no judgment in her look (for once). It's more like she simply asked a question and wants an answer. Not so long ago, I told Peggy that she couldn't understand what it was like, to be out there, day in, day out, scared, fighting, desperate. So I didn't bother explaining. But now, with Li, words start to form.

"You want control," I say. "But when we fight, we're in a dark place. The kind of place that most people don't want to admit they have inside. Where they're savage and brutal and can hurt and kill."

I stop, because I feel my voice crack. Li is absolutely still, watching me. I clear my throat and speak again.

"We all believe in the work we do for Athena. But some of that work is dirty. And maybe we should stop trying to pretend that it isn't."

Peggy's chest rises and falls with the air pumped into it through the machine beside her. Li says nothing. I touch Peggy's hand as a goodbye before I turn around and leave.

When I reach my landlord's front door, there's old-time country-and-western music playing loudly inside, so I knock hard enough that the thin window next to the door vibrates. The music drops in volume and the landlord opens up. He grins and beckons me in, locking the door firmly behind us. Then he leads me down a hallway lined with carpet that was once green but is now almost black with dirt, and into a tiny rear bedroom where the sole window is barred with thick iron rods. There's a tiny bunk bed in the corner. It looks exactly like a prison cell, except for the fact that the bed has pink princess sheets on it and a ton of furry stuffed animals.

"You have a daughter?" I ask. I think I'm safe to assume that even in this day and age, few men have the self-confidence to decorate their son's bedroom entirely in pink.

He nods. "Divorce," he says. I guess what he means is that the kid doesn't live with him full time. I think about my own bedroom in Kit's house, also covered in stuffed animals when I was very young, presents that Kit would bring back by the armful when she returned from a tour.

What Kit *didn't* do, at least, is keep an arms cache in a locked drawer in my room. My landlord kneels down beneath the pink sheets of the bed and pulls it out, opening it up to reveal a sniper rifle. Better specs than I could have hoped. I kneel next to him, pull out the parts and check them over.

"Good?" he asks.

"Yeah, good."

He gets up, complaining about his knees as he does so, and holds out his phone, which has the crypto account for me to transfer the payment. I show him the proof on my screen and then his. Then I indicate that I need a bag to carry my purchase in, and he pulls out a proper rifle case, which is not ideal. It might as well have a sign on it that reads, "Look in here for illegal weapons."

I look around the room. In the corner there's a black guitar case, covered with more pink princess stickers. I ask the question silently, and he hesitates, but a fifty-pound note helps to make up his mind. Carefully, I take out the guitar and lay it on the bed. Then I load the case with the rifle pieces and use one bedsheet to cover them up and another to stop them from rattling around. I glance at the clock on my phone. There's no time to waste, so I nod goodbye and leave.

■ ■ ■

As I stalk through the streets of Belgrade with my guitar case in hand, I can't help but hear that song from *The Sound of Music* running through my head. "Cream-colored ponies and crisp apple strudels . . ."

Kit sang that to me a couple of times when I was really young. I loved it, that list of favorite things wrapped up in a song. Even though I had no time for ponies and liked Lego more; even though I'd never eaten a strudel; it just *sounded* like happiness, and Kit's gravelly voice singing it to me *was* happiness.

My apartment is not even a fifteen-minute stroll from the parliament building, which they call the House of the National Assembly. It's a good name for what's happening outside today. Even from a few hundred yards away, I can feel a buzz of excitement in the air from the low babble of the crowd. I stop some distance from the steps, far from the loose cordon of police who are stationed around, and far from the security cameras that are mounted on the outside of the building. Kids are hoisted onto their parents' shoulders, people are waiting, chatting, jostling for position, making sure they get a good view of Aleks when he arrives and makes his speech. It feels a bit like a British royal wedding, like a day off. Everyone wants a hero, I suppose. Someone who does the stuff they're too scared to do themselves. Someone to stand up to a Gregory Pavlic, whatever the consequences.

There's a bitter edge of distaste in my mouth as I watch the gathered crowd. Until now, they were fine to just let things carry on; to look the other way, knowing Gregory is crooked, knowing he traffics women. What if all these people hadn't looked the other way? They have ideals and skills. They could write about what men like Gregory do; they could demonstrate, vote out the bad politicians, build shelters for girls who want a way out; they could find ways to keep their teenagers in school, instead of on the streets for people like Gregory to exploit and recruit.

But none of that is easy. And most of the time, it doesn't feel like all those little things, the small sacrifices, even make a difference. But what if they do? If enough people made the effort? Maybe we need thousands of smaller heroes every day instead of just the occasional big one.

Turning away so that my back is to the parliament building, I pause and look upward. Right across the wide street from the National Assembly is a vast green space, and set back behind that park is city hall. There's not much chance of me getting in there easily. But to the right of city hall is a small street with a row of businesses and a few shops, and above the shops are six-story blocks of flats. I look at the sun, where it's sitting now and where it will be in a little while, and I make my choice. While I walk toward the apartments, I pass a rundown café and stop to take away a coffee and a doughnut. For a moment, I imagine Li at my shoulder, shaking her head unhappily at the way I've fallen off the wagon of her ideal diet—but sometimes you can't find a green smoothie, and even if you could, you don't want it.

Each storefront in this row has a small doorway next to it that leads up to the apartments above. I approach the second door and buzz on all the bells at once. Nothing happens, so I lean on them all again, for longer. This time a man's voice snaps onto the intercom, and the front door clicks open for me.

Inside the entrance foyer, it's 1965. Or how I imagine 1965 looked. Little metal mailboxes with people's names handwritten on them, some in Cyrillic script. A milk bottle outside the ground-floor apartment with a note pushed into the top. A tiny, red-painted tricycle. All very quaint. A couple of floors above, a door opens and a man's voice calls out, most likely the guy who buzzed me in. There's an ancient elevator, so I send it up a few floors, so he won't expect a reply. At the sound of the lift rising, he closes his door again and I start running lightly up the stairs.

Why do all stairwells in old buildings smell the same? Like cats and vegetable soup and stale carpet. The corners are so tight that the guitar case bumps against a couple of walls on the way up. But soon enough, I'm at the top fire-escape door and pushing through onto the roof. I jam the door shut behind me, so no one else can get up here. I edge past a big TV satellite dish and walk to the edge of the roof. Here, I kneel down and lay the guitar case beside me.

Far below, the road is sealed off in anticipation of Aleks's triumphant arrival and, far across the street, more people move toward the wide marble steps and magnificent statues, to join the crowd that's already there. A broadcast van from the main news station trundles around the corner and parks next to another one that's already set up. A tech crew jumps out of the back, unwinding cables and setting up handheld cameras.

A little boy goes from person to person, trying to sell sweets to the crowd. It's like a festive holiday, and all to celebrate the man who has put Peggy, his *friend*, into a coma that's killing her. The man who was willing (before I drove a knife through his hand) to let hundreds of women suffer and die to fill his bank account so he could pay his bills and then retire to Monaco. I'm not one of those people who have an issue with wealth. I'm surrounded by it. Although Kit maybe doesn't have the millions she once had, Li has enough to buy a small country. But they both built it all themselves. They gave the world something in return. Unlike Aleks, who's only been blackmailed into doing the right thing. If there's one thing I hate, it's a hypocrite.

It's like I'm psyching myself up to open the case and fit together the pieces of the sniper rifle. The cool metal weighs heavily in my palms. It feels solid, substantial, true. It gives me power. The same power that people like Gregory and Aleks have, although I'm using that power for something better.

Placing the rifle on its bipod, I slide down so that I'm lying flat on my stomach. I lean in to place my eye against the viewfinder. It's really crisp and clear, a lovely lens, with light crosshairs that don't cover everything so I can have a good look around. I examine the faces of the people waiting. They're happy, content to stand about chatting. A couple of officials jostle for position near the podium where Aleks is supposed to give his speech. Then a sort of ripple passes through the crowd, like a breath of wind disturbing the air. Some kind of message is being passed around, and people turn to look up the wide boulevard.

So do I. I swing the rifle around and, sure enough, Aleks's black limousine is on its way, crawling slowly up the street. The windows are tinted, but I can see him, dimly, inside, with some other men. Possibly security guys. I follow the car along in the rifle sight, hardly breathing now. It pulls up outside the wide marble steps, and the door opens. I swallow. I know I'm doing the right thing. I know I am.

A bodyguard steps out of the front seat and holds open the back door for Aleks. Another guard, wide, barrel-chested, exits the back, forming an effective shield for Aleks to hide behind as he emerges.

"Coward," I mutter. Because there's no way I can get him at this moment without taking out his escorts. But then Aleks hears the cheering, the applause, the welcome, and he's tempted. His men are forming a tight shield around him, but he pauses and turns to wave at the crowd and press a few hands.

I have a shot on his arm, but that's all.

Move, I tell the guards in my mind. Move!

That's why we have a protocol, Jessie . . . To protect, not to kill . . .

Where Peggy came from in my head, I don't know. My eyes fill suddenly, but I dash away the tears. She wouldn't approve of revenge—but I can't let Peggy's advice derail me now; it's Peggy I'm doing this for. I hunker down, because when Aleks turns back for the stairs, he will be exposed, if only for a moment. But the chance is short, and I don't want to lose it; I can't lose it.

With a weird suction sound that I feel even from up here, a bullet flies out and into the back of one of the bodyguards. Right between the shoulder blades—it's a perfect shot, and he is down, slumped on the ground, and Aleks has turned to look at him. It's strange, but it takes a moment for anyone to realize what's just happened. Including me. My heart is pounding. I check my rifle, because I was sure I hadn't fired yet. I take my finger off the trigger, but I keep my eye on the scope, and now the second guard is pulling Aleks back to the car, shielding him, gun out. That guard is shot too, twice, in the chest. Leaving Aleks exposed. I can see him in my crosshairs, the target that I've been waiting for; but it's not me shooting.

I swivel the rifle around to my right and there, on a rooftop two buildings across from me, is another sniper. His head is bent, his finger is on the trigger, and on instinct, because I know he will kill someone else, I shoot. The bullet hits him in the shoulder. He gives a yelp and looks across and sees me. He turns his rifle on me, so I shoot again. He falls off to the side, away from his weapon, and doesn't move.

Back on the ground, Aleks is going for the car. Panting, stressed, I swivel the gun back and have him in my crosshairs for a moment, such a short moment, and yet long enough for someone like me— but I don't pull the trigger.

He dives into the car, the door shuts, and the limo screams away. The police have their weapons drawn, everyone is crouched down, the two bodyguards lie sprawled and bleeding and it's remarkably quiet. Everything has happened so fast that there's nothing but silent shock.

Without thinking, I'm packing up the rifle, unscrewing it, fitting the pieces into the case, and then I'm heading for the door, to take the stairs down. But I can hear wailing starting. Wailing people, wailing sirens. I stop and look back over at the other rooftop, at the other sniper lying there. The gap between buildings is tiny—these are old brick structures, packed close together. I run back across my roof and jump across over to the next and then to the next, where the gunman lies, unmoving.

I check his pulse, but there isn't one. My second kill in less than a week. But it was me or him. Somewhere, a phone starts ringing, muffled. With an effort, I roll the sniper onto his other side and check his pockets. In the background, behind me, sirens are going mad, police cars and fire engines are closing in. There are also armed police inching carefully across the street, edging nearer and nearer to where I am.

Still the phone rings. Thrusting my hand into his jacket, I find it, one of those old, tiny, plastic things with no screen. Disposable. I press the green button and hold it to my ear.

"Hello?" says a voice.

I say nothing. I just wait.

"Did you do it?" repeats the voice. It's a female voice that makes me gasp inside. Because it's someone I recognize all too well.

22

I SAY NOTHING, OF COURSE. I just wipe off the phone, leaving it back in the sniper's pocket. The police have figured out that there's only one strip of buildings that the shots could have come from, and they're heading toward me.

Grabbing my guitar case, I run, crouching down, over to the next roof. Already, I can hear men emerging onto the first roof in the block, the one that I was on a few moments ago. I jump down onto the roof next to me. It's a bit lower, and it's a commercial building. Through the skylight in the middle, I can see desks and files and computer terminals. I push at the skylight with no luck, but at the rear of the roof there's a thin fire escape ladder that zigzags down the back of the building, all the way down to an alleyway. How long will it take for the SWAT team to reach this street? Between the raid on the hospital and the shooting at Gregory's home, they can't have had a busier day in ages, and yet there seems to be more of them arriving all the time.

I clamber down into the alley and turn quickly into a small street and then into another. The guitar case slows me down, but I can't risk dumping it. The main danger is from the rows of windows all around me. I'm hoping everyone inside all these apartments is glued to their front windows, watching the drama outside the House of the National Assembly, but the truth is that anybody could have seen me climbing down that building just now, and it will take just one of them to say something to the police for me to become a suspect in Aleks's attempted assassination. It will help when they find the sniper's body, but they could still view me as an accomplice, and that doesn't thrill me, because what I feel like after this trip is a year in a spa, not a decade in a Serbian jail.

My feet move as fast as they can without actually drawing attention to myself by running. Blood is pounding in my ears. The voice I heard on the end of that phone was Paulina's, and I don't know what to think, except that she hired that sniper to avenge her father. I keep my hands thrust into the pockets of my jacket, where I take a bit of comfort in the familiar feel of my folded army knife and the bag with the solitary blue pill.

There is so much confusion around that I make it out of the area without much problem. There's still a high chance that someone is currently giving my description to the SWAT guys as they go from door to door, sweeping each apartment, but for now, I'm clear.

A block away from my apartment, I circle around for a bit to see if anyone's watching the place. On the way, I spot a rubbish truck,

parked outside a greasy café. The driver's probably having lunch. I
toss the guitar case into it and head toward my room.

There's a white van a couple of doors down from me, a nice one,
but not dressed up as a phone company van or anything. I hesitate.
There's no one in it, which is good. And the rear windows are darkened glass, which is bad. My options are limited. I don't want to go
back to the hospital or to the Athena house, not while I'm a possible
suspect in the shootings. And I can't go straight to the airport without my passport, which is upstairs.

I decide to risk it and head up to collect my stuff. It'll only take
me two minutes, because I have everything packed. The key sticks
in the lock in the familiar place and everything feels the same as I
walk in. I'm relieved. For about two seconds. Then a massive set of
arms grabs me from behind, pinning my own hands to my waist. I
wrench myself to the side and get a glimpse of a broad chest behind
me level with my eyes. Whoever's grabbed me is *huge*. I'm struggling
like mad, lifting my legs off the floor to make it harder for him to
keep hold of me. And then I remember to scream. One of his hands
comes up to muffle my mouth. He's smart enough to grab a pillow
off the bed and slam it over my face so I can't bite him. But I also
can't breathe very well now. I twist as hard as I can and wriggle my
left arm free enough to hammer down a fist on his inner thigh. He
cuffs me so hard on the temple that I stagger across the room. Even
as I get up, he's on me with a hood. It smells like it's been used on a
lot of people before me. But I can't stop it from going over my head.
As I struggle, I stumble and fall, hitting my head on something. The

last thing I feel is a searing pain at the base of my skull, and then the relief of blackness.

My brain feels like jelly as I start to emerge back into consciousness. The first thing I register is that the hood is off me. My eyes close again for a moment as I recall what happened in the apartment. Snatches of the fight come back to me. And I strain to remember what I was doing before that . . . leaving, because of the sniper, because of Aleks . . .

I open my eyes. There's a stained ceiling above me. Black, oozing, dripping patches of mildew. I'm lying on a mattress, but I'm up high off the floor. I try to bring my hand up to rub at my eyes, but my arm is trapped. Moving my head sideways stirs up a shooting pain, and I blink till it subsides. My arms, both of them, are tied down to a bed of some kind. And they look bare. I realize my clothes are off, and a worn blue smock is covering me instead. My feet are lashed together with a reinforced fabric strap, like an airplane seat belt but without a buckle.

I look sideways and Paulina is sitting there, watching me. I close my eyes again, then blink them open. Her eyes are clear and watchful, and she's sitting so still, so silently, that I think I must be dreaming her.

"Paulina?" I say, and my voice sounds like someone else's, croaky and weak. I clear my throat and say her name again. If she doesn't react, I'll know I'm hallucinating.

But she moves. She uncrosses her legs, gets up from her chair, and comes over, standing tall above me. Her eyes look sad, disappointed. I can see better now, and the fog in my mind is less thick, but I'm still confused. She needs to be careful or they'll get her too.

"Paulina, you need to get out. It's dangerous here," I say.

She smiles slightly and nods.

"That's the first true thing you've ever said to me."

I watch her silently.

"I trusted you, Jessie, and now my father's dead."

This is not good. On instinct, I try moving my arms again, but it's pointless. I glance around. On my left, on the other side of the bed, a looming shadow solidifies into a tall, broad man in a polo shirt and jeans. Most likely the hulk who overpowered me in my apartment. Behind him are double doors, and a row of empty metal beds like the one I'm tied to. It finally dawns on me where we are. Gregory's abandoned hospital. Apparently abandoned by the police too.

I swallow a surge of panic and look back at Paulina.

"Your father deserved it," I say.

"He was my *family*." She practically spits the words at me. I guess the honeymoon's over, then. "Maybe it's not like that where you come from," she continues, "but here your family is the most important thing."

"He buys and sells women," I point out.

"They all have choices. They just made the wrong ones."

"You can't really believe that! Paulina?"

I look at her; into the eyes that I had found so captivating before.

There's nothing there that I recognize. No warmth, no humor, no kindness. Just rage, and it's burning cold.

"He was planning to kill people for their organs," I say, just to jolt her into *something*, some acknowledgment of what's been happening.

She smiles. She actually smiles. Disbelief? I wonder, with a shred of hope, but then she speaks.

"And because of that, many more people will live."

Even if you suck at math, that just doesn't add up to a good deal, but Paulina's on a roll, so I keep my mouth shut and let her go on.

"Aleks Yuchic could never stop this by killing my father. He did that for show," she says angrily. "And then he had the nerve to try to make a deal with me, blackmailing me with information stolen from my home. From my *room*."

She looks at me accusingly. Safe to assume she figured out what I was up to during Kit's concert, then. I think it's probably best not to get into it now though. I keep eye contact and listen, while still pushing at my wrist and ankle straps, trying to find out how they work so I can find a way out of them.

"I will finish what my father started," Paulina continues. "And leave here with the money from that first harvest."

There's a word that's been ruined by the illegal organ trade. *Harvest.* It should make you think of farming and food and wheat and stuff.

"Where are you going to go?"

Paulina ignores that question, but then, I wasn't expecting her to spill her future address. I'm just trying to buy time.

"Who buys these organs?" I ask. "The Victory Clinic?"

She looks surprised that I know the name. I hold eye contact with her, trying to connect, trying to find some way in to that other part of her, the part that must know that this deal is just evil.

"You don't have to do this, Paulina," I say. "You already started selling art. It pays well. Why risk your freedom for this?"

Even before she smirks, I realize what an idiot I was for believing that those huge chunks of money in her account were from art dealers. And her next words confirm it.

"I made some money from art, but not enough. And Victory already gave us a down payment," she says. "These are not people who you let down."

She looks away from me. So, she's scared for herself too.

"But I saw them release the girls from here. On TV," I tell her.

"A few of them," she says. "Enough for the cameras."

My heart sinks. "So your plans stay the same?"

Paulina nods, then smiles at me. "With one exception. *You* are going to be my first donor."

I stare at her. Frankly, I'm terrified. Paulina sits down on the edge of the bed that I'm lashed to, right next to me. I can feel her leg touching mine as she perches there, and I try to move away but I can't. She watches me, but I can't stand to look at her. Gently, her finger touches my chin, raising it up until my eyes are forced to meet hers.

"Your eyes first," she whispers. "Then kidneys . . . liver . . . lungs.

And finally . . . well, we'll see if you really have a heart after all."

Her finger touches my chest, and I recoil, pulling away as far as I can, but she leans in even closer. That perfume that used to make my head spin now makes me want to throw up. Her breath touches my ear as she whispers.

"I can't believe how you betrayed me, Jessie."

She pulls back and looks at me, and the mask is down, just for a second. Her eyes look real, like reflections of true feelings, and I know she's been hurt by me.

"I really felt something for you," she says.

I look at her squarely. "I wish I could say the same."

Then I spit at her, which is maybe not the smartest move, but it gives me a moment's satisfaction and considering how close I am to death, I might as well take what I can get. Paulina wipes her perfectly draped shirt, where my spit has landed, and turns to the incredible hulk beside me.

"Kristof," she says. "Tell the doctor his first patient is ready."

I don't know where Paulina disappears to, but there's plenty of commotion in the wards next to this one. Low-level sniffling and crying; then I catch the tones of Paulina's voice, barking instructions. To my right, double doors lead into a brightly lit room where there is a whole lot of activity going on. I catch glimpses of doctors and nurses, heads moving back and forth past the single round window in the door. One man flips on an overhead lamp, another pulls on a face mask. Looks like an operating room.

I start to shiver, despite myself. It's cold in here, but really, dread has taken hold of me. *Nobody* knows where I am. Li, Kit, Hala, and Caitlin are at the hospital, watching over Peggy. Amber and Tom are back in London thinking that these organ harvests have been stopped, as does the entire population of Belgrade.

Paulina strolls back into the ward, through the double doors at the end. Composed and calm, she comes and sits down on my bed. She even takes a moment to straighten my hospital gown, which has gotten twisted in my vain attempts to break free. A regular Florence Nightingale. I keep my eyes fixed on the mildew patch on the ceiling. Prettier to look at than her eyes.

"Who do you work for?" she asks.

Seriously, does she expect me to just tell her? I ignore her and, for the tenth time, look around the place for any sign of a weapon I could use, in the unlikely event I can figure out a way to get my four tied-up limbs free. There's still nothing in sight.

"Is it British Intelligence?" Paulina says.

Now I look at her, scornfully. Like, could she have made a dumber guess?

Her right hand is closed in a fist. She lifts it up to my face and slowly opens her fingers. There, on her palm, sits my blue pill.

"Then why do you carry this?" she asks. "If not to avoid breaking under torture?"

She's so proud of herself and her genius deduction, I could throw up. But I make my eyes meet hers as if she's rumbled me.

"You're so clever," I say admiringly.

And before she knows what's happening, I thrust my head forward and bite down on her hand, swallowing up the pill into my mouth. It's down my throat before she can even react.

Paulina screams and jumps up from the bed, holding her hand. I seem to have drawn a lot of blood and I wipe my mouth on the shoulder of my robe while I watch her hop around the room, yelling for help. An alarmed nurse rushes in from the operating room and goes straight back for antiseptic and a bandage. Paulina glares at me, incandescent with rage.

"However long you have left, I'm going to make it painful," she says.

I believe her. Terror hits me again, and I feel the contents of my stomach rising. But I breathe, almost panting. Anything not to throw up. I need that blue capsule to work. And fast.

23

THE UPSIDE OF WORKING FOR a team of socially conscious women is that they take invasion of privacy seriously, even for their agents. It's why they never wanted to tag us with permanent trackers. They didn't want us to feel like criminals, or to feel that they owned us. So all I can do now is rely on that blue capsule.

I imagine it floating inside me. The coating wearing away in my stomach acid, just enough for the tracker that it contains to be activated. I visualize Amber, in London, getting a notification. Alerting the entire Athena team. I picture Hala jumping on her motorbike, Caitlin joining her. But here's the thing. They're focused on Peggy. They think the mission here is over. They think I'm off somewhere feeling sorry for myself. Who knows if they'll even be on the Athena comms system?

The doors to the operating room are propped open now. There are two teams of doctors waiting. None of them look over at me. At the foot of my bed, Paulina's hand is being carefully bandaged by a nurse, and Kristof has a hand grasping my scalp, gripping my hair, like the caveman that he is, presumably to stop me from biting his boss again.

For a moment I imagine my funeral. You know when you're young, you do that sometimes, when everyone's on your case. I used to do it so I could enjoy how sorry Kit would be that she was on tour when I died, but now that my demise is looking more imminent, I actually feel bad at the idea of my mother in so much pain.

A crashing noise in the operating room makes us all look up. Another "patient" is being wheeled in, screaming, a patient I recognize—Dasha. I jerk my head away from Kristof and call her name, struggling harder with my restraints, every ounce of frustration coming out in a desperate attempt to get free.

Dasha looks over at me, and our eyes meet for just a moment before Paulina instructs Kristof to close the door between us. He kicks away the doorstop, and it swings shut with a shudder. I can hear Dasha calling out to me, terrified, from the operating room. Except she's calling me "Daisy," which is the fake name I gave her. It would be comical, if it weren't so mixed up with impending death.

Paulina's watching me with a small smile.

"I heard you made a friend, when you broke in here," she says.

"You said *I* would be the first donor," I say fiercely.

"We have two medical teams. Because time is money. Don't worry. You'll be right beside her."

The door of the operating room opens again and two nurses

come in. They release the brakes on my bed and turn it around to wheel me inside. Paulina watches as the doors swing shut behind me, and just before they do, she raises her bandaged hand to wave goodbye.

Inside the operating room, nobody pays me much attention, because Dasha is going nuts. She's clearly kept her spirit, because she's fighting, kicking, screaming, giving it everything. The nurses assigned to me have to rush over to Dasha and help restrain her.

I know that I'm next. As long as I'm conscious, there's some scrap of a chance I can survive. While they all crowd around Dasha, I look at the tray of surgical instruments beside me. I can't reach them with my hands. But with a small twist of my upper body I can grasp a scalpel with my mouth. But I have to be careful and just take hold of the handle. It slips precariously between my teeth as I try to grip it, and so I have to drop it onto my chest, in full view of anyone who cares to look in my direction. But Dasha is still keeping them busy; she's moaning now, weeping. The sound of it breaks my heart, but it also helps me push down my own fear. I jerk my body to get the scalpel off my chest. It slides down to my side, where it's out of sight, but also out of my reach. Great.

I glance over to the other table. One of the doctors is prepping a syringe of something to calm Dasha down and now they are holding her arms, trying to get the sedative into her. I feel the cold metal of the scalpel against the underside of my arm. I keep working my hand, but gently, trying to ease that blade into my palm without slicing open my own veins in the process.

Dasha goes quiet suddenly, and there's a general muttering of relief from the doctors. I feel sweat start to form on my forehead. Poor Dasha. I can hear them firing up a small bone saw. Tears of frustration touch my eyes as I think about how badly I'm failing here. The team standing over Dasha start swabbing her, ready to operate.

In the meantime, my lot of doctors come back to me. I arch my back, desperate to move the scalpel within reach. It helps, a bit, and they all just think I'm trying to escape. Another one of those anesthetics is being prepared, and a nurse swabs my arm. She says something to the doctor, and they both tap my elbow, looking for a vein. They ask me to make a fist. Really, like I'm going to make my own murder easier for them? I don't oblige, of course, and so they start looking for a vein in my hand—but I keep moving my hand, so much that the needle scratches me a few times. But at last, I feel the cool metal of the scalpel touch my other palm. Is it the blade or the handle?

Outside, something is happening. We all look up. I can hear Kristof's walkie-talkie and a couple of cracks in the distance that I wish might be gunfire. But it's far away, and not only is that needle going to hit me very soon, but over on the other table, the so-called medical team is starting the operation that will end Dasha's life.

I move my other forearm back and forth, and the blade scrapes against the ties holding me down. It's a beautiful sensation. But now the doctor looks over his instruments and notices the scalpel is missing. He makes eye contact for the first time, suspicious, and I pull my left arm free—the scalpel has cut through enough of my restraint for me to rip it open. I stab the doctor with the scalpel, right in the bicep. He yells and retreats.

I cut through the restraint on my right hand and use my fist to slam into the face of the approaching anesthesiologist.

"Stop!" I yell at Dasha's medics, as I cut through the belt across my ankles.

I'm up and on my feet, scalpel out, ready to take on the room, but they're not fighters. They drop back, and a couple of them even seem relieved. Outside, I can hear Kristof grunting, and someone crashes against the door, falling into the operating room. It's Caitlin. Her head has taken a bad crack on the door, and she's sprawled on the floor, stunned. I run to help her, but Kristof gets to her before me and kicks her so hard that she is lifted six inches off the ground, landing farther inside the operating theater. Kind, brave Caitlin, attacked by a monster twice her size.

I lunge at him with the scalpel, hooking it into his leg and yanking it down. He roars, but he shakes me off. I feel like a fly attacking an elephant, and he's over by Caitlin again in a heartbeat. She's still dazed, still lying there, and he's so much stronger. He lifts her head to smash it onto the floor, as the skylight above us breaks. A shower of glass shatters into the room like a lethal hailstorm and, with it, the black outline of Hala descends.

She uses the momentum of her fall to land on Kristof and knock him over. With four well-placed swings of her gun she knocks him senseless and turns to me, breathless. She takes in my hospital gown, the scalpel in my hand, the gurney behind me. But she doesn't move. Her eyes go to something behind me.

On instinct, I freeze, even before I hear the click of a gun safety releasing. Followed by the touch of cool metal against my head. Behind me, Paulina breathes into my ear.

"Don't move, Jessie."

Hala glares at Paulina. I swear, she almost bares her teeth.

"Drop the gun," Paulina instructs Hala.

Hala's eyes move to mine, a look to assure me that I'll be fine. She starts to lower the gun toward the floor, but I hold her gaze and she stops, understanding what I'm thinking. She takes firmer hold of the gun.

"Just shoot her," I say, for Paulina's benefit. "It's worth it."

That freaks Paulina out, because Hala nods, like maybe she would sacrifice me for the greater good.

"Are you sure?" Hala asks, completely deadpan.

"Yeah."

Hala raises her gun at Paulina, who now thinks that even shooting me is not going to save her. She has no choice but to turn her gun toward Hala, which gives me the split second I need to knock my fist backward into Paulina's face, elbow her in the stomach, and twist her arm till she's kneeling on the ground. Her gun hits the floor, and I go to kick it away, but someone gets there before me. Hala's boot smashes ferociously into the gun, sending it skidding into the corner of the room. Then she grabs Paulina by the back of the neck and yanks her up and away from me, pushing her forward to the gurney that I was so recently strapped to.

Paulina whimpers under the force of Hala's rage. Hala holds her down with one arm while she reaches for a scalpel with the other.

"No!" I yell, but she can't hear me. She can't hear anyone right at this moment. I know, because I've been there.

I run forward just as the scalpel pierces the side of Paulina's throat. I pull Hala's hand back.

"Get off me!" Hala shouts. She's panting with the exertion of subduing Paulina, but I keep my hand on her own. Not fighting with her but calming her down. Gripping the hand with the scalpel firmly enough that Hala can't make a sudden move.

Hala looks at me, angrily, but I keep my hand over her fingers.

"She would've *killed* you," Hala says, and when her eyes meet mine, they are moist with tears. It takes me a moment to realize that Hala's not doing this because she's full of rage but because she's full of fear. Fear of losing me. Under the blade, Paulina's throat is exposed and a trickle of dark blood makes its way down her pale neck, where the scalpel has punctured the skin.

"I'm fine," I tell her, and Hala's other hand comes up to grasp mine in a moment that tells me how much she cares; a moment she'd probably deny for the rest of her life if I ever mentioned it again. Which I won't.

"She isn't worth it," I say. "Trust me."

A long moment. Hala pulls away, tossing the scalpel back onto the tray. Then it's like she's back on track suddenly. Following protocol. She uses a cord from her jacket to tie Paulina's wrists together, pulling the knot too tightly; but I figure I can let her have that much.

Caitlin is coming round, trying to get up, and I reach her in time for her to lean on me as she pulls herself upright. She is badly bruised from the fight, bleeding and limping as well. But she looks at me with a flicker of a smile.

"Peggy's okay," she whispers.

I take a breath, and it catches in my throat, like a gulp. For the first time in a while I can breathe properly, and it feels good. I take a last look at Paulina's angry eyes, and then I turn away. Caitlin needs my help, and so does Hala. And Paulina was right, in the end. Family is the most important thing.

24

"I KNOW WHAT YOU THINK of me," Li says. "You think that I cannot really know what it is to be under pressure, the way you do. The fear of death that takes a year off your life every time you survive it; the depression of waiting alone in an apartment in a place that smells like nowhere you've been before."

I listen. I'm sort of intrigued, to tell you the truth. I've never had this much time with Li. During my first interviews here, she fired questions and I did the talking. Since then, we've only communicated through briefings. Other than that small interaction at the hospital in Belgrade.

Earlier this evening, Li and I bumped into each other at Peggy's bedside. We all arrived back in London three days ago. Since then we've unpacked, debriefed, taken turns visiting Peggy at the private clinic that Li transferred her to, and mostly, we've slept. Peggy is doing well—sitting up, reading newspapers, talking a *lot*.

And when we left her to rest, Li asked me to join her for a drink at her apartment. It's not the kind of thing you refuse.

And, actually, I don't mind listening now that Li is talking. She is eloquent, and speaks in long sentences, with a precise and formal way of describing things that feels almost old-fashioned. We are sitting alone in her kitchen, which is very clean and white, with stainless-steel appliances and ice-colored cabinets and not much sign of food. Above our heads, high on the wall, a round, mahogany clock with Roman numerals and Chinese symbols ticks. Maybe it's an antique, or a family heirloom. But it's a strange timepiece for a woman who deals in the most futuristic technology.

"And yet," Li continues, "I have survived a lot, from the time I was a small girl. I grew up in the Chinese countryside. In the early years of the Cultural Revolution. I watched my father die. He died of illness but, truly, he was broken by unjust rules, rules that men with more pliant characters learned to bend to their own needs."

Li pauses, and I nod. The ticking of the clock is the only sound touching the silence between us.

"A year later, I was separated from my mother. I was fourteen and sent with hundreds of other children from my district to serve my country. I was a soft, shy child, attached to my mother, kept safe by her like a flower bud protected in green leaves. My heart screamed for years."

It's a devastating image. A heart screaming. Up until now, I hadn't really considered whether Li even had a heart. Or feelings. I look down at the polished wooden floor. A long pause ensues, as if Li is waiting for me to respond.

"Why are you telling me this?" I ask.

"Because you have a right to know. You have risked your life many times for Athena, and you should know why we ask that of you. Why we will continue to ask it. I don't believe any government wants to help the people we want to help."

"So Athena will continue?" I sit forward in my chair, eager.

Li nods. "I was so busy trying to teach you lessons, Jessie, that I made the mistake of arrogance. Of thinking there was nothing I could learn from you."

"What did you learn from me?" I ask, surprised.

"That, whatever the experiences that Peggy and Kit and I have had in our lives, we cannot quite comprehend what you three endure. But we want to help you endure it. And become better because of it. There is a Chinese saying—that precious stones need sculpting before they become gems."

That kind of touches something in me, and I feel a lump rise to my throat. I look down and wait, not sure of what happens next. Li sits erect on the chair opposite, watching me.

"I owe you an apology," she says.

Well, that's a shocker. I shake my head and try to shrug it off. Li gives me a glimmer of a smile and says nothing more.

Still, the clock marks off the changing seconds. I glance up at it.

"It troubles you, the ticking?"

I nod.

"Time is passing," Li says. "I've always felt it."

She nods at me, releasing me from my chair. And so I get up to leave.

While I've appreciated the talk with Li, it's a relief to be back in my own home. The lamplight is warm, and Kit comes out of her bedroom in a blue silk robe and a towel wrapped around her just-washed hair and asks me about Peggy. I fill her in, but I'm sketchy about the meeting with Li because I don't know how to describe it. But it did sound to me as if Athena would continue and, when I ask her, Kit confirms it.

While we talk, Kit brings over a bottle of antiseptic and some new bandages. I cut my wrists and ankles trying to get free in the hospital, and I think it makes Kit feel better to do a bit of the old mothering routine. There's a short silence while she unwraps the bandage, and I feel like she's working up to something.

"Listen, about Paulina," Kit says, dabbing at me with cotton wool.

I'm wary. "What about her?"

"You felt something for her."

I look down, say nothing, and try to ignore the warmth in my cheeks.

Kit tries again. "I didn't know you were attracted to . . ."

"Human traffickers?" I ask, still not meeting her eyes.

Kit smiles. "Well, I was going to say, attracted to women."

My face is burning. I don't know why. Not being heterosexual is probably the coolest thing I've ever done as far as Kit is concerned. I think it's just *talking* to my mother about this stuff that makes me uncomfortable. I want her to know everything about me and be okay with it and yet, what if it's just another thing about me that she doesn't get? I wait, in a sort of agony. But she doesn't say anything else. My head is down, and I can feel her looking at me. And, suddenly, her arms are around me and she's pulling me close to her and hanging on tightly—

"Jessie," she says quietly. "My Jessie. I love you."

It takes a few minutes before I can come out of that hug with any kind of control. Kit sees that I'm sort of emotional, I suppose, because she sits back a bit and gives me a minute, keeping herself busy putting the tops back on antiseptic bottles and whatever.

"Jess, I wanted to talk to you about Jake Graham," she says after a minute. I look up. That's out of left field, and my heart sinks. Jake the intrepid journalist. Did he find something more about Ahmed's killing? Something that could compromise Athena? But Kit holds her iPad out to me, bringing up a newspaper article.

"My PR team sent an advance warning. It's coming out in print tomorrow," she says.

I take the tablet and read:

MONEY GRABBER: KIT LOVE SINGS FOR SLAVERY BARON

I feel sick. Below the headline is a picture of Kit with Gregory and Paulina, and below that I search for the name of the person who wrote the piece: Jake Graham. I look up at Kit, horrified. The picture must have been sold by that photographer Gregory hired at the party. Once the boss was dead, he probably realized he could make some money without having his legs broken. And as for that so-called journalist, Jake . . . but before I can spew what I think of him, Kit interrupts.

"No, Jessie. He's a good reporter."

"But it's not true."

"He doesn't know that."

I pause, frustrated. Then I look at my mother with something like complete admiration. Talk about taking one for the team.

"How can you stand it?" I ask, looking back at the article. The things he's written make me feel sick.

"Look on the bright side," Kit says. "It's the best cover I could ever have. And we need it, because Jake's already written about, or connected, three of us. You, me, and Peggy. He might not see the links, but we have to be careful of him, going forward."

I nod. "It must hurt though . . ." I say. "Reading all this."

"Yeah, just a bit." Kit smiles. "You know what we need?"

"Vodka?"

"It'll be a cold day in hell when I let you follow me down that path," my mother says. "I was going to say a hot drink."

I watch Kit disappear into the kitchen and think about Li, sitting in her white, antiseptic world. One thing I appreciate about living with a mother from South London—there's nothing that can't be made better by a nice cup of tea.

A week later, and the early morning is soft and warm, with a gentle breeze. I'm leaning on the wall inside the back entrance to Athena. Hala and Caitlin are already inside the building. Peggy's coming back today, so we're having a celebration meeting. But I'm hanging around here, in the shadows, waiting for Amber. My pass has been restored, and I'm back on the team, so I don't need help accessing the building. But I haven't been able to get Amber to say anything more to me than yes and no since I got back, which I take to mean that she's still hopping mad at me for breaking into my lockbox. In one hand is a carefully chosen bouquet of roses that I hope will break the ice a bit. In the other hand I grasp my backup plan.

Right on time, three minutes to eight, Amber appears around the corner, turning from the brightly lit street into the darkness of the entry area. With the sun behind her, she's nothing more than a silhouette. I can see the spiked ends of her hair and a set of huge headphones over her ears. Moving her head to whatever vintage music she's undoubtedly listening to, she dances. Just a few steps, but really good ones. Then it's like she senses someone's watching. She looks over her shoulder just as I step out right in front of her.

Amber jumps, startled, and now I'm really in trouble, because she knows I must have seen her secret dancing.

"What are you smirking at?" she demands.

I'm trying *not* to smile—really—but it's hard.

"Nothing," I say.

I hold out the roses penitently. She pushes them back at me and walks on, briskly.

"It's going to take more than a bunch of flowers to say sorry for what you did," Amber says.

I hurry to keep up, holding out my left hand instead.

"How about a limited edition Kit Love album?"

Amber slows down and peers sideways at the LP record in my hand. Everyone has their price, I suppose, but I'm careful not to ruin the fragile peace by smiling again.

She scans herself in, and I follow hastily. I stand beside her while we wait for the lift doors to open.

"I've installed a lot more security in the tech cave," she says huffily. "Just so you know."

"I don't blame you."

Silence, as the elevator doors open. I sniff.

"You've changed your perfume, Amber."

We both walk into the enclosed space, then watch the doors slide shut again.

"I like it," I say.

"I don't remember asking your opinion."

This time, I do smile. I can't help it. And I hold out the record to her.

"Is it signed?" she asks.

"No. But I think I can arrange it."

Through the glass panels of the situation room, I can see Peggy, and she's looking almost like her old self. A fair bit thinner and a little gaunt in the face, but her eyes are smiling as she chats with Kit and Li. Both Caitlin and Hala are missing. I can see Hala in a corner of the ops area, chatting with Thomas. Well, maybe "chatting" is a bit of an overstatement. He's talking, and she's nodding while inhaling a muffin and throwing him the occasional smile.

I walk into the situation room, and Peggy looks up, her eyes lighting.

"You shouldn't have," she says.

I realize that I'm still carrying Amber's rejected roses, which are a bit crushed. I feel guilty, but I can hardly tell Peggy they weren't meant for her. I hand them over and give her a hug, so relieved that she is back with us. Behind me, Hala comes into the room, wiping crumbs from her mouth with her sleeve.

"Where's Caitlin?" I ask.

Kit looks up at me with a frown.

"She went to the bathroom a while ago. Maybe you should check."

Just as I go in through the bathroom doors, Caitlin comes out of a toilet stall. Her hand is at her jacket pocket, and I know she was about to take out the pills. She smiles at me, but she seems a bit shaky. Her face is cut and bruised from the fight at the hospital.

"I never thanked you for fighting that overgrown hulk to save me," I say.

"Hey," she says. "It's what we do."

She looks away from me and washes her hands, and I get the feeling she wishes I would leave.

"You don't have to be embarrassed to have PTSD," I say suddenly.

Well, she wasn't expecting that. I can tell she's upset with me.

"It's nothing to be ashamed of," I continue.

"Jessie, leave me alone."

But I plow on. "I messed up by not following orders, with Ahmed," I say. "All you did in Iraq was follow orders."

She glares at me, but I stay calm for a change. We look at each other for what feels like an age. She's blinking a lot.

"You didn't hurt anyone, Cait. You just learned you can't trust everyone who gives you an order."

Caitlin steps back. She looks angry and disgusted and upset. At herself and maybe at this whole, chaotic world.

"But sometimes you can," I add. Which sounds like a contradiction, but I'm realizing there are no easy answers. The older you get, the messier it gets.

"How do you know the difference?" Caitlin asks. She takes a breath, emotional.

As it happens, I've had a lot of time to think about that in the past week.

"I think it's something to do with who's giving the orders and why," I say. "In the army, they just sent you off to a war zone. They didn't ask you what you thought of the war, or if you believed in it. But Peggy and Li and Kit—they told us what we'd be doing and why. And we chose it. We chose it with them."

It's funny, but I look at the Athena founders now and I think that they must have been like us once. Maybe not fighting for an underground agency, but young, uncertain about things, finding their way through the stuff life throws at you. They've just learned how to get through it with a little more wisdom. Maybe all you can ever do is keep going and try to do a bit better every day.

"Anyway," I say. "That's why I'm planning to listen more and mouth off less."

"That'll be a nice change," Caitlin says, and we both smile.

"So what's happening?" I say once we're all in the situation room again.

The Athena founders are diplomatically ignoring Caitlin's red eyes.

"Paulina's in jail," Kit says, glancing at me.

"Good," I say, meeting my mother's gaze. "And Aleks?"

"Arrested."

"For attempted murder?" I ask.

Peggy shakes her head.

"Corruption. The cryptocurrency keys you found were the hard evidence we needed to prove that he was taking bribes for some time. But we can't go for the other charge without opening a can of worms about what I was doing there."

"We've also built quite a case against the Victory Clinic," Peggy continues. "And our embassy in Moscow has exerted enough pressure to close it down, along with another clinic that was planning to get organs through them. They didn't want the publicity, so they agreed to do it fast if the press didn't hear about it."

"Who were those organs for?" Caitlin asks.

"Wealthy Russians who are sick and don't want to wait.

Russia does very few transplants compared to European countries, so there's a high demand. Whatever names we gather through Victory will be reported to the authorities."

"One more thing," Li says, looking at all of us in turn. "We're sponsoring Dasha, the girl you rescued, to come live in London. I'll give her a job at Chen Technologies, but really, if she's as strong as you say she is, we should look at training her to join us here. She should certainly be motivated."

There's no doubt in my mind that Dasha will be an asset to Athena. You can train weapons and fighting techniques, but you can't train that kind of courage and willpower. You either have it or you don't.

I clear my throat. There's something that's been stressing me about my own performance on this mission.

"About Aleks," I say. "I should've found out his son was sick. And found the crypto stash."

Peggy looks at me kindly. "His son hadn't started treatment there yet. It needed a big deposit that Aleks was hustling to gather. There's no way you could have figured out that link. Maybe I shouldn't have been so quick to trust him."

It's like I can breathe freely again. I guess the weight of the worry was heavy on me—that I could've prevented Peggy from coming so close to death.

Li takes a sip from her cup of green tea and flicks on the big screen, breaking the moment of reflective silence.

We all watch as a snapshot of a dusty village comes up. It shows a new school building, with a crowd of families outside it, and it takes me a moment to recognize Kit, Peggy, and Li among them. In khakis and hats, smiling at the camera.

I exchange a look with Caitlin, then Hala.

"This is northern Pakistan," Peggy says. "Two years ago. You all know what happened there."

We nod. Li switches the picture on the screen and brings up that terrible shot from the newspaper. The charred building, the rows of white-sheeted bodies laid out . . . We all look away, and Li clicks on to the next photo.

"The deaths of those girls impelled us to start Athena," Peggy continues. "And the man who started that fire was arrested. The evidence against him was overwhelming."

The face of a man in traditional tribal clothes appears on the screen, along with stats—name, associates, recent contacts, last known sightings.

"But he was released without charge. Because the local police were either threatened or paid off. So he has never been brought to justice. Until now."

"Our next job?" asks Hala.

Kit nods. "Yes. But you need to take a bit of time off, all of you. We'll meet back here in a week and go over it in detail."

The moment feels solemn, like we've been entrusted with something extra meaningful. Slowly, we all start to pack up our things, ready to leave for now. But then Hala speaks. She looks at Peggy shyly.

"Is there any news about my brother? I know it's only been a couple of days, but . . ."

That's out of the blue. So Hala must have asked for help on Omar's immigration file. Peggy and Li exchange a glance; a moment of silent communication that doesn't make me feel good.

"Let's talk alone," Peggy says to Hala.

We all move faster to clear the room, but Hala's voice stops us.

"No. You can say anything you want to in front of them."

That's huge, for Hala. Someone who thinks talking about the weather is too personal. My eyes meet hers in a silent question, like—Are you sure? She nods, and we all sit down again.

"Omar is on a terrorist watch list," Peggy says. Li pushes a thin file across the table, but Hala doesn't touch it. She just stares at Peggy.

"It must be because of where we're from, our Arab names . . . ," Hala says.

"No doubt," Peggy says kindly.

"He's not a terrorist," Hala protests. "He saw what they did to us. . . . You don't understand the pressure that young men are under there. To join one side or the other, or die . . ."

Peggy listens, and I can see she feels terrible about it.

"I'm sure that's the case," she says. "But it makes it incredibly difficult, if not impossible, to help him with an asylum request . . ."

Her last words are lost under the scrape of Hala's chair. Hala pushes open the door and runs out. From across the ops room, Thomas looks up, but I'm already right behind her. She seems disoriented and heads to the bathroom.

When I go in, Hala's leaning against a sink, hands gripping the bowl on both sides.

"Hey," I say.

But her shoulders are shaking, and I realize that she's crying. And not just crying, but weeping. As if everything she ever kept held inside is pouring out. Without thinking about it I go straight over and hold her. It's not easy, because she's pressing her palms against her eyes and her elbows are out, but I find a way just to get my arms around her. She sobs and sobs, and I don't know what else to do but hold on. She's probably understood that she may never see her brother again. After a few minutes the crying subsides.

The door to the bathroom opens and Caitlin is there, obviously sent to check on us. And behind her, over her shoulder, Thomas waits, worried. My eyes meet theirs over Hala's shoulder.

Hala herself takes a shaky breath and turns away from me to wash her face.

"Listen," I tell her. "If Omar's being pushed to do something, we can find a way to get him out. We won't leave him there."

Hala starts to tear up again. Maybe it's been too long since any one of us took the time to be kind to her. But she gulps a breath and leans back down to the sink.

"Our next job is in Pakistan, anyway. We'll figure it out," I say.

She nods and looks at me, a glimmer of hope in her eyes.

"Do you want to go home, take some time?" I ask.

She splashes her eyes, wiping the water off her face with that all-purpose sleeve, and shakes her head, refusing the offer.

"Good. Because we need you."

For the second time this morning, I shepherd one of my team out of the bathroom. I'm really hoping this is the last I see of that place for today. I wait for them all to go ahead of me. Caitlin walks alongside Hala, a protective hand on her back, and I follow them out. Ahead of us, in the situation room, Kit and Li are standing up, worried, looking out for us.

When they catch sight of us coming back, they glance at each other, relieved. And then Kit looks past the others, straight at me. I pause, because for a moment, it's just her and me, communicating, even at this distance. I feel like she's proud of me. I don't know why, but I can tell. She holds my look for a long moment and then she smiles. And for the first time in ages, I smile back.

ACKNOWLEDGMENTS

About two years ago, a group of builders showed up at our front door with a pile of planks and a truck full of equipment. They proceeded to create a cabin in our back garden—a fully lit up, warm, cozy room with big windows. It remains one of the best presents I ever received. Frustrated with my low writing output (in my defense, I had been writing and directing movies), my wife, Hanan, decided to gift me a room of my own, a quiet space with a desk and piles of film reels from my movies for decoration. I finally had no excuse not to write a new book, and *The Athena Protocol* was the result.

My deepest appreciation to Hanan for being the anchor and meaning in my life and my constant champion. To our beautiful sons, Ethan and Luca, for their love and support, and for the unrelenting critiques that make my work better. And for understanding that their mum spends all day making up stuff about people who don't exist, and that sometimes she forgets the stuff that does exist as a result.

Thanks to Hannah Patterson, who I met at Amazon Studios in LA, and who introduced me to my fantastic agent, Sophie Hicks. Thanks to Sophie for her immediate belief in this book and the characters, and her intrepid, entrepreneurial spirit.

Patrick Ness—not only are you a beautiful writer and person, but also a very real inspiration to me as I learned to believe in the huge opportunities that are open to us as storytellers. And to Marc

Nowell—with Patrick, they are amazing godfathers to my boys, and true friends.

My thanks to Tara Weikum and Sarah Homer for really excellent edits. I was sure I had delivered them a masterpiece, but they delicately showed me how to lift this story to new heights. And sorry that it took me so long to figure out where to properly use an em dash.

Thanks to Guy O'Keeffe who helped me early on with information on Peggy's poisoning and also organ "donations." Wanda Whiteley helped me to find a voice for Jessie and encouraged my first foray into the young adult genre. Holly Valance made sure my Serbian translations didn't make a mess of my entire plot.

It feels like the right moment to say thank you to the myriad of friends/family (you know who you are) who have been part of our fun and insane forays into storytelling—for showing so much support, buying so many books, attending every screening, throwing launches, and generally making me feel like a genius. What a gift that is.

In the end, it is my readers who make *The Athena Protocol* come to life by picking up this book and interacting with it. I appreciate you taking the time with this story, and thanks also to the thousands of amazing, passionate fans of my past books and films, those who've championed me and stuck with me through every story I've cared to tell. Writing is a privilege, but it's also a lonely business because you never really know if anyone will connect with what you want to say. You all have made that so much easier for me in the past fifteen years. Thank you.

South Lake Tahoe